AN ORDINARY ECSTASY

Also by Luke Carman

An Elegant Young Man
Intimate Antipathies

LUKE CARMAN

AN ORDINARY ECSTASY

STORIES

Published 2022
from the Writing and Society Research Centre
at Western Sydney University
by the Giramondo Publishing Company
PO Box 752
Artarmon NSW 1570 Australia
www.giramondopublishing.com

© Luke Carman 2022

Designed by Jenny Grigg
Typeset by Andrew Davies
in Tiempos Regular 9/15pt

Cover art: Imants Tillers, *Kangaroo Blank*, 1988
oil stick, gouache, oil paint and synthetic polymer paint
on 78 canvas boards, nos. 16231–16308, 213 x 195 cm

Printed and bound by Ligare Book Printers
Distributed in Australia by NewSouth Books

A catalogue record for this book is available from the National Library of Australia.

ISBN 978-1-922725-24-0

All rights reserved.
No part of this publication may be reproduced, stored in a retrieval system or transmitted in any form or by any means electronic, mechanical, photocopying or otherwise without the prior permission of the publisher.

9 8 7 6 5 4 3 2 1

The Giramondo Publishing Company acknowledges the support of Western Sydney University in the implementation of its book publishing program.

This project has been assisted by the Commonwealth Government through the Australia Council, its arts funding and advisory body.

What is apparently absurd may have some deeper meaning.

Hans Küng

Contents

A Beckoning Candle

Two fine filaments of light crept under the blinds, ghosted through the curtains, refracted on the dresser mirror, converged at a single point on Joseph's shiny pate, and by slight increase of that dome's warmth, caused him to wake from a dreamy sleep. Margaret snored lightly beside her husband, with lips parted, her small body motoring in private gasps beneath the sheets tucked to her chin. Of nature's endless consolations, Joseph pondered, is any fairer than a loved one beside you in repose? He formed the question in the crepuscular light, his eyes boggy with sleep, and as if to abide by his own ruminations, rolled over towards his wife's tender breathing. He made a formidable effort in manoeuvring around, groaning and cursing at the pangs of morning's first indigestions, and effected a deliberate rattling of the bedsprings, but Marg's sleep was undisturbed. Heavy sleepers, he thought, watching her deep-set eyes quivering beneath their lily-white lids. Her family sleep like spring lambs, the whole brood of them. Old Peter Miller could rehearse his sulphur-crested circus at our bedside, and she would keep steadfast as dreaming stone. He recalled a famous definition to share with her when she roused, 'Nothing, my dear, is what rocks dream about – so said Aristotle.' Or was it Plato, that one? I should worm the old Peripatetic into more conversation, with Michelangelo when I go to Woodville later. If I mention such drivel to the wife, she'll advise me to keep my nonsense to myself, but then let me ask, my dear Marg, what was the point of all those days, weeks, and years I sacrificed in rote memorisation of civilisation's footnotes? Supervised by barnacled nuns who drummed into our heads every word of each infernal line of every book that their pale curled claws might conjure up, with cuts of the canes for dim learners and crude mnemonics for the rest of us? Should I shed my mind like an onion whose outer layers are turning parchment yellow, and consign the skinned content to a peremptory oblivion? What say you, dear Marg? Come to mention dreaming, there were infernal visions erupting all through last night's sleeping. Joseph eased his grey tufted dome back on the floral patterns of the mounded pillows in motions that were achingly slow to avoid the stiffness of morning, and he lay utterly still to revisit what he could salvage from the night's liminal projections.

It begins with a fragment, Joseph saw, and he thought himself back into the dream world, clambering up the steep incline of a chalky cliff-face, with a wide clear morning sky around in all directions. How hard that long ascent was on his ancient body. A mistake in looking down exposed him to the toothy abyss of silent treetops and jutting rocks below, and he saw a world beneath him waiting to catch and break his body apart. If I should slip and fall, I'll go spinning down and be impaled on those horny branches or smashed to meaty slabs upon the stones under the cliff. A stream of blood leaked from a throbbing cut on his knee he hadn't noticed, and one fat droplet twirled down into the wide grey-green oblivion. It's all that Catholic imagery that makes the world so dramaturgical, Joseph scolded himself, pressing his face hard against the cool cliff-face to calm his fear. Those nuns have a reckoning to answer for, filling children's heads with sulphuric lakes and fanged hell-mouths erupting from the earth to swallow sinners in their hundreds. Still, one foot wrong, and I am lost. With fingers digging and shoulders throbbing with a fiery heat, Joseph scrambled up the last of the climb and came upon the summit, and collapsed like a sack of wet rags upon it. There he lay, recovering his wind with a dreamy efficiency, and when he rose and looked upon his triumph he saw only a small field of dried shrubbery, and a clearing circled by patches of fine yellow sand leading into thickets and brambles. Beyond, he spied a familiar shabby cabin with a tin-pot chimney, partially hidden behind the ironbarks that lined the clearing. That's Old Tom's cabin, he saw. The very same it is, there, behind that bark and bramble. Joseph had seen the shack often as a boy, when the family was visiting his grandmother's house on the Riverina, down south of her Red Shadow Lodge. With an instinct stronger than the illusions of dream, Joseph knew that the cabin did not belong on a mountaintop. Has some higher power placed it here? Its true locality was far away, Joseph knew, on a wide expanse of flat land, near the commons south of Henty, where the saddle horses stood in their leather coats, their black-maned necks bent in the pale grasses – calm creatures at a distance those horses, though their black marbled eyes brimmed wide in terror when he or his brother, Bobby, came too close, and they whinnied and bucked in fits of sudden fear like something loosed from the underworld when their pop wandered into the field with his saddlery swaying at his uneven hip. Some days, under an immensity of cumulus cloud, they hunted and skinned goannas pulled out of burrows by their mud-slick tails. Those lizards had speckled, beady scales bronzed by the ochre burrows, and their dad would skin rabbits too, stretching their furred coats off with a shucking sound and revealing the red wet flesh under fur and skin, the pungent smell of their ribbed carcases leaking, and the stink of plucked birds in the afternoon warmth in the air like unwashed feet fresh out of old workboots, until the fire turned the grimy creatures into a salivating assemblage of hocks and hardening crusts, their juices dripping and crackling into the open flames, glowing brazier-bright under the descending country twilight. In the dimming hours, stars were like quicksilver spilled out over the night, and he spied his mother with her legs tucked modestly under her Sunday dress, smiling at him like she would at times, wearing her love plain in her keen intelligent eyes. She beckoned to him, her soft hand patting at a spot beside her on the coloured patches of the picnic rug. The patches! Those expletive heathen *patches*, Joseph thought, rubbing the crust of sleep's shock away from his face and out of his beard.

It was those cursed nicotine patches that had made his dreams so vivid of late, and this morning's reveries were no exception. There was one of the varmints stuck to his shoulder this very moment, obviously the cause of his recalling long-gone days down south. And such a charming side effect, it is! Little wonder they never mention the possibility of unsolicited memories in their phonebook of side effects. Chemists are like to lawyers in the ranks of deceivers, let me tell you. Old Dante in his inferno will sort the tricksters out, with his whirlwinds and practical jokes in the circles of Hell. One genteel demon on a lower level of Hell played a trumpet with his rump, the nuns explained, to rob the damned even of their dignity. For all we know, it's the bad dreams which cause the common rashes and the dizziness, too. And moreover, the more crucial point is, Lord Father above is well known to take a sour attitude to sins committed while in rapid-eye-modality. A bad dream can show you hell, as they say, but it's the pleasing dreams that'll get you there.

Joseph peeled the nicotine patch from his shoulder, and it

plucked some grey hairs off as it came away. The doctor's ordination is for me to quit, he considered, tossing the hairy crumpled square into an ashtray by the side of the bed. But has he an explanation for the fact that there are more old smokers than old doctors? Joseph heard the doc's proscriptions running through his mind before he could prevent them, 'Joey! My brother! Come, come, let's fix you up! How are you? How is your wife? How have you been? Are you taking your medication? You see what I told you now? It's time to quit! How many times have I told you? This time you're ready to listen to me, yes? Nothing more serious! Let's check your blood. Hold still. That's the way, Joey! That's the way! We'll fix you up, my brother! Hold on, I'll make you a script, wait here, my brother.' A good man, Joseph considered – beloved by his community – as people liked to say about decent men today. They ought to put the man's name on a plaque outside his practice, on a plinth by the Woodville park, so that one day I can point at it with reverence to my grandchildren on our way to the TAB, and the council can add it to the tours that come in from town for their charcoal chicken safari, 'If you look to your left, you will see the grounds where miracles of healing were conducted for generations innumerable, and to your right, the halal snack packs you've read about in the latest issues of *Metropolitan Weekly*.' Perhaps when he retires, I'll petition the council. That's the proper time for honorifics. Should be a parade, like in days of old. When someone died there'd be a procession through the mourning streets, all comers out to signal last respects. You can't imagine it now. Mourners in old-style hats and coats, hands to breast with low voices confiding to their neighbour, 'Oh well, there goes Terry O'Quinn, between the salt and the city, he was. Liked a fortnightly drunk, of course, but what's that against a man? Christ himself was fond of his dram. Poor sod owed no one more than a pinch, enjoyed a punt, was neither a borrower nor a lender except by and by as all men are, and what's to speak against him but he raised thirteen and lost three in infancy, not to mention he healed Mrs Custard's rheumatoid down by the creek while speaking in tongues with a Jefferson Bible in his hand, so help me he did! And end upon end, his soul will see ours in eternity.' What would people say now if you ran through the trouble of a walking wake down main street, but 'Who's that proverbial blocking the road? Who are these mourners holding up the living daylights?' And let's not get started on 'The Community'.

The peeled patch Joseph had tossed into the ashtray was unfolding like a dead spider returning to life on the counter, beside a bowl of rings and chains where his wife's earrings were kept. He avoided glancing at the old man reflected in the mirror as he rose, and the sight of prayer beads hanging on the mirror's edge. Pale blue pebbles linked by a chain of tiny silver, the colour fading from them despite a terminal lack of sunlight in the bedroom where the curtains and blinds were always drawn. In the name of the Father, Son, and Holy Ghost. He prayed, and then kissed his closed fists to sign off from God. I'll need all his help to face the coming day, Joseph knew. 'Some days are diamonds,' he muttered as he collected himself with a grunt for the effort, gazing quickly again at his wife in peaceful rest, and twisted open the bedroom door to welcome whatever waited outside the sealed hermetic gloom. 'Some days, quite different, are a river of shit.'

The rest of the house was plunged in darkness, but a small rectangular window in the toilet presented the still silence of their yard and the backstreets beyond where the scene was illuminated by orange streetlights, and a few scattered houselights in the maze of the neighbourhood's angles. The obscenity of the day-to-come was out there too, where his property abutted the building site behind his still-wounded fence. There was nothing of the mess to be seen through the window, but the thought of it was enough to bring on a nauseating dizziness, and he turned away, unable to contemplate the effort required to remedy yesterday's events. What would Aurelius say about this? I should know my Emperor Marcus by heart. Learned that from Father Penrose, the pillow-biter. Old pervert tapping his cane like a metronome to catch the mnemonic metre. 'In the morning, when you awake unwilling, think on this: I rise to do the work of man. Why else was I into this world brought? To lie in pyjamas and sheets and be by cushions comforted? Do I not see the small birds, the ants, the spiders, the bees, all work to put their house in order? He who does not love the work of man, loves not the whole of nature. Why, present to me the burdens of a man, and I will make of them the living art.' Joseph took his ablutions with these words ringing silently in his head, and as he stood in the semi-darkness performing this act of man, he turned aside all thoughts of the dysfunctions contained in his yard and dreamed instead of consummation.

Something with a gravy sauce to soak on buttered toast, he decided. That'll serve as a general theme. Eggs, something with eggs. The thought of empty eggshells reminded him again of Pop. He was an old gentlemanly style of bloke, with a moustache lacquered black beneath his plump nostrils, a stalwart Saint Nicolaus with a sweet sibilant voice. Heard him sing in the choir at Christmas. Oh, that time he over-fed me at the Lodge! Gran was out with the washing drum, left me for hot breakfast with him getting about the kitchen in his striped breeches and woollen cap. She came home and saw me eating a seventh boiled egg out of the shell with an oyster spoon. She must have counted the empty shells on the sink-top because she shrieked to Hades. 'Jesus and Lord of All Creation! Have you lost your instructive bonnet? Are you trying to kill the boy with indigestions?' Old Pop's face dropped, the moustache with it. 'Well,' says he. 'The boy kept eating them, so I kept cooking them!' She was like a mad devil after him all the rest of the day to poke his posterior with her fork. It was always Pop who took me to see Old Tom's cabin. Pop would stir me up at sunrise, one of the dogs with him, swishing its tail mad with excitement, and we'd set out under a morning sky so blinding on the green hills that the dawn seemed another country fallen on the lonely earth. Pop took him east across the flats of the commons, their solitary hike over the plains beset by insect choir and birdsong from the gumtrees and elms and the craning figs bordering the plains, and the trembling leaves bristled in the yolk of sunlight pressing hot against the two travellers' skins, brushing it a coppery colour. When they had crossed the commons and made their way up the ash-white track, they came to the door of the quiet cabin set in swathes of sword grass, the very same cabin Joseph had seen in his morning dream. Pop knocked on the iron hinge and entered. They found Old Tom inside, flummoxed, like a loose pile of shag against the farther wall. He was lying straight and flat as a railway sleeper, on a sack of rags in an upturned cot. The bushman's jacket and coat and his beard were all hoary with an old bushies' fizz, and his hair was the colour of wire bleached white by the beating sun, though his skin had been sun-blasted in the opposite direction, cracked and crusted as a parched mud-flat. 'Well, Tom,' his pop announced, taking off his hat and folding it under his arm. 'Young Joseph here is down from the city and has come to see us lot. Chuck your coat on and let's get some hunting in before the sun's too buggery hot.' Old Tom stirred under the ragged cloak he used as a blanket, his eyes flecked silver as they drank in the pouring light. The lone hunting dog they'd taken along with them for the day began to whine at the door but made no move to cross the threshold and enter. Old Tom rose slowly, first to his hands, then from his hands he lifted his knees to the floor, and then he was fit to rise one stoop at a time, putting his patched day-coat over his breeches without word, slipping into a pair of button-hooked overalls which were nursed together with stitches and patches. Those damnable patches again! Joseph cursed. I'm prone to sentimental excursions this morning thanks to those diabolical squares. Stick to the larder with your thoughts, my man. Avoid distraction while you can. Now do you see what danger there is in dreaming? Sitting down to breakfast on eggs-in-purgatory, Joseph raised a dribbling fork to his mouth and was consumed by a mental rehearsal of the previous day's calamity.

Of course, it was Marg who spotted the catastrophe first. She'd gone out to hang the washing under the garage awning and had come up panting, her bright blue eyes wild. One look at her face and Joseph knew enough to raise his hand to prevent her gleefully announcing the horrors that were unfolding outside. Something from hell itself, if that excited awe on her face is any indication, he thought. A brief exposure to the disaster outside saw Joseph standing out in the backyard, on his mobile phone, an eschatological tone in his gravelled voice. 'I beg your pardon?' the site manager replied.

'I said,' Joseph repeated in calm resignation. 'I'm calling you about a river of human shit, over which I am currently standing, which is running from the sewage pit on my property, downhill into your worksite, with all the vigour of a young Niagara.' The site manager seemed unable to comprehend it.

'Let me put it this way, I stand here in my back garden, looking at a gushing stream of effluent, pouring out of the ground, as it swallows up my backyard. And I must tell you, I'm seventy-three years of age, and it is not until this wretched day I ever thought to see my lawn be swallowed by a flood of the neighbourhood's shit.'

The site manager, Nate, seemed a decent enough bloke, and when the penny dropped there was nothing but sympathy from his end of the call. Marg had secured his number from the Community Relations woman, whose name and contact details were on the letter the department had sent about the planned development months before they knocked the old commission houses down. 'Dear Resident, this is a letter to inform you in advance of essential housing development scheduled for commencement under approved application number 201210007 for the below listed properties directly adjacent to your address.' The correspondence was replete with the usual assurances, that the proposal had been vetted by the council's careful contemplations committee, reinforced, of course, by a laundry list of the beneficial consequences of the development's proceeding. 'If you read the way they laud their own designs,' Joseph commented to his wife, 'you'd conclude every building of high-density housing to be merely a singular instance of the modern world's inexorable transition into general architectural utopia.' It's their Orwellian world, he thought, we're just living in it. They say, 'increase shade' when they mean, 'dismantle the sun'. This polite propaganda was sealed with the beguiling invitation to peruse the plans at their leisure, a schema of the development showing the dimensions and scale of the buildings, fences, trees, driveways, walls, parking spaces and sewerage systems included for their inspection. Ah, yes, the sewerage system. Well, they hadn't accounted for the delicacy of those under-organs, installed by better men, after the war. Those old clay pipes would have been left to lie in peace but for the greed that drives lesser men to meddle with the foundations of the world.

'Listen, mate,' the site manager explained. 'The thing is, I've got no one coming out over the weekend, but I'll see what I can do and call you back.' As it turned out, what they could do was send out a pump truck from the Water Board first thing next morning. Joseph hung up in resignation to the situation being out of his control until then, shut the back door on his slowly swamping backyard, and stripped out of his soiled clothes in the old shower recess in the laundry. Marg was sitting quietly at the dining table, reading something privately on her phone, her eyeglasses balanced at an odd angle on her expressionless face. 'I told you there'd be more trouble,' she said when Joseph wandered out wrapped in his towel, his hair in a mess of discombobulation. 'You said the fence would be the end of it, but...' She shrugged and sighed, resumed her reading. Blind Freddy could have seen it coming, he thought. The sewerage systems were old and connected along the entire block, and they had been pounding away at the ground with machines loud as collapsing scenery, like madmen with a longing to scourge the earth itself with a sadistic fetish for destruction.

It was true that Marg had voiced her concerns, two weeks prior, just as the men had finished tearing down the old housing homes behind their property to make way for the foundations for the unit block-to-be, filling the couple's lives with such a steaming, pumping, shovelling racket. Marg was the first to notice the damage they'd made that day, too. She was putting cheese out on the veranda for the magpie larks nesting in the tree over the garage, when a bobcat had smashed its way through the fence panels. She tossed the fragments of cheese, called out Joseph's name, and stood in front of the flyscreen, barring his way to the yard. 'You're not gonna believe this,' she warned him with a frightful light in her blue eyes.

There it was, Joseph's fence, crumbled in rigid disassembly, and not a sign of remorse in the machines as they raved on unabated. 'What are we going to do?' Marg asked him, an odd high-pitched delight in her question. What am I going to do about it, she means to say, Joseph thought. Well, I'll show her what I'm going to do! Joseph donned his old hi-vis top and walked all the way around the block and down Brussel Road, to the accessible side of the building site where the cement truck was parked on the footpath. Marg watched him from the kitchen window as he marched round the long block's corner and disappeared behind the neighbour's place, only to pop up again a moment later, heading down Brussel, chugging his way towards the side access on the adjacent property, his arms swinging wildly as he huffed and fumed his way towards the building site in his spotless boots and shining vest. 'Why's he off the long way? He could have just gone over the broken fence, the silly thing. Unmanly, using someone else's hole? Hope he doesn't go off his rocker, get punched on the head. Might not see him coming and roll over the top of him with their machines.'

When Joseph turned the corner, he realised he'd not walked

down Brussel Road in years. They used to come down this way twice a week when it was still safe to visit Swan Park. Now that's a long time gone. Not had reason to walk this street since Jude was a boy. Oft wanted to feed the ducks or play cricket by the creek. Never had much coordination. And there's the house they shot at in a drive-by, just last week. Bullets missed a mother-of-six sitting in her lounge-room, she was watching *Home and Away*, the poor fat goose. She said so, on the news, and Jude called saying he could see our house behind the reporter talking. He asked if we'd heard the shots, 'No, only the sirens,' I said. And the helicopters grooming all over the skies around us, and for what? They'll make a television series about these streets, a few years from now. Can't see any holes left in the house, or did the bullet go in the window? They found a severed head in Swan Creek last month, just where we used to play cricket with Jude. The helicopters came out flapping then, did they what! No wonder I don't come down this street.

Joseph came to a gap in the loping wire gates that separated the worksite proper from the footpath. Where the four commission houses that had been home to many a beloved neighbour over the years once stood, there was now nothing but upturned grainy soil, damp and steaming where the machines were busiest. Here and there Joseph saw the first signs of the new foundations stamped on the dishevelled grounds, around which bobcat and digger spun and churned in a frenzied motion. Near him on the nature strip beyond the gate was a white cement truck, splattered in dried sprays of its own mixture, its barrelled gut spinning with a high-pitched whine, spewing sludge down a crusted pipeline while its engine trembled and three large men in yellow helmets and filthy boots stood watching the porridge-like concoction splatter past them while they communicated with one another over the racket with broad gesticulations about the adjustments that needed to be made, or stood staring at the cement flowing into the catchment with their hands on their hips.

The ground under Joseph's feet shook with the heavy-duty oscillations across the nearby earth. A sign pinned to the wire gate cautioned that protective equipment must be worn beyond the fence – earmuffs, hard hats, boots and vests. Joseph had his boots on, he'd bought them from a sale at Aldi. You really can't get better value for money, I told Jude he should get his shoes from there, but he doesn't listen. Anything I recommend he remainders by default. Won't listen to the Lord about his immortal soul, why should he listen to me about footwear? All these men should be buying their boots from Aldi. But why should I care if these fence-wreckers throw their money away? Joseph's good boots sank into the soft disturbance of the worksite soil, as he crossed into the yard beyond the fence. A large man whose paunch was pressing up against the gears and levers of his earthmover lurched to a stop when he caught sight of Joseph waltzing over the boundary. 'You right, mate?' the man bellowed out above the clamour of his own machine, wiping crud away from his eyes as he called to Joseph. Joseph replied by pointing to his mangled fence, the panels lying bent and twisted behind the earthmover. The large man had trouble twisting in his cabin to see over his shoulder at what the pointed finger was supposed to indicate. Keeping the digit levelled at his loss, Joseph marched across the uneven surface of the soil and sand, and the demarcation stakes with little red rags tied to their tops, and the rudimentary piping markers sticking out of the steaming earth, and the heaped mounds of broken terracotta pipes, and upturned roots, and unearthed rocks, and little pagan altars of broken bricks, and walking very close to his own ruined fence panels, he stepped directly up to the bent neck of the excavator's muddied bucket. The operator, whose black beard was a nest to a large family of tiny contaminants, instinctively took his earmuffs off at Joseph's approach, the latter calling out in answer to the former's now forgotten question, 'To tell you the truth mate, I was doing a lot better before you blokes knocked a bastard alleyway along my property line! You see that house there, the one with the immaculate lawn and the carefully manicured garden and the flowerbeds, which, although lacking ostentation, seem to be a simple source of pride for its owner? That happens to be my house, and my garden, where I've tried to live in peace and goodwill to all mankind for almost forty years, and this morning, as I woke to undergo my usual daily labours in hard-won retirement, I step upon my balcony to see you blokes have made a ruin of my domain.'

Seeing the encounter kicking off from a position on the far side of the site, another bulk of a man in an orange vest, with sweat and flecks of dirt lodged in the severe folds around his eyes, began stepping over the rubble with a careful familiarity, and hearing Joseph's lamentations over the machinations of the cement truck and the bobcat, waved his arms to grab the elderly man's attention and began devising a plan to assure him that all was well. 'Hey mate!' This large man, who turned out to be the site manager, called out. 'It's okay, mate! Don't worry about your fence! We're gonna have to replace all these fences anyway. All along this fence and that fence and then these ones here. We're gonna knock 'em all down as we go, and we'll fix them up before you know it. It's okay, mate!' To this Joseph replied, 'If it's all the same with you, and with all due respect, I think I will worry about it.' Joseph turned his full attention to this second man, adding, 'Again, with total appreciation for the task you blokes are required to undertake here, I don't think it's unreasonable to ask, that if you're going to knock a man's fences down, it's fair play to either offer a verbal warning in advance, if the action's intentional, or if it's done in error, to provide him with some timely words of reassurance that the injury isn't being done with total disregard for his life, liberty and pursuit of happiness. I'm seventy-three years old, I'm not young and fit like you blokes are, and a man my age has concerns, not only for his own safety and the safety of his loved ones, but for the safety of his property, too. You blokes might not be aware of this, but we tend, as we get older, to see things from a perspective different to that of a man your age, who's young and in his prime. We old farts don't have the luxury of throwing our hands up in the air when disaster strikes and hoping for a bumper crop come next spring, we can't shrug our shoulders and conclude that here's nothing to worry about in the short term. The short term is all we have left! At my age a man has lived long enough to know he has to sweat the small stuff, if you know what I mean. To give you some indication, consider that I don't want scrappers or carpetbaggers coming here in the middle of the night and getting curious about my garage long after you blokes have gone home and are sitting on your recliners watching the footy. An intruder on my property, by the time my security light comes on and I drag my old bent body out of bed, might well have kicked my garage door down and made off with half a lifetime's worth of tools and equipment and other odds and ends. This might sound like spilt milk to you, but for a man my age, on a pension don't forget, replacing a broken padlock puts me in an irreversible arrears, let alone a new lawnmower. My time of acquiring is long gone. I only have what's left to me, and so at my age every loss is eternal. Or consider how frail an old person is in their bodily dimensions, and say a stray dog comes onto my property at night, and takes up residence under the house while I'm sleeping, and the next morning my wife comes out to hang the washing on the line, none the wiser, and she gets mauled to death by the stray when she stumbles onto him in her slippers and dressing gown because she's too deep in her infirmity to defend herself from a vicious mutt, whose only crime, by the way, was doing what comes naturally when someone disturbs its slumber – because without the fence how was the dog to know it isn't welcome? Or maybe some kids coming round and sniffing about after school start peering in at the missus' clothes on the line, and thinking falsely that they belong to a younger woman, they find it funny to snatch her knickers off the Hills hoist and do a runner? Are you going to come out and accept a laundry list of unmentionables from a seventy-year-old woman, and take her shopping down at Merrylands to pick out underwear in her preferred colours and styles? I mean, for heaven's sake, there are things a man my age entrusts a fully functional fence to prevent, and so I think it's common courtesy that when you begin knocking down fences you apply some consideration in your imagination as to what others might be keeping in and blocking out.' The site manager, being thus harangued, assured Joseph they would plug up the fence every time they knocked it down with their usual unavoidable destruction, and Joseph went back around the corner with a certain straightness to his back, and a length in his stride, and he proudly announced to Marg that all would be well from here on out.

'I've heard that before,' she said to the warm water in the kitchen basin, scrubbing mugs and plates without turning to face her husband. A cloudless sky outside in the window above the sink set the golden crown of her hair about her like a halo and the blue dressing gown that was slung across her slight shoulders flowed down like a soft chasuble, wet at the cuffs with warm water spilling down her ruddy hands into the sleeves. Look at her glowing in this kitchen's liturgical light. That's how the old priests gave their sermons when I was a pup, Joseph thought, as he observed her disapproval in the minor round of her back, and he felt the depth of his disgust for those hypocrites in robes at mass not far from the surface of his instincts. They used to keep their backs to us, until it was time for the body and blood. What was it the priest said when my father was buried? After the funeral, while Bobby helped my mother down the stairs of St Johns where the abbey stone was slick with moss, I thought the church itself was crying ancient tears. That nauseating organ hummed adagios and I watched the Father come towards me over the slippery footpath, his alb's white edge stained grey from his crossing over the lawn to farewell the lady mourners, and the purple cincture was swinging from his shoulder like an elephant's bollocks, and his bony fingers caught together like a snare upon some invisible orb. 'We've missed your family's presence at mass on Sundays of late, Master Joseph. I believe you have something for me,' the old buggerer said, eyeing the envelope in my hands. Is that all the finesse in you, Father, for one of your own dear flock? The butcher's hands have known more finesse in slaughter. What did I say to him? 'My father's lying in a box under the earth, you've only just flung the mud down on his corpse, and all you've got to say to me is "Where's the money"? You old ghoul, here is what I have for you, and with these pieces of silver I free myself from your hypocrisy.' You should have seen the look on his buttery face, with its bucolic jowls aquiver. 'Behold, Father, the chapel is erect with gold, that it might please thee to squat upon it.' How little reply he had for me, and my tardy cousin, Liam Watts who, overhearing all, took me quickly away from that hallowed ground.

There was a storm that sent the shutters reeling the same night, and the wind was haunted with howls. Or was that the following week? Hard to remember. I was already a man by any measure, worked hard hours with my father down at the lumberyard helping splice the wires and holding the nails for his sledgehammers to blast down upon. He was the midnight watchman, too, patrolling with a torch whose slim light was not much fit but for disturbing feral cats under the wood piles, mousing for rats in the dusty air of the yard, and the black crabs come in from the bay scattering at our boots, little alien saucers pantomiming with pincers in the dark. The lumber boss told Dad to wear a gun, so he bought a cap shooter from a two-bob shop and kept it in his belt. Wouldn't carry the real thing, swore off the use of them on his fellow man. Asked me to shoot a bird once, though, a little wren, bobbing on the branch of a poplar tree, rocking the leaves with its tail feather against clear blue light behind, tiny eyes like black beads. I can still see the dotty speckles of its under-feathers, its needle beak angled to the sky. I raised the muzzle up, you know I don't remember the feel of the gun, and fired, the pellet passed by his breast into clean air, an echo, and I missed. 'I know what you're doing,' Dad said. 'I told you to shoot him.' My cheeks were hot when I aimed again. Why didn't he move? Didn't he hear the ringing echoes? The beginning of tears coming on. 'I won't do it,' I said. He who harms the...shall never pass the...I forget the words. William Blake, the nuns would make us read him at our desks, the waxy smell of glue on the old reference books. That barking storm after the wake, or the next week, whenever it was, that was when that cur, Billy Robertson, he came round to the house and made a nuisance of himself. Could smell the metho on him through the window, like pissy sour wine. And there was a stink like ash from his damp dirty clothes, soaked by the black rain that smothered his face in greasy long slicks of hair. My mother was crying and cowering away from his silhouette as he beat on the door, speaking garbled through the keyhole. 'Only to quickly have a word with yeh,' he was saying, his nose pressed up against the misted glass. 'Out of here, Robertson!' she commanded him, no coward soul was hers, but more of his butchered face shoved against the glass and his thick pissy breath in the room. That was it, the death of youth.

Marg slipped a sudsy white plate into the dishrack mounts without turning back to observe her husband, who had stood watching her domestic liturgy by the window light as these stray scattered thoughts had pressed about him. 'I'm going out,' he said, and made to march off without turning back to see how his wife would react to this sudden heresy of her husband's. Gathering his keys and cards, and some thirty dollars from the dresser by the bed, Joseph closed the heavy front door behind him and stepped out into the bright street, feeling strangely free and guilty as he headed up to Woodville with no certain purpose in his mind but a throbbing flush of anger in his cheeks. There were piles of jacaranda leaves turning black in the driveway, and the paperbark tree outside the neighbour's place was growing into the powerlines with its bare prongs. Joseph's neighbour Geo, whose yard was jammed with the cars it was his business to detail, looked up from a green station wagon with a rag in his hand and waved a large hand vigorously. 'Hello, Joey!' the man called out, and received the same greeting in return. A good man, hard-working neighbours, here. Can't beat them, good children flow from good stock. A large leather-clad man on a white Harley Davidson roared passed Joseph on the street and the old man came close to covering his ears at its intensity. Jesus wept! Should be made legal to hurl bricks at them as they go by, in the name of auditory self-preservation. Grown men so desperate for attention, bad as young girls at a discotheque. Now look at this place, he thought as he passed another housing commission joint that had not changed a dot in fifty years. The old duck that lives there, I forget his name, haven't seen him wandering round like he used to do. Before his wife died, she went round with him, on the frame. Could both be gone for all I know. Yard needs work, all overgrown thistles and dandelions. Sad paradox, that this ruin of a place sits side by side with Michelangelo's masterpiece. There he is, bent down at his hedge, little garden gnome fellow. What was it I was supposed to tell him? Ah, will you look at what he's done with this old joint, born green-thumb sorcerer!

'Michelangelo!' Joseph called out over the hedge, and a small man, curled up like the shell of a snail under the shrub with a pair of barber's scissors in his hand, looked up blinking into the light, holding a trembling glove across his pale eyes to observe the shadowy figure addressing him. 'Oh, Joe. Hello, my friend,' he said, breathless. A cluster of bright mauve daisies were arrayed at Joseph's feet, like a coloured collar round the hedge which served as a fence for Michelangelo's frontage. The faint blue flowers bobbed against the boots he'd put on to intrude on the building site, now caked in grey mud. Behind Michelangelo, who was slowly rising to his full bent height, was a grevillea tree in red flower, and Joseph's admiring eyes gazed upon the fiery combs of the bright display with such intensity it might have been the portrait of a long-lost friend. 'Michelangelo! How you manage to make this yard so resplendent is one of the great mysteries of the modern world. A thing of beauty is a joy forever, and if your lilly pilly, your pandorea, your pigface, if they were ever to wilt, I'd know all eternity was on the verge of surrender. Believe me, I'm no slouch in the mechanics of gardening myself, but what you've managed here shows such brilliance that a lesser man is reduced to awe. You should be on television, my friend. That's no joke, either! What you've done here in this small square of nurtured space should be studied for years to come by botanists and scholars alike, and beamed, in the meantime, directly into homes around the world. Believe me – ask my wife when you see her, and she'll tell you – I've always said, when the yearend comes around and the powers-that-be tell us all to huddle at our television screens and marvel at the Harbour fireworks display, I turn to her, and I ask, "Why?" I ask her, what is any given fireworks display but an instantaneous act of spectacle gone up in smoke and out of mind? Sound and fury that signifies nothing to the average punter on the street. Imagine an alternative world, Michelangelo, where we ring in the New Year with displays of wattle and tea-tree, or rock orchids and desert pea. It may sound ridiculous at first, but is it so foolish?' Joseph turned away from Michelangelo and looked about him for some tall trees above the rooftops to illustrate his cause, and seeing none, pointed down with both hands at the small mauve flowers bobbing by his feet. 'Take a moment to study the intricacies of a fine flower's countenance, or the organic complexities of a flowering tree's reaching branches, and tell me if that's not a subject fitter for inspiration and awe than popping powder and illusion. What is a tree but organic eruptions of colour and form in arrangements of perfect aesthetic complexity determined by a million years of propagation? An immutable portrait of bounded beauty that apprehends the very substance of life in subtle motions imperceptible to man? If this land were truly civilised, as is so often claimed, then we should celebrate the statesman-like steadiness embarked upon by living breathing organisms which manage to be both under the earth with ribbons of sturdy roots and simultaneously reaching for the sky like an emergent and unsinkable Icarus. Then as if to enhance the generous expression of their casual maestri with one final aplomb, they bless us with their shade for seasons without end, and hang hives of honey from their boughs, and call the owl to perch on their levers to scatter rodents and snakes from our doorways and hearths. All that is consubstantial in every tree that ever lived, though we curse their roots when they trip us up and lay them low by the billions for our factories and furnaces. Why did the druids of old draw faces in the trees? Only so they might speak to us and grant us the secrets of their subtleties. It is to them that we should kneel and praise, come the end of the year. Instead, what do we do? We gather in the darkness to gasp at a battery of banging candles, the choking crowds covered in stinking soot and ash, shoulder-to-shoulder for destruction's pretty, sparkling party tricks. That's the folly of man, Michelangelo, but we might yet make ourselves whole again, if we only turn to what grows in solid air beside us, in the fiery flowers of a neighbour's humble garden.'

Michelangelo, who had been nodding earnestly throughout this discourse, coughed and swallowed a large disturbance – a bug had flown into his mouth. 'Did you eat those oranges we gave you?' Joe asked, and Michelangelo nodded more vigorously at this change of subject, coughing a little more. 'And were they to your satisfaction?' Yes, the older man said, and he thanked Joseph profusely, tugging at the gardening gloves on his fingers as he did so. 'Those were Marg's oranges,' Joseph stated very slowly, as if the man were not following. 'And if they aren't the sweetest, juiciest oranges known to man, I'll give the ghost up.' Michelangelo continued to nod in a steady flow of agreement. 'Very good fruit,' he agreed, with another quiet cough. 'Next week,' Joseph remembered to add. 'I'll have some of *my* oranges to give you. Not as sweet as my wife's. Tart, but that's more akin to my taste. In general, sweetness isn't my particular forte. I prefer a powerful taste. Give me something with a passion, I say! Something that'll supply a reason to get out of bed in the morning and cry "Come to pappa!" I promise you, Michelangelo, you try my oranges, no citrus on earth will ever compare. Like a satyr to Hyperion, as the saying goes.' 'Yes,' Michelangelo nodded more, smiling as best as he could, and he raised a finger, now out of its glove, to signal a momentary break in conversation, then he shuffled off towards a shady spot by the driveway. What's he doing over there? Joseph wondered as he watched the older man bend down behind a yellow bottlebrush. When he rose again, there was a small potted plant with white and purple flowers in his hands. 'What have you got there?' Joseph called out. Michelangelo shuffled back with the pot in both hands and made such motions as to indicate it was for Joseph to take. 'You give to your wife,'

Michelangelo added. 'Yesterday, today, and tomorrow,' Joseph identified the plant correctly, as the older man nodded once again. 'You're giving this to me?' Joseph asked in stunned surprise. Michelangelo reassured him with a furious nodding. 'You beauty!' Joseph declared, laughing out loud and showing the plant around as though there was some unseen audience observing this gifting. 'In that case, I'll have to bring you twice as many bloody oranges!' The two men smiled and blessed each other for a while, passing on expressions of love to their extended families, though they'd never met them, then began a series of farewell waves, during which Michelangelo made the labour of putting his trembling fingers back into his gloves, and then slowly curled back down behind the hedge, returning to the weeds.

With his small potted plant beneath his arm, Joseph continued along Woodville Road where next he spied an old fibro house on the street ahead that had lost at least a dozen terracotta tiles in its passing age, and a rusted Santa Claus weathervane leaned up against the brick chimney. The faint curtains of the house were drawn, and Mrs Cotter, a once buoyant presence in a floral summer dress who tended to red and purple petunias growing in the hanging pots above a picturesque lawn, now bereft of colour but for weeds and grasses, looked out with increasingly vacant white eyes from the gloom of her easy chair, her face so close to the window that her respirator mask's tubing pressed against the glass. There she sits, paralysed force, gesture without motion. Her eyes, you dare not meet in dreams. The nativity-like sight of this unfortunate wretch pushing at her window revealed a secret to Joseph – while he honestly believed he had left the house with no intention or direction in mind, he recognised now that he had formulated an unconscious plan to wander up the street to Ling's supermarket and purchase a pack of cigarettes. The sly stratagem of his sub-awareness, he saw, included even a sprinkling of theatre – he would have wandered into Ling's convenience store whistling a tune to emphasise his innocence, distracted all the while with internal monologues of no particular significance, observed the various detergents, fruits, tin cans, and frozen pies contained in the multitudes of Ling's store, and making a show of finding nothing of particular interest, he would have whispered to himself, 'Well, I've come all this way and nothing takes my fancy, why not buy one small pack of smokes since I'm here? Haven't I been good? Haven't smoked at all for weeks. Think how much more robust my lungs and air sacs and blood vessels must be for all that steely abstinence! Strong enough surely, to withstand one small return to the purchase and consumption of two or three last smokes. What harm would be done after fifty years of fags without number? It's true that every grain of sand is numbered, but surely even heaven above forgives a lowly cigarette to a man deep in contrition. Jesus drank with the sinners, so he may well have been a smoker, too. What were the pubs of the Nazarene in the Aramaic days? Am I too good for one whose father laid the foundations of the earth?' At least now, Joseph thought, aware of his own deceptive devices, there would be less hypocrisy in the act – and since the thought itself was sin it hardly increased the crime to go ahead and carry the action out. If Marg made a fuss when he returned with smoke on his breath, he could say, 'Well you turned your back to me, and I've been good and healthy, and isn't it true that he who clings to the world of flesh hath no love of the Lord in his heart?' No, no – not that. Does no good sermonising to a woman who's conscious of the preacher's sins. Once they've seen a man naked they will not fear his gospels. Something about the sight of testicles makes a man ridiculous in their eyes. Still, doesn't sit well with me to have to hand the money over to Ling. Joseph had been victim to her tapping on the sign with her long fake nail as she announced 'Sorry, no credit Joseph. No credit.' He'd argued with her despite knowing it was futile and he pointed out the loyal custom he'd provided to her store for the last fifteen years, going back to the time when her husband had run the place. Mention of her ex, who'd flown the coop and burdened Ling with the shop, was a rhetorical blunder and only redoubled her resolve. She crossed her arms at this line of argument and, with a mild smile, explained to Joseph that he could easily walk back home and come back with the coin he claimed to have left on the counter within five minutes if his needs were truly as dramatic as he claimed. 'You live just up the street! Just turn home and come back, no worries.' Times had changed. He surrendered. A pack of Benson and Hedges 20s, or Holidays, would suffice for that first inhalation of balmy toxins and the smell of the gingery dry leaf burning in the stinging puffs of ivory air. The sweet disappointment he longed to experience, the livid anticipation coursing along his thrumming nerves, squeezing moist mandalas of sweat from the glands under his pits for that first flashing spark of lighter wheel leaping into the air. I'll have to buy one of those too. Or borrow one from the army of the damned who sit al fresco outside the Viet café in their footy shorts and thongs, their tattooed arms flapping as they extol the sage wisdom of yesteryears and blow their cavernous noses into tartan handkerchiefs while old dogs lie flat on the concrete with their leashes wound round the legs of the chairs beneath their masters.

Good old folk they were, if on the rugged side of the retired heap. They could spark him up for the cost of a few sincere questions about the missus and the good old days.

Woodville shops came into view just as Joseph walked by old Charlie May's house. A gentle natured chap was Charlie. Used to catch the same bus and train some mornings. An accountant in the city, he was always impeccably dressed, kept quietly to himself, but knew a joke when he heard one, and could return them on occasion. A baldy, he must have lost the hair at an early age, always scratching the dry spots on his head. Sat behind him once, in the morning, his little pale finger was digging around on the scalp like a mole snuffling for truffles, little flakes of skin all over the back of his collar by the time we got off at the station. His wife was always immaculate too, had that saintly quality of quiet women of certain age. Can imagine the two of them sitting of a Sunday afternoon reading different sections of the *Herald* on opposite sides of the sunroom while the cricket plays on the wireless, turning the pages gently with an occasional sigh and a glance at one another to ask about a cup of tea. Didn't know him to drink. Never invited them round. Must leave a Christmas card in their letterbox this year. Said the same thing last year but never did! How much a man forgets! Joseph couldn't help but roll out a similar train of associations and flashes of motley memories about old Charlie whenever he passed his house, not least because although the blue plasterboard walls and tricolour tiles of the place were of the ordinary postwar style, the yard around the house was something quite eccentric. Charlie's sweet wife – what was her name? Kathy, Karen, Katie, Vera, Venice? Sue. Her name was Sue, and she had made of that yard a miniature theme park. Whirling tin-metal windmills no larger than teapots, and semicircles of garden gnomes dressed in various painted overalls stood posing in groves, some carrying mushrooms or pickaxes under their beards, and there were statuettes of kittens too, with their tails upturned, and little boys in fishing hats sitting on hollow logs beside their faithful dogs, and ceramic ladybirds with smiling faces, and happy monkeys sitting with brown paws over their eyes, mouths, and ears. An old farmer was leaning on his shovel by the roots of a fir tree, a spotted dragon was being ridden by a boxing red kangaroo, and mighty Atlas held up a bubbling birdbath in the centre of the yard, his bare limbs mossy black. A loom of minute symbols stitching together the ends of the earth in all its ages, Joseph marvelled. Too risky for me, draws too much attention. Surprised nobody steals these things, or kids of an evening smash them up with a hammer and cricket bats and toss them through the window. Not my style. But then they seem to have made a 'go of it'. No harm seems to have come about. And who are they, Charlie and Sue? Two quiet, careful, elderly folk who have no children and live alone and keep to themselves but for the consolations of lawn ornamentation.

Not a moment after coming to his conclusions about the significance of the garden arrangements, Joseph spied the Sue in question, staggering down the street from the shops and coming towards him, struggling with the weight of a plastic bag she had grasped in both her bony hands. Seeing the lacquered look in her eyes and the pink flush of her face, Joseph abandoned his potted plant upon the footpath, marched towards the old woman with all his ancient vigour, declaring as he waved hello, 'Fancy meeting you here! I stop to admire the handiwork and lo and behold, the decorator herself appears in apparent distress!' The old woman's thin, wrinkled mouth let out a trembling exhalation then smiled, showing her delicate dentures and she announced a wavering 'Oh.' Sue required the last remnants of her strength to offload the plastic bag into Joseph's hands. 'Good Lord,' he exclaimed loudly on receiving the trade. 'This thing weighs a tonne! What have you got in here, Sue?' It turned out to be a litre of milk, some mixed birdseed, and five hundred grams of raw sugar. 'Old dotty bitch! I left without my trolley thinking, oh, I'm only going up to get the milk, and when I got there, I remembered the seed and sugar and thought, oh, it's only a little walk I can make it, but I think if you hadn't come along, I would have expired on the street.' She gave a breathless sort of laugh, rubbing her hands along her sides to shake the tingling numbness from her crooked fingers. 'Well, that would have been a terrible shame for me, as I'd have been the first responder to your poor body waylaid in the street. I don't want to be the one to have to break it to old Charlie that his bachelorhood days have been thrust back upon him. Not at his advanced age.' Sue lifted her crooked fingers up to her eyes as if blocking out a painful glare. 'Oh Charles!' she whimpered, her jaw springing up and down in her soft face as if it were tethered to some unseen spring, and without further ceremony, two slow tears leaked down her trembling face. She chased them with shaking fingers.

'My word, the poor mite hasn't passed away on us?' Now you've put your foot there, Joseph! 'What,' she mocked, fingering the wetness in her eyes. 'No, Joseph. The poor sod should be so lucky.' Joseph gathered her together as best he could and directed the old woman towards her own home, saying, 'Let's get you inside, unpack these things, and you can tell me what's become of Charlesworth.'

Inside the house was as Joseph imagined. A lounge room

dedicated to the television, some lapis statuettes of ballerinas and an albino tiger watching the room from beneath blinds closed to keep the afternoon heat from accumulating. There were pictures of Sue and Charles over a liquor chest in the hallway. Not much younger, must have been the last ten years, Joseph thought. She wasn't smiling in the largest photograph, their faces somewhat blurred by their closeness to the camera, but it was evident that grief had aged her terribly since. She hurried the milk into the fridge, made mention of tea over her shoulder and insisted that Joseph sit at the dining table while she put things in their proper place. Joseph continued a private inspection of the place, ending in a slight sunroom replete with paintings of sunsets over the sea which led to the back door, shut up with two padlocked bolts set to keep the outside where it belonged. These locks Sue opened with a key in her unsteady fingers, and the light passage of cool breeze rolled into the stuffy chambers of the house. The old woman seemed able to breathe easily at last. 'Now sit down,' Sue commanded, 'and I'll make some tea.'

Joseph wiped the edges of a dining chair with the palm of his hand and eased himself into it. Uncomfortably hard, not good for a long stay. Can feel where my coccyx broke pressing into the wood. That weekend at Sparrow's place, slipped on the pool deck and cracked myself in two. Still aches to sit. Sixteen years of sitting on a broken tail. Still, no need to be a martyr. Before any tea was set in motion, Sue placed a Tupperware container of assorted biscuits on the table and asked Joseph to pry the lid off for her. 'This would be a job for Charlie, back before his turn. Which is not the right word for it, to be honest with you. The state he's in, I don't fairly know what to call it but it's somewhere south of being deceased, in my way of thinking. Oh, when I see him now, all trapped inside himself, and I sit by the bed listening to him breathing, and that isn't the worst of it, mind you, but the way he breathes now, his mouth is hanging open all the time. For a while they put a little hose inside it, but they've taken it out. Have a biscuit, those are my favourite. Monte Carlos they are. Can't eat them now, though – break the teeth.' Sue began to shudder, her eyes rapidly moistening, and she dabbed at her face and buried her chin into the soft curtains of her neck. Joseph offered to fetch a tissue but she waved him be and the spell seemed to pass in an instant. 'Not right to see him now,' she said. 'And he's thinner than he has a right to be, never having had any weight to lose. Ate like a minnow all his life. And they put him on a bed beside a woman who's always moaning, and she curses, awful sounding thing, and you have no idea the smell in the halls as soon as you walk in, it hits you ungodly rotten. And there I am, I sit by his bed. Used to read to him, but now I stay a while, till the nurses come and do God-knows-what to keep him hanging in, and I sit there thinking how much better it would be if God would take him up. If God would tell me, take the pillow and put it over his mouth and press it there, well, not that I have the strength, you'd need some weight to press it on. He'd be better off, and as to who can speak on that subject, well, I knew him since he was seventeen, so tell me what's that worth? Better than most I'd say. Hardly a soul in this world could know a man better than a wife of sixty years, I'll wager. Could pick out the sound of his bowels digesting in a line up, if they'd like to test me on it. Like watching someone you love turned into a piece of furniture, for strangers to sit on. I want to say, well yes, you may well be a carpenter, but don't you tell me what's what, because I've been sitting on this man for sixty years and I know he doesn't like where you've put him, even if he can't speak it himself.'

'It isn't easy looking after them,' Joe agreed. 'And believe me, I know how you feel. I nursed my mother at her end, and I was a young man. Let me tell you, hard as it is to be old, and I know all about it, being young doesn't help to ease the pain of losing a loved one in slow decline. Loss and grief are as immune to the charms of youth as they are to the dignity of our late stage. Still, I managed to discharge my duties as my mother's keeper, best I could. We nursed her on the couch of our house at Leichhardt. My brother Bobby and I lived together there, but he's another story, that brother of mine.'

'What was your mother like?' Sue asked, still dabbing slightly at her eyes.

'She was loved by all, and she had love for all,' Joseph began without hesitation. 'Was known as a woman whose heart and soul could outshine the light of heaven, though she didn't suffer fools and wasn't slow to part a dolt from his misconceptions if he rehearsed them in her presence. Married late for the time, now that I consider it, and she had only two boys, myself and my brother Bobby,' Joseph shook his head at mention of his brother and then continued. 'She was a gentlewoman, wise, and intelligent, and sophisticated, especially for the time when women could be condemned for their inner resources. A beautiful woman, dignified, and dignifying, in equal measure. And even as I say these things about her, it occurs to me I'm speaking abstractly of her to you. There's a reason for that, I think. You ask me what she was like, and it seems as though you're asking me to talk about the greenest valleys of my childhood, and when I try to think on them again, away from strict routines and roads I know by rote, and try to give an account of the woman that she really was, it is like describing old forests I crossed in my earliest days, holding her hand, and the smell of dew on reeds and golden dawns over hillsides ringing in birdsong and distant wood smoke from unseen cottages comforting in air over shining fields. I can hardly pay my mother more mind as a woman than to say that where her absence sits inside me it is the blackest emptiness on my soul, and to look there again after all these years is as sharp a memory to hold as ice is cold to touch.' Joseph replied with all this, his eyes drifting as he spoke, to fall upon a painting that was hanging on a wall of the kitchen, portraying a herd of brumbies fleeing through a dense woodland weighted with deep snow, and a jackaroo with a lasso high above his head, urging his dray in hot pursuit behind the horses as a cascade of light shone through frosted gum trees. The interplay of light is the genuine subject, Joseph considered. If you look closely at the figures of the horses and their riders, or the distant cows and the leaves in the branches, they are paid scant attention. The figures don't even wear faces, the finer details don't seem to matter.

'You must be an educated man, Joseph. You're too smart for a place like this, that's for certain. You're all full up with words, like a piñata. Charlie was always good at Scrabble, and all the games we played, but he didn't like anyone to know how smart he was. Should have seen him answer the questions when we watched the quiz shows of an evening. You're more like my brother, he's got the golden goose in his mouth, doesn't stop with all his quotations and things. He's the prodigal son. Went to the university in Melbourne, became a doctor. Talk, talk, talks till you can't remember where he started. Like listening to a conversation in a crowded room, even when it's just you and him. Now his children are all transexuals, or some nonsense. I'm not saying one thing leads to another, but they say there's a fine line between brilliance and misery. I should be happy as Larry, then, silly old cow I am!'

'Not at all,' Joseph frowned intently. 'That's another one of those tools of modern propaganda they club people like us in the gob with – the volubility of a man and the quality of his thoughts are ships in the proverbial night. We might say speech is a form of thought, but what comes out of the mouth is only the fluttering shade of the infinite internal thing that has its range and scope outside conscious introspection. Though I can speak with as much deliberate cogitation of our mutual language as the next man, I can confide that I never even finished my Leaving Certificate. I put no stock in formal education. Generations of youngsters dulled and processed in schools like numbered cattle, no better treated than mindless beasts led into grey slaughterhouses of the spirit. And yet, lucky us – back when we were knee-high to the echidna, the schools still managed to fill our heads with facts and figures. For instance, I can tell you that it was Romulus and Remus who founded Rome on the Palatine Hill, and that it was Romulus who slew Remus, and he gathered unto him hordes of exiled and unwanted Barbarians so that they might multiply at the Sabine women's expense, taking them forcefully in their hundreds, as depicted in art works hung in the great galleries of cities that are the jewels of the civilisation founded by those very rapists and murders. The machinery of systemic mental dismantlement was not yet at total efficiency when we were kids, and so you and I were able to know a few useless things of that nature, with which we can at least frame a picture of history.'

Throughout this analysis, Sue had been fiddling with one of the Monte Carlos, and hearing a break in the flood of his account she remembered the tea, at last. 'I'll just get you that cuppa,' she said with a delighted smile.

Sue retrieved cups and saucers from a low cabinet, and tea from a tin box above her head as the kettle trembled and steamed. 'You're so clever, Joseph. I love those quotations of yours, they make you sound like a learned man if ever there was one in this house. And to think you didn't even finish your Leaving Certificate! Oh, imagine what you might have done with that brain of yours if you'd gone into university and studied like my brother did. For all the good it did him. You'd probably have been a doctor yourself, or some Queen's Counsellor with a powdered wig, changing the law and protecting the innocent. And why was it you left school so young? Of course, boys did that all the time, and girls, too, but for different reasons, naturally. Did they need you working at home?'

The kettle's bubbling was growing louder, and it was difficult to hear the old woman as the steam began to swirl up into the air around her. 'My father,' Joseph said, 'who was the hardest working man in Glebe, who worked three jobs to keep us fed and sheltered, succumbed to a lifelong weakness and died of a heart attack, leaving me, the eldest son, to assume the responsibilities necessary to keep the family solvent. My father came from the country, and people from the country of his generation knew no limit to exertion other than the one six feet below the soil. He worked the lumberyards in Glebe, splicing the wires with his bare hands and the frequent use of a tempered hammer. He'd take me sometimes, to work on the logs that were always floating on the bay's calm waters and I'd break out in a cold sweat leaping from one log to the other in early morning light, thinking that if I should lose my footing and go down between the logs they'd close up and crush my ribs, or else trap me down deep in the waters of Blackwattle Bay, scuttling under with a lungful of air, searching for the shimmer of daylight between the flotillas of pines spread out over the waters, which at the time were rank and rich with the slurry of butchery from the slaughterhouse on one of the islands. That rotten meatworks was forever spewing pig's blood into the black bay around it and you could smell the rendering fat for miles. And when he finished his shift, we stopped at the tucker shop with the other men and he always had a cold meat pie, and then we'd set out with lines and hooks and snatch the crabs from under the rocks of the bay, as big as your arms, with great fat pincers gleaming red and barnacled that could take the nose off your face if you weren't alert. Though the sun was setting and we'd been up at dawn, we'd haul them in sacks back to the house as soiled and stained as if we had crawled up from the mud of the bay ourselves. We lived in a mansion, like all the working families did then in Glebe – great big colonial mansions – filled with other families all clumped together, trying to make ends meet, and everybody knew every dog and cat in town, let alone one another's business. When I walked down the street with my father, everyone from the Lord Mayor to the local cutthroats and bootleggers and winos in town would nod their head and say, "G'day Tommy." His muscle, nerves, and sinew were as strong and tough as the wires we used to splice. He'd make me hold the nails when he brought the sledgehammer down to strike those great splints. Could have crushed all twenty-two bones in my hand flat as Peck's Paste with a single swipe. But he never did, and I never flinched. In my waters, without a shadow of a doubt, I knew that his aim would be true, because that was the nature of men in those days.'

''Course, yes,' Sue agreed, pouring boiling water into teacups. 'So many things have changed since then, you wouldn't know it was the same world except we're still ourselves and we're still in it. Least, I think I am. It's hard to prove it, the more I look into the mirror, the less sure I get. Old photographs hurt to look at now. Can't say it gives me much consolation to stick through to the ending of the days, and when I see what it got Charlie for his pains, well, that's that, and I'll say nothing more except it's even little things that are in smithereens now. When you see the way the nurses keep him, and the way they talk to you. I can understand with him, he doesn't speak back, so there's no point in niceties and the like, but then they give me that same rough treatment, and they don't bother keeping track of his clothes! I take them down once a month, with his name writ in the collar, and they disappear, and what's a man who doesn't move except to breathe losing his shirts and pants for? Tell me how that happens. You'd think they were stealing them for pennies, but you wouldn't get even that for Charlie's clothes. I've still got his shoes packed up inside his cupboard there in the bedroom. No more need for them, I suppose. Still, it takes a bit to toss them out. But listen to me batter on! It's all coming out now, isn't it? But it's bound to happen, an old fossil who has nothing much to speak about can't stop herself. Give me attention and this is what you get. Heaven help me if I haven't forgot my decency! Let me bring this cuppa to you, Joseph. It's the least I can do.'

'As for complaining about the way things are,' Joseph said, helping the trembling teacup to the table without a spill, 'what other pleasure have us old goats got left?'

'Oh,' she said, taking her own cup away from her lips before she'd even had a chance to sip from it. 'And let me ask you, since you know a thing – what's the point? What's it all for? After the denim stitches and the shopping trolleys? I don't know, and I don't believe it when I hear otherwise said on the matter.'

Joseph looked at Sue with his deep, keen eyes. 'Old age might be a haunted house by my account, but don't we all keep our house as best we can? Old Michelangelo, down the road, is that why he keeps his garden neat and radiant? Is that why he waters the flowers? And you, you set the gnomes and windmills you keep assembled and presentable in the yard, what do you work on them for? We might think it a curse to go on in the face of ordinary calamities, confined by a prison of skin and overworn tendons. We can make all kinds of excuses for our continuation, but in the end we are no different from the movement of the spheres around us, and the consistency of the silent heavens, and the trees whose branches take shape in their intuitions, or the fish that leap in the flowered streams, and the little concessions of pollen breaking into faint air when bees stir the multifoliate form of a flower's painted face. We are the same awkward agents of the humble hour, and we do our best. And I think that's what heaven is: heaven is when God gives you a task you can accomplish, no matter how insignificant the duty might be.'

''Course, yes,' she said to this. 'Though Charles and I never put much stock in the Church. We never wanted much fuss for us when we die, either. No funeral, no fuss. It's all the same to me, he would say. Save the money. Put it all to fitter use than messing about with a plot. Not for my sake to invite our few remaining friends, have them all limping around on the uneven grass worried about their hips. No good comes from that. Damn them for keeping him alive.'

Tears welled up again in the old woman's eyes, and Joseph saw her reaching for what he thought was a tissue from a container on the bench, but when she pulled it out he saw she was rubbing her face carefully and softly with a wet wipe that left the skin around her eyes and cheeks a ruddy colour. Then she tossed it into a basket half-filled with more of the same. 'I cry so much,' she said, seeing Joseph's eye on the wipes. 'All the tissues are too harsh on the face, after a while, they dry out the skin. These things, the wipes, they help keep me comfortable while I'm busy crying myself to a miserable death. Oh, Joseph, if you'll allow me one more dose of self-pity, let me say there's nothing left in living, not one thing, not taste or touch or joy or happiness, not even the fear of pain and preliminaries of dying. Just one endless evening-time sitting in my armchair by the television light. A silly parade it is for me now. Goes by the window, like a circus, and under those conditions you'd think, what's the use of crying. And yet it happens on the quiet evenings, in the mornings, afternoons. While I sit here every second thought seems to bring out a little water. I don't know where they are inside me. Must be a well somewhere inside. This basket gets filled up, emptied, fills again, and one thing seems like another.'

Sue had pointed towards the lounge room to indicate some unseen television set, and Joseph happened to turn about, and it was then that he saw, on the wall behind him, a framed print of Elvis, on stage with a microphone stand at an angle in his hand, his white suit ablaze in the glare of stage-lights. The King's signature was printed on a golden plate beneath the image. Fake, of course. Joseph had seen the posters sold at the markets in Merrylands. And yet, casting his eyes upon that image hanging on the wall, he felt a sudden spirit rise inside him.

'You never told me you were an Elvis fan,' he said as though this had been a terrible dereliction on her part. 'Yes,' she admitted, adding how silly she was to have talked their tea cold. 'I'll get some more hot water,' she said, and slowly made her way to the kitchen sink and set the kettle on again. 'I had all his albums,' she called out over the rapid return of the kettle's bubbling. 'Charlie bought me the picture for Christmas, one year, I don't remember. He was never a fan, but I owned all his records and back when we had a record player, I'd play them every Saturday morning while I vacuumed up and did the ironing. He was my first love. So handsome.'

'You know,' Joseph called out over the boiling kettle, 'I was one of the last of his supporters. I remember, 1968, I was young, still in my twenties with a full head of hair, and me and Mike Sorensen and Toady Wilson, and a few other blokes came round after knock-off for a few drinks at my place. It just so happened that on the television that night, there was to be broadcast a show called the *Elvis Comeback Special*. I made everyone follow me into the lounge room when it started and said, "Now you blokes check this concert out." And to a man they groaned and grumbled and rolled their eyes and said "Elvis Presley! What are you, some sort of retrograde?" They spat when they spoke his name, 'cause in those days, as you know, the popular thing was going down to a nightclub with your winged collars and your flares to pick-up young women under the disco balls. Elvis, by contrast, was a fat, washed-up relic, and I said, "I'll tell you what, I'll make you blokes a bet. If what we witness tonight, when that man comes out on stage, if it doesn't impress you, if you're not blown out of your chair by what the man does on the screen tonight, then I'll strip naked and run back and forth on Leichhardt Road until they put me in a padded cell."

They laughed, shook their heads at me, said I was a madman, and that was fine with me, because I can still see him, much like he looks in that portrait of yours. He came out in a bright white suit with nothing but a void black at his back, and he walked out and looked at us from the emptiness of the stage, into the camera, and gathering up all the tenderness residing in his spiritual heart, and with a grace given to him by his creator, Elvis began to sing, and he bent down so that his voice had to will his body to straighten up, and when he did rise there was a power you could feel in the depth of its timbre, from the deep darkness of universal despair his voice reached out like a dancing ember's glow, and before our very eyes the light began to increase, so that he seemed to cast out that dark star that resides in every heart like a saint might draw demons from a tortured body, and as he sang, sweating and shuffling on the stage, rocking and wracked like a man whose ghost is trying to overcome some enmity, every eye in the room was transfixed on the act, and every ear in the room was filled with his power, and across the world, in every home, on every television, the same mystical conversion was underway, and he sang like a preacher whose sermon was the promise that out there in the vast darkness, there was an eternal candlelight, one fine filament of sustaining tenderness, as real and indivisible from all mankind as the spheres in the heavens.' And Joseph looked up with an eerie longing into the flat portrait of Elvis on the wall behind, and he stood up, taking on the bearing of the King, and then, loudly, and with a quavering voice unaccustomed to the act, which pressed painfully against the tight scar over his heart, he began to sing, 'And while I can think, while I can talk, while I can stand, while I can walk, while I can dream, oh please, let my dream come true, *right now!*'

Joseph bellowed the final words so that even the neighbours might hear them, and turned to Sue, who was standing very still as the kettle filled the room around her with its steaming vapours. 'And as the music rose around him,' Joseph continued rapidly, 'and his brow was dripping with sweat, he belted out one last refrain of the chorus, and he thanked us, the invisible audience, an exaltation across his smooth brow, clear as the crystals in a lit chandelier, and he marched off stage into a commercial break. Stunned silence was in the room with us. You could see the hairs standing on every man in the house. Tough, hardworking men, uncouth and without pity, brutish men, you might say, men not much more refined than beasts, and there they stood, transmuted into their higher parts, and you could feel the spirit radiating off them, hovering around us in all its infinite potential, and one by one, they turned to me, and the light we all shared for that unforgettable moment was like a fire in our eyes!'

No sooner had Joseph finished making these remarks than another thought took hold of him. What am I doing here, and taking so long? What am I talking about? he asked himself. Marg will be beginning to worry, and all for this poor woman struggling with the groceries. Sue seemed strangely bewildered by something Joseph had said, though she still managed to offer Joseph hot water for the tea that had run cold. 'No, thank you,' he said, repeatedly. 'Charity must begin at home, and I've got to see to my own needs.' Forgetting completely his plans to purchase cigarettes from Ling's, Joseph blessed Sue, invited her to visit them soon, thanked her for the tea he didn't drink, though she again attempted to insist on him staying for it, and walked out of the house, past the tiny twirling windmills, the gnomes, the toadstools, the obese frogs, the boys and their dogs and a small grove of wooden spoons with eyes glued on their bowls under a plastic sign reading 'Welcome to Spoonsville', and made his way back home, waving once again to his neighbour Geo as he hurried inside to apologise to Marg for his extended absence.

Joseph sat at his dining table with an empty plate before him, back in present time and space, as he let his remembrance of the day the fence had fallen slowly fade. There was only a trace of yellowy egg fleck left on the plate, with a slither of toasted crust, and his knife was neatly tucked between the prongs of his fork. I went too far, the other day, with all that Elvis talk to poor Sue, he conceded. And what did I ever do with that potted plant Michelangelo gave me? Did I bring it to Sue's house? To think talking to her cured me of my plan to buy the smokes, and I cooked and ate my meal with a head so full of that day's memories I can't say for sure if I enjoyed eating what I made. How odd the mind is! A further proof of the dangerous nature of dreams. Dreams are to be endured and forgotten on first awakening, or else should forever keep their peace.

An almighty rapping on the front door caused Joseph to jolt upright and out of his chair. Throwing on a jacket over his flannels, he flung the front door open to find a giant mechanical monstrosity slowly advancing onto his property with a great yellow belly and three sets of immense wheels coming on over the driveway as its operator made a painstaking attempt not to crush the hedges on either side of the drive and to avoid the low-hanging branches of the jacaranda tree as they scraped up over the windshield and broke off at the smoke-spewing port of the exhaust. 'Good morning!' the site manager said, a black-bearded and Bluto-shaped man, who stood beaming in the doorway in a smeared yellow vest, his hard hat and green rubber gloves shining in the early light. Marg appeared behind Joseph, peering up over his shoulder in her soft blue gown and slippers. 'Oh my goodness!' she declared at the sight of the septic truck shuddering to a halt on their property, its great rugged wheels sinking into the manicured lawn on either side of the drive. When Joseph's power of speech returned, he found himself too overawed by this sudden appearance and made the instinctive mistake of offering to shake the site manager's gloved hands. The site manager took a step back and held his hands up in the air and replied, 'Nah, trust me mate, you don't wanna shake these hands. I'm wearing high-grade industrial shit-shovelling gloves, if you'll excuse my language, miss. You wanna open that gate of yours up and gives us a look at your overflow issue, and we'll see what we can do for you, aye?' Joseph turned to Marg and asked her to fetch the keys, and when she returned with them in her hands, her blue eyes wide at the sight of the beastly piped contraption the crew were unfolding at the rear of the tanker, Joseph took the keys from her without a word. He nodded to the yellow-vested team of men, all large and bearded besides the driver, who was rail-thin and whose arms displayed ribbons of heavy veins as he climbed out of the cabin and leapt down to the lawn with his boots caked in grey mud. The driver and the site manager followed Joseph through the unlocked gate and into the backyard. 'Beautiful garden you've got yourself, mate,' the site manager said, observing the Balinese thatch, the pink rose bushes, the rows of succulents, the Buddhist statues, the pebbled stones, the marbled birdbaths, the citrus trees heavy with lemons and limes, and the netted veggie garden punctuated with wooden stakes set beside tomato plants, passionfruit vines, and uprisings of silverbeet. 'It's not bad if you can get over the smell,' Joseph replied, regaining his full sense at last. 'That's what we're here for,' the driver stated. 'And believe me, mate, if we can't clean your issue up, then the next number to call is an exorcist.' At once the three men inhaled the first scent of the sewage in the air. 'She's ripe,' the site manager noted. Closer still, they began to see the dark trickling flow of coffee-coloured water running in a thin stream in the corner of Joseph's yard. 'That your old barbecue area?' the site manager asked. Joseph said it had been, in years gone by. 'There was a brick barbecue there in the seventies, and we cooked with sticks and logs with an open fire under a steel hotplate. Hard to fathom now. All that smoke we sent into the air. Never even gave the sewers a second thought back then.' The stench, as they came to a closer inspection, was viscerally repellent, and the consistency of the flow was alarming to behold. 'Take a look over the fence,' the driver said. 'Your site's a fucking swamp.' The site manager swore, peeking through the dents in Joseph's fence to inspect the state of his worksite. 'Well, thank fuck you got us out here, 'cause you weren't wrong, Joe. This just might qualify as a literal shitshow. If it went on any longer we'd be up on charges of biological warfare.'

The driver, whose name turned out to be Wayne, and the site manager, Nate, each stood with their hands on their hips, in the mild morning sun, inhaling the rank air and discussing the situation. Wayne is the expert, Joseph determined. He must work for the Water Board, he has the greater knowledge about submerged infrastructure. Funny, he reminds me of someone, spindly, red-skinned as a Kakadu rock. 'Yeah, mate,' Wayne turned to Joseph, 'You see, the thing is, they built these pipe systems after the war, and they put them together quick and easy so all the sewers are just one straight line that kind of meets up in two directions underground, at a kind of intersection like you've got here in your yard. So when there's a major blockage anywhere along the line, all the water runs back to this low point, and then it starts to rise. That means there's probably a block somewhere, but you've got no way of knowing what it is, or which direction it's coming from.' What can I say to that? Is he going to leave this in my court? Joseph wondered, but Wayne wasn't finished. 'I'll show you what we can do,' the driver said, and he gestured to the other men to follow him back to the truck. Marg was on the back balcony now, arms folded, and she exchanged a strangely excited look with her husband as he walked by behind the younger men. 'See this?' Wayne said when they returned to the truck, holding up the wobbling nozzle of a rubber suction cap at the end of a great black hose hanging limply from the back of the tanker. 'We'll send this end down into your system, and we'll suck up whatever's blocking the pipes, and then fingers crossed, you'll be good as gold.' Wayne passed the rubber end to one of the other crew, who charged into the backyard dragging the fat hose along. 'Should only take a couple of minutes, you can go and relax if you like and we'll give you a shout when she's done.' Joseph explained that he'd prefer to watch, feeling something like a parent about to have his child undergo major surgery. 'Bit like your backyard's having a kidney stone removed, aye?' Nate suggested. 'Nothing that dramatic,' Wayne said, and the three men made their way out to the point in the yard where all the trouble was percolating.

The rubber hose was bent and buckled into the sewer outlet by one of the crew who, boot-deep in a small pond of foul water, called out, 'She's right!' The tanker's engine cranked into sudden life with a calamitous roaring and pumping effort that shook the ground beneath Joseph's feet. Geo, Joseph's neighbour, popped his head over the fence at the sound of the exhortations. 'What's going on, Joey?' Geo called out, and with something like a weary resignation, Joseph explained the situation as best he could without taking his eyes off the sudden bulge in the huge hose lying across his lawn that seemed to be writhing and convulsing under the duress of the tanker's groaning pump. 'Mind if I come over and look?' Geo asked. Soon he was there in the yard beside the other men, nodding a greeting to each and standing with his arms folded to watch the strange lunging and snaking of the hose. 'Hello, Geo,' Marg said, using his arrival as an opportunity to observe the phenomenon more closely herself. The worker deepest in the muck forced the end of the hose deeper into the pipe with stomps of his heavy boot, and occasionally a brown hiss of sewage erupted from the pit as he did so, and the exposed skin of his shins was awash with dripping spray, and his shorts and vest were likewise splattered. Marg held the end of her sleeve up to her nose to defend against the waves of foul air, and she made a pained expression and waved hopelessly at the stinking breeze. I should have had a coffee this morning, Joseph thought. It's too late now, and that caffeine headache is coming on. Who knows how long this will all go for? Knowing my luck, they'll suck the very pipes out of the ground and stick me with the bill for rejigging the whole suburb.

'Hello!' came a sweet voice, and Joseph turned to see Johnny, Geo's youngest son, standing beside his father. 'Johnny!' Geo scolded, 'What are you doing here? Go back inside the house,' he said, pointing home. 'It's alright,' Marg added. 'I'll take Johnny inside, we've got some cakes for him.' Johnny smiled. 'Thank you!' he said. ''Cause it's too noisy out here and it stinks, too!' Geo shook his head, 'Sorry, Joey – he's a curious boy.' Joseph said it was no trouble, his eyes fixed on the enormous hose as it shook ever more fiercely on the ground, as if fixing to explode and shower them all with its contents. Unsettling, reminds me of something malevolent, an awful, dying thing. The sound of the pump was becoming harsher, as if there was a loose stone in the machine, caught up in one of the gears. 'How long does it last?' Geo asked Wayne, who grimaced and said, 'Dunno mate, how long's a piece of string, y'know?' That trembling sight, like a death rattle. A horrible expression that one. 'Ah, fuck!' the worker with his boot on the hose cried out when an expulsion of thick gunk flung out of the pit and splattered along his cheek. 'Nice shot!' Wayne laughed, as the worker spat and wiped his face along his shoulder.

What was it my old pop used to say, Joseph wondered, when things were at their worst, and nothing was to be done? Said it when Gran came back and found me eating those eggs. That's it, he would say, 'Saint Fairy Anne'. His little prayer. I wonder what it meant. Did he ever stand in his yard, though, and watch something like this? Did the men of his day reckon with overflowing sewers? They didn't have sewers then, did they? The bucket man would come round in his cart, collecting pots of waste with his horse blinkered in the lane. A dirty milkman in a wide brim hat, he was. Other men wouldn't stand next to him at the pub for fear of his grubby coat. 'Course they didn't shower till they got home in those days. What am I saying, they didn't shower at all! Remember the old days, collecting wood for heating our bathtub. One batch of bath water for the family, per day, only one lot of hot water for four people. Father would go first, sinking into the steaming water, and all the scum would rise off his body like chicken soup on a simmer. He'd be in there, with his eyes closed, black hair and grease and swirls of sweat and clumps of sawdust. Then out he'd rise, his body steaming, and in we'd go, Bobby and me. Family stew. Had that one battleship they got me for Christmas, Bobby broke it to smithereens in a fit of temper one night. Ah, but he's another story, that brother of mine. All the while, his heart was overworked, our father. Hardest-working man in Glebe. Would put this lot through their paces. Look at them, one fellow with his boot does all the work, the rest are here paid as witnesses. Big beards and broad shoulders and full of guts, the lot of them. The old man was a piece of twisted iron compared to these loafers. Sad day in Glebe when they buried him, all the folks out on the street with their hands on the hearts, talking to their neighbours in hushed reverence. Me and Bobby in our Sunday best. The priest coming towards me with his hand out, his robes wet and muddied on their ends from the moss and mildew of the holy ground. Had his envelope for him, alright. Hypocritical buggerer with his keys to heaven. There was such a calamity in the skies that night. Or was it the week after? Whenever the storm came on, it was one to be feared. Lightning flaring through the old mansion's windows. Then that cur, the stinking metho and ash-daubed critter, he came round that night, knocking on the door of the old mansion, eyes red and yellow like a gutted blacksnake. Mother was crying with fear by the hallway, she said, 'It's that Billy Robertson, that bastard's come by now your father's gone, the coward.' My father would have cracked him apart from apex to cockles, no bones about it. I was fifteen years young, what did I know about how to shoo old rummies off from my mother's skirts, but what I knew was to go and take the rifle out of the chest and load it fit to kill the bastard. I'd faced off the other dirty beggar with his sanctified collar when he asked for the bob for the funeral, and I thought, what's a pickled bum to stand against me now that I've chased off a reverend? That foul bastard Billy Robertson was there alright, bleating at the doorway in the storm, and calling after my mother by her name, and I swung the door open into the whirling pitch-black rain and there was the rifle, aimed right at his temple, in my very own hands, and I was a snarling lad and told him squarely what a howling the night winds would make in the tunnel I desired to blow through his skull. 'I'll put a cave through your expletive face, you unholy maggot.' What wildness to be prepared to kill a man, but he staggered back a way, into the rain and the shadow of the street where he slipped in the mud near the footpath. Strange to think, I felt he was robbing me as he went away, into the night, and looked like he was sobbing, but it might have been the downpour blasted in his eyes. Somewhere there's a fire in me that wishes evil for my soul, I've seen its face in deeper dreams, its eyes two fixed pinpricks of light, like pale unflickering stars in an empty darkness too deep for living sight to hold upon. I fired the rifle into the emptiness after him, like another kind of thunder echoing through the watery lanes, and he got up all soaked hat and mired coat and ran like the filthy mangy dog he was, the poor cretin. Well, that was the end of childish things for me.

'Here she comes!' the man with his boot on the snake's head called out. Just then the hose coiled out of the sewer, retreating towards the tanker for several feet and then came to a dead rest, oozing and dribbling a trail of sludge from its mouth, from which it released upon the ground a golden orb that had been stuck in the nozzle. Joseph's eyes bulged at the sight of this huge chunk of solid gold, and his mouth fell open. Wayne walked over to the rough golden sphere, covered in slick oily water, and he struck it with a small hammer taken from his belt, splitting it perfectly into halves. 'What in hell is that, Joey?' Geo asked. 'You've struck gold, mate!' The worker who'd been holding his boot to the hose kicked at half of the golden orb. 'Oh fuck me,' he said. 'She's a bunch of wet wipes all congealed up.' The driver, Wayne, added, 'Some fuckwit must have been flushing these things down the dunny. Happens all the fucking time.' From the sewer, where the pipe had so recently emerged, there was a loud gurgling sound. 'And there she goes!' Wayne said to Joseph. 'All going back to normal now, mate. All your troubles are over.' He patted the old man on the shoulder, his face was skeletal thin, a gold tooth bright in an ugly smile. 'Yes,' Joseph said. 'God willing, they are.'

An Ordinary Ecstasy

'Well, HELLO lovely. Here's a question for you...what's the MOST beautiful THING you've ever seen?' There was an emoji at the end of the question, a little monocled yellow face looking upward, with furrowed brows, and a gloved finger and thumb resting where its chin might be. Holly read the question several times in the blurred disturbance of eyes still coarsened with sleep. It's far too early for these modern dating indignities, she protested to herself, and lay with the phone pressed against her chest. The late morning light was coming through the shuttered blinds, parcelled out in panels of bright blue between the unit blocks over the street. There was an old globe from an op shop on the bedside table near the window, aiming a pale map of Australia in her direction, and a disposable face mask laid across the miniature Earth, covering the northern hemisphere like a religious cap. Someone was mowing the shared lawns, and a vacuum was whistling and scuffing in an upstairs bedroom. Her match's name was Will, and he was young, only twenty-seven. And what is he really asking, here? Holly wondered, rethinking the clumsily playful question he'd sent. There was a mandate for something called 'banter' on the dating apps. You were supposed to communicate using a coded substitution for wit and charisma, ideally peppered with clichés and puns. 'Hey babe, are you corona? Cause you're taking my breath away! If the virus doesn't take you out, can I do you the honours? You can't spell quarantine without U R A Q T!' Just the thought of this so-called banter was enough to get her day off to a lousy start. All sorts of curmudgeonly indigestions crowded in on Holly's consciousness. She heard her father's voice coming on, the old professor, exhorting her with his belief that we are witnessing the technocratic enslavement of depoliticised and alienated populations, whose shared humanity has been beaten out of them by forty years of neoliberal class warfare, made ideologically invisible by manufactured pseudo-cultural contestations amongst a demoralised citizenry, where even love has become an algorithmic automation reduced to fit an app on a screen, et cetera, et cetera. Holly heard the old man's voice in her mind whenever a grim mood took her in, but she tossed this morning's funk aside with a laugh at her own expense, thinking, don't become the old underground man this early in the morning, not before the morning coffee. The phrase 'morning coffee' made her think of a mug that was always visible in the staff kitchenette at work – she'd see it in the washing rack, Monday to Friday – a large white mug with a picture of a hideous cat on the side beneath the droll caption, 'Before my morning coffee, I might as well be a f###ing dog.' The mug had mocked Holly for years from its upside-down crevice in the tearoom rack. Teachers are always trying to make use of irony to get by, she'd noticed. Once someone had placed a sign above the staff kitchen's doorway that read, 'Due to budget cuts, the light at the end of the tunnel has been removed.' Holly had taken the sign down immediately on arriving at school, tugged and pulled at its invincible laminate, and finally shoved it into the bin with the used tea bags and sugar packets.

I can't think of the most beautiful THING I've ever seen in a mood like this, Holly thought, whatever was meant by Will's capitalisations. Do events count as things? Are happenings part of that category? Childbirths, holidays, love affairs, long walks on the beach with the mermaids singing each to each? Animals, plants, minerals, major modern generals? Categorisation isn't as easy as people think. She remembered the whale-skeleton reconstructions hanging from the ceiling of the museum lobby she'd visited once as a girl, for instance, or eating bleeding mulberries off the neighbour's tree, or being woken in bed one morning by her old dog's chugging tongue lapping at her face. These were all beautiful things, but they were moments, too. It was easier, far easier, to call to mind the worst thing Holly had ever seen. Too easy, and now it was coming on. The memory began as a tableau set on a neat cemetery lawn. The occasion, the event, was burned brutally into Holly's mind, and it sprang up without much resistance, as it did most mornings, when her guard was down, setting headstones at intervals along a distant hill bordered by motorways. She remembered the sight of a father, approaching a small white coffin as it was lowered into a square hole, the tall, dishevelled man, dressed in a crumbled black suit, wearing a grey spotted tie, poorly arranged, with a handful of dirt crumbling from his fist. The funeral scene came to life like an old carousel being powered up in an empty fair at night, the same obsessive moments of recollection, the father leaning over the deep wound in the ground as though he is afraid to be sucked inside, and then the terrified man snapping along the legs, and the people behind catching his arms as he staggered back. She didn't realise until that very moment that people's knees actually 'gave out'. It was an awful glimpse of grief, almost absurd in its intensity, but happening at a distance. Holly was not even sure where she had stood to see it occurring, as if the memory had been told to her, second-hand, and she'd only imagined the details. And now these recursive images, dimmed by obsessive use, were part of the present day too, like a familiar stain seeping in from a case of rising damp you can't quite cover over. Remember all of us are suffering, in our way, Holly told herself, remember the parable of the mustard seed. There were equally injured mothers and fathers out there, and little children too, going about their business this very moment. Perfect pristine children in school shoes and white socks. Holly supposed there must be countless folks out in the quiet streets and in the silent houses, bearing their grief upon their backs, going on living. Outside she heard the light sibilant voice of a young girl from the unit upstairs, singing at an open window, 'The snow glows white on the mountain tonight, not a footprint to be seen.' Holly drowned out the voice by reciting a poem in her thoughts, as she did whenever she needed to silence the world. What was her favourite line of the poem, 'I am moved by fancies that are curled, around these images, and cling: the notion of some infinitely gentle, infinitely suffering thing.' The girl at the window did not sing for long, and Holly turned her attention back to the question Will had asked.

The best thing Holly had ever seen, she frankly admitted to herself, was the birth of a child. The little creature – having not yet attained a human form – came headfirst into the world, as purple and plump as an eggplant with limbs, summoned into existence by its mother's labours. The mother herself was also red and swollen, her hair wet and swept about her face with the terrible effort of creation, and her eyes were glazed with an exhaustion so extreme she seemed doped and dreamy, straining and sweating and crying all at once, and the doctor loomed over her and placed the baby squealing on her chest. The mother marvelled at the living thing bobbing in her arms, gaping at its tiny red face and its bright eyes with utter disbelief. There, Holly had confessed it, the most beautiful thing, she'd dared to remember it, despite the morning's difficult start. But she couldn't give this answer to Will, of course – it was not a fit subject for a potential lover to receive. Best not to discuss the results of intercourse at all. Childbirth, Holly thought, was the ultimate anti-aphrodisiac. And anyway, enough of children. I'm not going to think myself into the glooms about that anymore this morning! What had she seen in recent days, weeks, or months? There must be something in these last ten years? This bedroom, mostly, with its dusty ceiling fan, a stack of books on the floor by the bed, a faded *Guernica* on the far wall in a plain white frame. Not fit material for transmission. Yesterday was nice, she'd seen the sea moving over the rock-shelf on the local beach, green weed waving in the clear waters and small blue crabs darting under the stones, half-sunk in the wash, scuttling fast as shadows. Holly couldn't type these things into the phone for Will, they were too 'random' she supposed, and she stayed leaning over the quilt, holding her head up, like an emoji made of meat. The question stayed there on the screen, unanswered. Someone was smoking outside on the street, the smell of tobacco coming in through the window, and Holly pulled the blinds shut and carried the phone out into the brightness of the kitchen.

One memory came to mind as she stood by the sink, filling the kettle. Before her world had changed, she had gone to stay with a friend in the heart of the city, and decided to go jogging in Centennial Park, to fill in the idle hours waiting for her friend to finish work. It was spring, and the park was crowded with pedestrians and cyclists bustling around the park's grand circuit. What an odd thing a large park is, she thought, all that space set aside for the principle of leisure, built by people whose names remained only on plaques on statues, or screwed into empty seats beside the creeks and ponds where families of ducks move in loose formation, and a stray black swan sails proudly by, with turtles and koi fish bobbing up from under the calm silvery surface, in the shade of trees so tall they'd outlived the children of those whose hands had planted them. It is a kind of paradise, she considered, when the light is clear and you're passing a rose garden in its full bloom, or the roots of trees as ornate in their arrangement as a cathedral's buttresses, and so many happy children out in the light, kicking soccer balls on the grass and flying kites, with frisbees flung between sisters in blue skirts, and training wheels on the backs of bikes wobbling along the path beside parents with smiling, focused faces.

Holly had jogged round the circuit of the park with these inconsequential impressions in mind, when a young girl had ridden by on a grey horse with an ink-dark mane, its stiff cantering kicking clods of earth up into the air as it bounded past. How strange it seemed to Holly, that a girl so small and thin could command that creature's movement as it carried her, thudding between the old oaks and the children on their bikes crossing between the white fences and posts. When Holly rounded the end of the course a while later, breathing heavily and glistening with layers of sweat, the same grey horse came pounding past in the opposite direction, and she noticed people in the park were stopping to watch the animal as it went, wildly shaking its head and flinging its black mane, completely riderless. Two women in lycra bodysuits pointed to the horse, which slowed to a trot, seemingly confused by its own strange autonomy. Then one of the women, whose hair was tied in a tight strawberry knot under a black cap, walked slowly towards the advancing beast with her arms out lightly before her. The horse made a cautious stepping approach towards the woman's offering of hands, and then pressed its great twitching chest into her palms, bringing its long face down to have the woman nuzzle its neck. The little blonde rider, in her helmet and boots, ran breathlessly up with flushed cheeks. She grabbed at the reins and held them tightly and bowed her head, and the woman who had consoled the fleeing horse put her arms around the little girl too, who now had bright tears flowing down her purpled cheeks.

Holly had watched this misadventure unfold, and then gone and sat inside her car, damp with her cooling sweat, and drank from a bottle of water, contemplating those strange moments where life seemed to be portraying itself too openly, as if aware of its mystical excesses. There were often moments like these, where life appears as it does in great art, all the secret inner organs laid bare in their splendour, too vast and tender to endure for long, before the more mundane necessities regained their primacy, and some gateway of perception swung shut. There was a portrait in a Canberra gallery that Holly had seen as a girl, two white ghostly gums leaning on each other, like mother and daughter, and behind them the sweeping plains and valleys framed by stony red earth and pale-yellow grasses, a landscape flowing to blue mountain ranges. What was it called? That intolerable excitation, when art reveals passion beyond measure? Passion, Holly knew from her study of the German poets, back at university, was seeing an infinitude in a finite thing – perceiving, in other words, what is not there. It was irrationality, like love. To select, without reason, or worse, to have thrust upon you, a belief that one person, animal, mineral, THING, out of the vast array of ordinary multitudes, is the holiest one, for all eternity.

Holly put the phone face down on the counter and flicked the kettle on. She stood, and waited. The kettle boiled slowly, and against her will, memories came upon her, from every angle they pressed towards her. She moved closer to the window and looked out at the purple leaves of the potted plants trembling on the neighbour's driveway, and the shadowy grain of the building's yellow bricks in the late morning light – she even tried to return to the poetry that had worked so well against the little girl's singing, but the impinging memories would not be repelled. She went a long way back, far beyond the times that hurt her most, way back to when she was a girl, and she thought of the white glare of sun on green lacquered leaves when she had climbed the soft paperbarks in her great aunt's yard, hunting cicada shells, clinging barbed to the branches. A helium balloon had snaked its way up into a milky white sky after a Christmas party in the same yard, and sparklers that had been sizzling on top of pastel-coloured ice-cream cake left a metallic aftertaste in the air. Holly's great uncle had dressed as Santa Claus, with a sack full of toys for the many cousins, the foamy white beard hanging loose around his own greying whiskers, and his hard lump of nose sticking out as he rang a gold bell and bellowed to the laughter of the families gathered on the lawn with open bottles of beer and lit cigarettes in their smiling faces. A fresh packet of Crayola crayons, glossy and ripe, was under the wrapping he gave her. The curl of the old man's tongue, as he whistled to the grey myna birds playing in the mulberry tree was a fascinating thing, and the tree itself, with a purple-stained moat of fruits, as its branches shook in the cool afternoon breeze. Her old uncle's scars of an evening, a fierce jagged line between his sagging breasts as he smoked a fat cigar in the darkness of his veranda, a glass of scotch and two ice cubes in a calloused brown hand. The release of pulling carrots up from the ground in the morning, and brushing the soil from twisted roots to reveal their bright orange stumps, and the curled eyelashes of Charley the horse who would put his snuffling head over the fence from the back paddock of the old man's house, smelling of warm earthy sweat. Charley would sometimes find half-rotten apples in the compost heap piled high near the fence, and he'd crunch into them, dribbling pulp and juices. Holly would sneak out of the house to bring him fresh apples and feel the hot breath of his great nostrils on her skin as he took her offerings with probing lips, and the words of her great aunt ringing in her mind, reminding her, 'Make sure you keep your hand flat, so he doesn't bite your fingers.' Charley's eyes, dark and terrible as a gypsy's crystal orb. Holly would bite corn straight out of their husks in her great uncle's garden, their taste sweeter than syrup with the juices running down her elbows, and the leafy scent of the herbs and tomatoes and the piquant soil in the morning air. The cousins would go out together, gathering driftwood on a beach for bonfires, and in later years these fires were accompanied with plastic cups of cheap bourbon, poured by local strangers, boyfriends of older cousins, long-haired coasties with guitars playing easy chords to familiar songs. Glowing teenage faces were lit by flames at night. 'I'm cold,' a boy with long black hair said to Holly one holiday evening. 'Come closer then,' she told him, mouth finding mouth in the warm flickering light, the taste of tobacco and salt. What happened then? Stars. Silence along the sands, waking up in a thousand strange rooms to soft morning's filtering brightness. The old man sick in a hospital bed, a hole in his skull where the treatment had been pumped into his brain, his hollow eyes and his withered limbs. The silhouette of a woman, leaning on a balcony, looking out to sea and watching the waves. Her great aunt's grandfather clock, the pendulum ticking and chiming in the middle of the night while she lay awake, wondering. All the aunts in the little kitchen late in the night, singing and dancing together with their arms wrapped around one another, smiling and crying while the music played in the far room, and the moon hung over the houses on the street.

Holly looked at her phone, that little black screen laid on the bench, and was swamped with utter contempt. For the first time in many months, she wanted tears to come. She'd hadn't thought of those days with her family in years, they were like someone else's memories, from a time before her world had changed forever, immutably, eternally. Holly wanted to pray at the remembrance of these long-gone things. She might ask the higher power: what had it all meant? What purpose had it served? There would be no answer, she knew, but with questions of this kind, perhaps it sometimes helped to ask the wind. She scolded herself – don't give these thoughts any more attention! There was a cup on the counter, she'd poured coffee grains inside, and a little sugar. The kettle on the bench was beginning to shake, then it shook terribly, and was so inexplicably loud in the small confines of the little tiled kitchen that Holly stared at it with a kind of rage, daring it to get one decibel louder than it already had, to be any worse than it already was. At last, the boiling water sounded a click, as if a light had been turned off from another room. The kettle gurgled, sputtered. Slowly settling into a steaming wake.

Jason and I sat outside on an extension of Darren's porch fashioned to resemble a public bar, complete with a tin plaque documenting the licensee's rights and responsibilities, beneath which was a shelf stocked with hard liquor and, further below, a fridge full of local beers and vodka cruisers. We watched the footy on a plasma screen fastened above the bar, drinking whatever we wanted, lazing in large recliners while the two dogs trotted around our feet, and the meat-smoke from the charcoal barbecue behind us set my guts to gurgling while we reminisced between the motions of the game. At half-time, from a shoebox hidden under his chair, Darren produced a contraption that I soon understood by its whirring to be a tattoo gun. Darren looked closely at its tiny engine, wiped some greasy muck from it with a rag, and asked Jason what he'd care to have added to his skin for all eternity. Jason thought a while without taking his eyes from the recap playing in slow-motion on the screen and said, 'I should think...well, how about a penguin...brandishing a straight razor?' Jason took a drink after this suggestion, still attentive to the game's replay. 'For shaving?' Darren asked. 'Or is the penguin armed in self-defence?' Jason shrugged, finished his drink, then turned his attention directly upon Darren as the commercials began playing. 'Porque no los dos?' he replied.

Darren dipped the droning tip of a fresh needle into a small nub of black ink and said, 'In that case, Jason, I'll give the penguin a hat.' He put the gun down and took a swallow of Jameson. 'A sailor's hat,' Jason added. 'Very well,' Darren concluded, 'The Donald Duck special it is.' Reaching his long, tattooed arms down to grasp the bottom of his chair, Darren slid close to Jason, who was pulling a leg of his tracksuit pants up to expose his thigh. 'While I'm doing this mongrel,' Darren added, looking intently at Jason's bare skin, 'you start planning what you're gonna have.' I sank back in the largesse of the old chair, sculled the remainder of my beer and saw in my mind the tattoo Darren had given to our old friend, August Augustine.

'You remember it?' I asked Darren, picturing the inked insignia on August's right foot. 'August Saint Augustine!' Darren said to himself, as he pressed the gun's needle into Jason's thigh, a dribble of ink and blood running down towards his knee. 'How is old Augustine?' Darren asked, not taking his eyes off his work for an instant, adding, 'I haven't seen that Fijian bastard in years.' This question brought me to a strange remembrance. 'Last I saw of him,' I said, 'we were on a trip up north. As far north as I've ever been. All the way up to the Northern Rivers as it happens.'

Darren dabbed with a rag at the mess of ink and blood he was making on Jason's leg. 'That far aye? It's always a weird one with old Augustine,' he said. And he was right, the trip had been a strange one, as every encounter with that queer fellow was fated to be.

It was only a couple of weeks after my second wife left for good that August called to propose his road trip to the Northern Rivers. When he began to expound clichés about change and holidays being good for the broken-hearted, I insisted that such a reset of circumstances was unnecessary and stressed that the whole separation had been far less traumatic than my first divorce. There were no children to consider this time around, and barely any promises to break since the vows we'd recited at the wedding had been quite noncommittal.

Sensing I was not going to admit to a secret despair, August side-stepped my assurances and began criticising what he imagined was the sorry state I must be living in, seeing as no one with a domestic consciousness was now residing in the dwelling with me. There was no way to deny that the living quarters had gone to the dogs since I'd become the only occupant – for one thing, the 'chair' I was sitting in as we spoke was actually a pile of damp laundry, and my feet were lain over an empty carton of Carlton Dry that was serving as an ottoman – but I could report with some genuine relief that being left with so few possessions after the split had rendered the place virtually immune to clutter. Save for the things I was currently sitting on, an old dumbbell, and a copy of David Mamet's *A Whore's Profession*, which I had lost the inclination to read, there was very little lying around which might be considered out of its place. Exasperated by these unassailable assurances, August at last began to reveal a quarter inch of his true agenda, declaring that this road trip was 'a once-in-a-lifetime opportunity' to right *two* independent wrongs. This caught my attention.

The first of these 'wrongs', he explained, was the already-broached subject of my broken heart, but before he rehashed this failed topic I cut him off by explaining, once and for always, that my heart was not in need of mending, largely because it had long since been removed, and I was much happier without the rotten thing anyway, its absence occupied by more meaningful objects, like wheels of cheese, and frozen pizzas. Hearing this nonsense, August quickly moved onto the second 'wrong' in need of righting, which was, evidently, his true motivation. This proposed road trip to the state's north was a chance for *him* to settle a long-standing personal vendetta *he* was holding against a man named *Cain*.

The 'vendetta' August bore against Cain Rivera was well known to me. The feud went all the way back to that primordial time when we were junior rugby league players for the local Mounties football club. August 'Saint' Augustine, as a prodigiously tall and broad teenager, was the star player of the club and more than made up for his lack of technical exuberance by being bigger than most his age and more naturally athletic than anybody, anywhere. The most obvious exhibition of August's innate talent was when Coach Phillips ran us through the dreaded 'beep test'. For the uninitiated, the test requires participants to run back and forth across a given distance in time with an audible 'beeping' sound. The cruelty of the test lies in its acceleration: every minute the time between beeps is reduced, so participants must 'shuttle' back and forth at an ever-increasing speed. Failure to put a toe over the line in time with a beep results in elimination, and so an entire team of footy players can be run through this ritual, until only one individual remains. At this exhibition of stamina and speed, August was the undisputed district champion, until, that is, the arrival of a stranger named Cain Rivera, who turned up for try-outs in the early months of the year 1999.

Cain set a bum note with me the moment he came upon the scene. As tall and broad as August, Cain explained to the coach that his family had moved in that year from Penrith, where he'd been a representative player of some repute, and he was now looking to make his name in our town. Coach Phillips, who had kept me on the team for years – despite my fumbling hands and weak heart, for the sole reason that he was enamoured with my mother – took one look at this strapping young prospect, asked what position he played, and hearing that it coincided with my own, stripped me of my jersey and handed it to this newcomer with all the sentimentality of a guillotine. Despite losing my place in the on-field squad, I maintained close enough contact with the team to perform the duties of 'water boy' – a calling made somewhat more embarrassing thanks to a recent Adam Sandler film – and so I was there to witness the team's progress that year from the safety of the sidelines and the musty locker rooms at home and abroad.

Throughout the season August and Cain fought a duel of rival talents that elevated the whole squad's performance, and to the disbelief of the entire region, Mounties' under-16s made the semi-finals, though a bout of fisticuffs broke out between the two star players during training for the semis. A rumour circulated that the fight started when Cain muttered 'shitskin' at August, under his breath, and so to settle the build-up of athletic enmity, a showdown was proposed. The face-off was to be a two-man beep test in which either August Saint Augustine or Cain Rivera would emerge from the beeping and cheering to be declared the ultimate under-16s rugby leaguer. Once both claimants had agreed to the contest, much hype and fanfare circulated through the town, and I, like so many others, turned up on the field behind Mounties to watch the events unfold, keen to see the usurper Cain taken down in the town's estimation.

The sun was obscured in an overcast sky, a crowd of parents were assembled about the field, some two dozen strong. The local skater kids had stopped their skating on the bowl to come over and observe, and the basketballers had left their hoops, and the tennis kids leant on the fences around their courts, and even old Ernesto, the local river-man who fished for scrap in the waterways that ran into the sewers near the field, ceased his trolling in the muck to come and spy upon the combat. August and Cain both arrived in their black-and-gold jerseys, slightly damp under the arms from whatever warm-up routines they had each conducted. There were cheers for each competitor as the club president, Wayne Thompson, bid them to step up to their positions by speaking into a megaphone that was barely audible over the calling crowd. A cap-gun served as a starter's pistol, fired in time with the first beep, and the challenge began.

For the first few shuttles there was a relative silence from the assembly, and both boys' faces were tense with grit and flushed with bloody focus. As the electronic beeps quickened, the crowd's volume rose alongside it, until the calls and gesticulations from the audience became frantic, and it began to seem that both boys were so committed to defeating each other that they would defy the very laws of physics. The shorter the space between the beeps, the more the two lanky, long-limbed contenders would dig their heels into the dirt to spin back for yet another lap, both managing their oxygen reserves with astonishing craftiness, so that when either appeared to be losing their wind they would find some deeper will to push on harder and faster. Coach Phillips stood at the head of the cheering mob as the beeping quickened, his eyes wider with amazement each time he glanced up from his stopwatch, until he looked like a man consumed by apoplexy. My own voice was hoarse with screaming, and the faces in the crowd all seemed warped with uproar and admiration for the duel which none could believe the two athletes were daring to maintain.

No doubt some world record was within breaking point on the field that afternoon, and had the people of Guinness been present, this fact would be set down in print for all eternity. People in the crowd began to jump and wave their arms like those drowning, or on fire, and the club president was red-faced with bellowing and shaking his fists so that his tie was up on his head, and younger members of the audience threw themselves at the grass in howls and shakes of excitation. Coach Phillips, his eyes now the size and colour of plums, began riding some imaginary horse, slapping at its non-existent hide with an invisible whip. Then the whole thing exploded into an outrage – August, when he reached the mark with another 'beep' perhaps half an instant behind his opponent, did not turn back towards the opposing line, as he had done in the hypnotic succession of shuttles beforehand. Instead, while Cain raced back towards the opposing line, August ran on in his own singular direction, bolting perpendicular beyond the bounds of the competition, and then split off in a zig-zagging course heading away from the scene altogether, far from the crowd, sprinting faster and faster from the contest while Cain continued his conquest unabated, apparently unaware that his opponent had shot off in a host of disqualifying directions. Parents, hermits, skateboarders – all began to yell August's name in their confusion as he raced out of the field, then into the club's car park, and then completely out of sight, into the horizon of Sunday traffic, service stations and roundabouts, leaving behind a cacophony of hollering.

Cain collapsed at last, heaving in a private exaltation with his eyes closed tight, and now bedlam was unleashed upon the crowd. Some celebrated, others ran off in search of August, or their cars, or an escape from the breakdown of order on the field. The president raved and ranted into his megaphone, trying to restore control of this shattered spectacle. When the chaos died down, with the abandoned witch's hats and empty Tooheys cans spread out on the field, speculation began to circulate that under extreme physical pressure, August's mind had snapped, and that his bizarre zig-zagging flight was the act of madness brought on by exhaustion. Others believed that August, realising he could not win, and ever the delinquent, had chosen instead to rebel against the entire event and smear Cain's win with his own disgrace. Increasing the whispers, in an age before the internet was able to answer every mystery, Cain Rivera disappeared in the days after the discord. August, likewise, never returned to the scene of his opprobrium, nor ever played for Mounties again. But it was Cain who seemed to vanish so unsettlingly from our lives and our town.

Since that shameful race meet, some twenty years ago, I had not raised the subject with August, and so as I sat upon a pile of dirty laundry in an empty house listening as August broached the topic directly, my attention was greatly piqued. August explained that he had recently used various digital platforms to track down Cain's whereabouts and, to use his own enigmatic phrase, the two men 'had established communications'. During these social media exchanges, August had discovered that Cain, having long since given up on football, had taken to mixed martial arts. August responded to this disclosure by confiding to Cain that he, too, had recently become a mixed martial artist, and although this was a bald lie, the two men arranged for an exhibition match to take place at Cain's local gym, up in Byron Bay, with the aim of 'settling old scores' in a competitive but friendly fashion. Hearing all this over the phone, and knowing something of the ways of vengeance, and the graves that get dug in its name, I declined the offer of joining August on his strange quest to rewrite the injustice of the past. Besides, I told him, I couldn't afford a trip to Byron and had things of my own to do. He scoffed at this but said he understood, was disappointed and so on, but the offer was open if I changed my mind. I returned to watching the wall where my television had once been. My part in this affair might have ended at that moment, but not three weeks later I was on the winning side of a class action suit against a robot working for the Australian Tax Office, who had defrauded me of a sum of 3,000 dollars by means of a faulty algorithm. Made anxious with the weight of this endowment, and looking around at the emptiness of my life, with its sodden laundry, empty bottles, and bare walls, I called August and asked him to sign me up.

When August arrived, it was evident from the outset how serious the business of revenge had become. When I gathered my bags and stepped outside at the sight of his white sedan pulling up out front of my place, I found him facedown in the driveway, performing an alternating set of one-armed push-ups with his bare knuckles on the uneven concrete. Startled by this impromptu display of exercise, I dropped my suitcase and waited for him to complete his routine. Once he had ground out the final reps he leapt to his feet, flushed and slick with sweat despite the cool April air, and stood there, as if posing, grim and solemn as the Colossus of Rhodes. What a spectacle it was to see him – the sun had not long been up, and it shone on his glistening form, revealing the most astonishing transformation of his physical proportions. August's limbs, which were now covered in copious tattoos – snakes, spiderwebs, angels, saints and other mystic miscellany – were thick and filled with muscle, and the skin beneath the ink was covered in vascular ribbons. Under the immediate exertions he'd performed in the driveway these pulsing channels were full of blood, pumping along the swollen form of his marbled arms.

I stepped up to give this transformed version of my good friend an embrace, despite the unappealing thought of touching his sweaty frame, but instead of returning my greeting, August grabbed my arms, spun me around, and captured me in what I would call, without consulting a combat manual, a standing rear naked choke. Some instinct in me for survival attempted to neutralise this attack by launching us both towards the ground. We landed sideways, thudding together on the still-dewy lawn. This countermove only worsened my situation, as August then increased his hold by wrapping his legs around my waist like a pair of tattooed pythons. What could I do but listen in wonder, as he said directly into my ear, 'You will learn to love again, now say it!' It was a command I could neither dissent from, nor submit to, having no capacity of speech or movement in anything other than my arms, which were busied in a futile attempt at pulling apart the chokehold wrapped around my throat. He loosened his grip around my neck and commanded again, 'You'll learn to love again – say it! Swear it!' Just as I was gathering the air to agree to this threat, my neighbour, an Italian with age spots where his black hair had once been, appeared at the fence between our front yards, armed with a hose. He demanded that the strange brute who was attacking his neighbour release me at once, or he would spray the devil out of him. Both of us leapt to our feet, August the faster for the obvious reason that he was supplied with oxygen, and when the power of speech returned and I'd coughed out some of the terror, I apologised to Tony and attempted to explain to the poor old man that this sudden assault which had just taken place before his eyes was an exhibition of skill rather than an attempted murder, an assertion I was not certain was true at the time.

'Where have you been?' Tony asked me, after accepting my assurances that the stranger was an old friend of mine, a deep furrow of concern on his weather-weary face, the ends of his tracksuit pants dampened by his gardening duties. 'Inside, mostly,' I explained. He confirmed this himself, saying, 'I never see you anymore? Where's your wife?' 'Ah, she's gone Tony, she left.' Tony nodded his head and closed his eyes, holding up an open hand that I took to mean 'Say no more.' August intruded into the conversation here, saying, 'Don't worry mate, I'll get that heart of his beating again.' From the expression of fear on Tony's face, I saw that he took this to mean something homosexual was afoot. 'Look after the place while I'm away, would you?' I asked, and he nodded his head and returned to watering his roses, but kept a leery watch upon the pair of us as we dusted the dirt and grass off our clothes and packed my bags into the boot of August's Corolla.

The first question I had for August, once we were on our way, was why he'd decided to dedicate his energies to addressing a slight he'd suffered back in ninth grade. I crowned my question with a quotation from Patrick White: 'Either turn your back forever on those who have seen your youth, or admit that even shame has some sweet melancholy.' August frowned, keeping his eyes on the road as he processed the question. 'There are no straight lines in nature, my friend. Your question reminds me of that story about the runner who can never reach the finish line because some lunatic keeps dividing the distance by halves. It's a paradox, you see? What appears to be progress in your big blue eyes is really an arbitrary measurement across an illusion of space. I've made that false measure myself, by the way – the measure of progress – and I've seen its implications right to the end, and now I'm getting into another kind of arithmetic – one that is taking me in a different direction and another way of being.' He put on his dark glasses then, so that I couldn't see his eyes. 'You call yourself a learned man,' he continued. 'I've noticed you doing so, it's in the way you carry yourself these days, but you need to re-read your Pythagoras, your Plutarch too, and failing that you ought to take up computer animation or some other career, rather than the one you're in. If Picasso were alive today, he'd be on a MacBook Pro drawing Mercedes advertisements, and I'll hear no dissent on that score.' This was all typical, and I reached back into a bag of road supplies I'd brought along to fetch out a whisky flask with a drowning man painted on it. 'What's that in there?' August asked. 'An ascension into the brain,' I said.

'Don't worry, friend,' he assured me. 'I'm not going to make this trip all about some primitive obsession with the past, and that race with Cain. That's what you're thinking isn't it? Well, you're truly out of your mind if that's what you're thinking. People of your sort like to say, "Oh, but the past is not even past," and then condemn others for living in it. You reserve the right to say, "Look at me, I like to go swimming against the stream of time," but you don't like common folk to think that way, do you? It's hypocritical, and a common pseudo-intellectual's fault. There's no point thinking about the past either way, because you can't help but repeat it, and even if you could, hypothetically, well the future never arrives, does it? So, what I mean is, don't get nervous, this week is going to be a genuine tourist experience for you and me, and when I'm a tourist someplace I'm a tourist all the way. Right to the roots.

I'm talking tie-dyed shirts, and drug-induced encounters with the great cosmic dingos. You don't want me to bring up your broken heart, so I won't, but that doesn't mean having a good time isn't important to us on this trip. You're my friend, and that's no joke, and I would never drag a friend away from their doorstep for my own amusement. You're not fun enough for that kind of thing anyway, because you don't seem to like fun at all. You're one of those people who says, "Fun is not fun, and if it was, I wouldn't admit it," but rest easy, we're going to do what every good tourist in Byron Bay should do. We'll walk on the beach, smoke some gunja with the old hippies, go hiking in a rainforest, get you laid, wear white corduroy, and take selfies by the lighthouse. We'll cry some tears into our kebabs at a late-night takeaway, and in between, I'll be revenged, after all this bloody time, all these storied years. And what's more, you'll be there to say you saw it all. What do you say, are you excited?'

I kept drinking from the flask, and for the first few hours entertained myself by listening as August gave an in-depth explanation of his latest get-rich-quick scheme, a plan to get into the booming Pick-up Artist business – he planned to become a guru of the 'Pick-up Arts' – assuring me that it would be easier than I'd suspect, since it was a field which involved manipulating only the most desperate and pathetic people on earth, involuntarily celibate young men, a demographic – and he was emphatic about this to the point of quoting some alarming statistics – that was ever-accumulating in the general population. And what's more, he said, these growing hordes of desperados were willing to believe anything they were told. The poor losers were willing to test any hypothesis, no matter how suspect. They would accept anything anyone promised them, to the extent that they would die defending what it was that you had persuaded them was in their best interests to believe. 'Grant a man an axiom, and he'll prove pink elephants amass on the moon,' August said, though I wasn't sure what he was talking about, and I wondered if that was, perhaps, the point of his endless babbling. Either way it passed the time, and the liquor was strong. 'When did you come up with this program of yours?' I asked as we sped along the highway heading north, over rivers and islands and mountain peaks, and we saw seagulls spreading along the expanse of national forest close to the roadway, and the occasional eagle flying above the emerald hillsides scarred black and bare from the fires that had consumed the countryside in the previous summer. 'Last week,' he said, suddenly irritated. 'I've had plenty of time to think lately.' There was a quiet in the car. 'They got you back working in the deli section again?' I asked. August checked his mirrors and changed lanes around two trucks crawling along in the left lane. 'Yeah,' he admitted. 'Back in the deli section.' I took another drink from the flask as two utes coated in bumper stickers overtook us before we could get back in the slow lane. 'That's no good,' I said.

We were crossing a bridge not far from Newcastle when August finished delivering his account of his new passion for helping involuntary celibates free themselves of their money. The afternoon had turned so grey that the waters of the great lakes to our east shone as flat and clear as runways of silver, and on the long surface of those waters small boats were anchored, and on them lonesome fishermen watched their floats until we reached our first stop of the trip, and I drank coffee as I waited for August to finish his ablutions in the roadhouse toilet, watching a silent family stand in line at the Hungry Jacks café. We passed through Newcastle without much ado, and its harbours were on fine display from what we saw. Coal freighters sat in a pale mist on the horizon, their distant immensities like seabound monuments to the mastery of man's will over nature, which was none of our business, so we kept right on going until we reached the convenient coastal and casual admixture of Coffs Harbour. August repeated his excitement at the prospect of visiting the Big Banana, and I warned him once more that it wouldn't be as big as he was hoping, but he would not hear a bad word said about the subject, explaining in an explosive whorl of passion that it had long been a dream of his to visit each 'big thing' in the country, except the Big Prawn, as he was allergic to seafood, or something equally absurd.

There was no one around when the great fruit finally came into view, so we stopped the car, stooped out with aching backs and cramping legs, and made our approach like riders who'd been too long in the saddle. When we came up to the body of the banana itself, August leant on its wooden pseudo-skin and bowed his head, as though attempting to commune with some site-specific energies the structure might possess. After a few moments of this, during which August kept his eyes tightly closed, he suddenly looked up at the banana as if seeing it with redoubled awe and announced, 'I thought it would be bigger,' and then we took turns standing in front of it to have our picture taken. 'Should I pull a face?' I asked, but August said it was too late, he'd already taken the photo. 'So? Take another one,' I said, but he replied that it wouldn't do to go taking a thousand pictures of everything we came across. A billboard on the side of the banana announced that there was a laser-tag range inside and a putt-putt course, but when I pointed this out it seemed somehow to offend August's sense of propriety. I became convinced he believed there was something spiritually significant about this big construction, in the same way that might be appropriate to a discussion of Uluru or Karlu Karlu, but when I pursued this conviction, as we made our way back towards the Corolla, August took the wind out of my pursuit by announcing, in what appeared to be a sincere tone of voice, that, in his opinion, the operations of the Big Banana should be given back to the local custodians. 'Traditional owners?' I asked. 'Are you serious?' He stopped and turned towards me, standing just outside the driver's door, and started tapping his sunglasses upon the rooftop of the car. No sooner had I made my remark than I realised the trap he had set for me. August reeled off a brief history of how Sikh immigrants had been the ones to 'make the banana great' in Australia, and that it was typical of an 'Aussie' to only want to 'give back' to Indigenous peoples things they had no right taking possession of in the first place. If such 'Aussies' were really serious about all this 'returning' they'd start giving away things they had some legitimate claim to, instead of only dealing in what they'd simply stolen. I looked at him over the top of the car, the cloudless expanse of the late-morning sky above him, as a cool coastal breeze moved through the tops of the gum trees on the other side of the Pacific Highway. Not a single car was on those four winding lanes of highway that morning as the two of us glared at one another in a silence marred by squawking cockatoos. There wasn't another soul in sight, as August tapped on the roof of the car with his sunnies, on the black surface of which I could see the Big Banana's reflection. 'Now look,' I started, and gave August such a steely expression so that he could see how serious I was. 'If you're going to make every disagreement between us about our racial differences, it's going to be a tedious trip.' I let August know, in no uncertain terms, that if that was his intention then he could leave me here at the banana, and I'd find my own way home.

It was quiet in the car as we drove away from the great yellow grin in the rear-view mirror, passing the many motels and banana farms and the quiet streets of Coffs with caravans parked at rest stops by the highway, and empty hills bordered by palms and bandy fences with rusty wire, and small mountains in the distance whose dense tree lines opened onto grassed escarpments scarred by colonial farms and old graveyards marked by crucifixes looming out from between the branches. August apologised for causing the tense atmosphere, and we stopped to eat and make peace at a KFC. Once we'd eaten our Zinger boxes and wiped off the grease, we discovered a coffee store chain called Zarraffa's near the main street marquee in a town called Corindi, and though neither of us were caffeine connoisseurs, there was no doubt in August's mind that a finer cup of coffee could not be found this side of paradise. We took a short walk along a wooden pier with our paper cups in hand, watching power-walkers pass us in their hot-pink activewear, and the sun glistened on the calm harbour's expanse. We stopped for a while to read posters for missing children on a tunnel wall near the water's edge, above which some vandal had sprayed the overwhelming question, 'Have you seen the three-metre flatty?'

Then it was dry grass and shrubs on the fields and hills around the road for hours, and powerlines and trucks and caravan crews that my folks back home would have called 'the grey-nomad brigade' as we chased the sun, hoping to arrive at Byron before the darkness swallowed us up. August explained to me as we drove that his favourite word was 'paradox', and he had seen a book called *12 Rules for Life* for sale in the window of a bookstore and underneath this book was a recommendation from one of the staff stating that the book had been on the bestseller lists around the world for over a year. 'Twelve rules is too arbitrary a number,' August explained as we drove by a series of sheds set up beside netted papaya orchards. 'Twelve months? Twelve Apostles? Fine, fine. But if you're going to have more than, say, ten rules, why not have a hundred? You let a system get too complex and it gets to be a waste of time – leads to error. If there's a rule *for life*, it ought to be useful in every situation – not one-twelfth of all your troubles. "Live your life like you're wearing maxims on your thongs," that's what my mother taught me. She used to say, "There should be an adequate equation in your body for every action you partake in." There's only one real law in my estimation; the law of contradiction. Where things confuse themselves – that's where the substance of existence is to be found.' He looked across at me, and seeing I was unconvinced he gave me an example of this law.

'Do you remember that time Cain and I came to blows out on the field, in the lead up to the semis? I claimed at the time that he had called me "shitskin" under his breath. Well, the truth is I can't remember if he called me that or not. Maybe I made it up, I don't know. Too much time has passed now. Still, it used to play on my mind, even if he hadn't said it, I thought the idea was there, just under the surface. And one night, not long after Cain and I had that fight, I fell asleep and had the strangest dream. I found myself standing in my mother's backyard, the house in Bonnyrigg, and there was a red-faced old man in a singlet and thongs, who was in the yard next to ours, looming huge over the fence with a beer in one of his leathery hands and cigarette in the other. And he said to me, "So you're the one I'm neighbours with, yeah?" And I nodded and said, "Yeah, I reckon I am," and then he laughed at me, laughed right into his can as he took a swig and said, "Don't you reckon it's a bit of a problem?" I knew what he was getting at, of course, and I thought to walk away, to go inside where it was safe, but then he was suddenly standing in the yard with me, this huge leathery man, his lips wet and his eyes yellowed, and he began railing at me, ranting on about "where my people were" when his ancestors settled the land. He spoke to me, like God spoke to Job, saying, "And where were you and your people, when the night crawled with goannas creeping through ironbark ash? Did you daub the wattle on cottage walls in the wildness of Botany Bay, in prison chains under the flesh-eating whip of the government men? And when the Mallee bulls moaning filled the unforgiving heat for miles around, as shirtless men in bullocky teams strained to pull broken wheels out of the caked earth under a sun that melted the very vision of the empty hills, were you amongst their number?" He went on and on, and it was so distressing to listen to him, and when I woke my heart was deeply troubled. For days on end that dream played on my mind, and I kept asking myself, "What does it mean to be me? How does one become what one is?" But of course, I grew out of such questions, and forgot my dream altogether. Then one afternoon, many years later, as I sat in the yard of my mother's house in Bonnyrigg, the same yard I'd dreamt about so long ago, drinking a rum and cola, a crow landed on the fence beside me. It was so black that the light in its feathers shone with a shimmer of blue, and its white eyes were on me. And then I remembered my dream for the first time in years, and suddenly, I saw that the fear and pain I felt in the dream was not my own. It was out there, in the world, in some interconnected global mind. I realised a paradoxical fact, which had nothing to do with the bird per se. That it is better for some of us to be outside belonging, than to be constituted by it. Looking at the crow, and his curious eye, I saw that all my life I had not been suffering from some repressed diasporic melancholy, but from the bittersweet experience of exile's consolation. I pitied, sincerely, all who belong, because I found myself free from the anxieties of contradiction, and the constant insistence of the world's wide and mystifying strangeness was my natural condition, it was a home to me no man could disturb.'

The story, August asserted with a vehemence I had no will to doubt, was an insight into the powerful rule of contradiction, which he claimed was as infinitely self-correcting as God in heaven.

We pulled into the caravan park August had booked on the outskirts of Byron just as the sun was going down and settled into our cabin. The accommodation was fine, except for a stream of ants coming up from the bathroom drain, crawling into the shower recess, emerging from the vent and marching into the air conditioner – which made so much clatter when we turned it on that it might have been a tin-pot orchestra rehearsing at the end of our bunks. We stayed up drinking beer and arm-wrestling, which was fine, until August grew tired of defeating me, and in his drunkenness took to wandering around the caravan park's circuit, knocking on doors and offering the stunned inhabitants fifty bucks to try and beat him. No one took him up on this offer, and against my advice, he began unzipping tents and poking his head in at startled campers, desperately looking for opponents. Eventually security arrived in a four-wheel drive with a pit bull painted on its side. August was excited by this, believing at last that a worthy adversary had arrived, but as it turned out the guard was old and feeble, with a hunched back. He scolded us, saying, 'Boys, we're in the middle of a pandemic here, you gotta maintain social distancing – that means no knocking on doors and opening up tents, and whatever else, for fuck's sake!' He repeated this over and over until we both agreed to go to bed.

First thing in the morning I went out to caffeinate away the excess of the night at the caravan café, and found the place busy with beautiful young people, who in the bright Byron morning were wearing very little clothing, so that their flawless skin glowed golden bronze, except where they were tattooed with mandalas and other mystic symbols, and every one of them was dressed in flowing strips of white linen over their bikinis and bare chests, and the only table free for me was outside, behind a bulbous fern. I began to feel like some strange pervert peeking out at these youthful folk from between the tree's fronds, listening to the breezy conversations as more young people crowded in from the street to drink green smoothies from glass jars and eat from açai bowls so large the waitresses handled them gingerly with both hands, and panting dogs and cats with collars lounged on a small strip of grass on purple cushions in the garden. August tracked me down there just as I was finishing off my third coffee. He was wearing black trackies and a green shirt that read 'Recognise' above a portrait of Beyoncé, and I could tell by the look on his face, despite his dark glasses, that he was agitated. As it turned out, he intended to travel into town immediately, and locate the gym where Cain trained. He believed that dropping in a few days early, unannounced, would give him the psychological edge ahead of their scheduled bout.

I agreed this sounded like a fine idea, so long as we stopped to get supplies at the local supermarket. August confessed he was curious to see how a supermarket in Byron Bay might differ from the sort he worked at in Sydney, and so we set out.

The store we located was stocked with an encyclopaedic array of health food tonics, trinkets, elixirs, kale combines, krill derivatives, turmeric extracts, almond essences, and seaweed corn chips with celery salt amidst a hoarding of Byron Bay brand biscuits, chocolates, ice-cream cones, and so on. 'This all seems rather corny, and frankly, a little tacky. I was expecting something more bespoke from the reputation,' August confided to me. But then moments later, as we rounded the corner towards the store's deli, August was struck by what he regarded to be a veritable cornucopia of processed meats and antipasti. He grabbed at my arm without taking his eyes from the counter, behind which a broad-shouldered woman in the white-collared shirt and cap of the store's uniform gazed at us with an expression of nonchalance. 'I didn't know a deli could be like this,' August said, still gripping my arm, standing in a kind of mortification at the counter while the woman, whose massive red dreadlocks were wrapped up in an enormous hairnet, began slicing cuts from a leg of ham. August let go of me and grabbed instead for his phone – I thought perhaps he was about to add this delicatessen to his catalogue of photographs, but instead he started calling someone. It turned out to be his mother, a fact easily deduced from the heavy Fijian accent he assumed whenever speaking to her, and I listened as he narrated the amount of cold meat he was looking at. 'They have everything Mum, yes everything – what would you like me to bring you? Okay. Okay. What about some guanciale, too? You want me to get you some culatello? Yes, and some cervelat? Okay, they have it all!' He went on like this, and I winced, realising it would be up to me to point out that we had no way of hygienically storing sliced meat in our caravan beside a small fridge crowded with beer bottles, let alone transporting it back to Sydney at the end of the week, and that all of this meat, while an impressive stock, was easily acquired anywhere back home, particularly for someone who worked in a deli. What it was that had provoked his excited phone order was not known to me, and I chalked it up to another of his endless eccentricities.

Having talked some sense into my companion, we left the shops unencumbered by slabs of exotic meats and made our way to the gymnasium August said was located on the outskirts of town. It was round the back of a rather dilapidated rural brick property with a shabby tin roof, windows barred with planks of wood and a front lawn with muddied patches of dried grass. The driveway led around the side to what looked like a storage barn, the only evidence of its association with combat training of any kind a flexing arm with a lightning bolt on the bicep painted along the sheet metal wall. 'Are you sure you want to rock up to this place unsolicited?' I asked my friend, who was studying the barn with a focused intensity. 'This looks the sort of place you end up tied to a chair while someone starts a chainsaw.' But August was too busy psyching himself into the state of a warrior-monk to answer any questions, and the determination on his face was frightening to behold. He unbuckled himself from his seat with the slow deliberation of a jungle cat preparing to pounce on unsuspecting prey, and I hobbled after him up the pebbled driveway, my thongs slinging the little stones in all directions as we went. I noticed the windows of the gym were barred and blacked out as we approached, and the only visible entry was adorned with a thick silver padlock. 'You were saying something previously about knocking and entering being the state of heaven,' I said, in a futile attempt at wit, but August was in no mood, and he banged heavily on the locked door. 'Can I help you gentlemen,' came a nasal voice from behind us. We spun around to see a tall, lanky man in a lime-green robe adorned with sequined dolphins. His dimpled scalp was polished clean by a case of alopecia so severe it had swept even his eyebrows away, and his pale face wore a bemused, unearthly expression. His thin fingers were extended sharply at his sides, as though at any moment he intended to begin flapping them and ascend into the air.

August explained our presence with an efficiency and coherence quite surprising for a man prone to excessive discursions, and evidently this stranger knew some of the story. When August mentioned the upcoming bout with Cain Rivera, the robed man, who gave his name as Graham Powers, laughed derisively, and assured us he was familiar with the arranged contest. 'I have trained with your forthcoming opponent quite often here,' he said. 'I am, I must say, most excited to observe the contest.' He added this with a lingering scan up and down August's body. 'The gym is closed today, I am afraid. If we had been forewarned of your arrival, we would surely have put on a welcome for you both. Here, many fighters, many trainers, come to visit on their journey. We like to think of ourselves as a way-stop for travelling combatants of all creeds, colours, styles and ages. Allow me to show you inside, if you wish,' he said at last, stepping between the two of us and patting us simultaneously on the shoulders as he did so. 'I confess, our gym is focused more on the body, mind and spirit than on aesthetic arrangement. You may find it somewhat austere, by your standards.' He seemed particularly amused at this thought and, producing a small key from a pocket inside his gown, he unlocked the place and let us in. He stepped into the darkness, hit the lights, and revealed an interior much like any other fighting gym I'd seen. There was a boxing ring, medicine balls, black punching bags of various sizes, benches, dumbbells, mirrored walls, and all the usual combat paraphernalia – though the facilities were in a shabbier condition than most. Foamy padding sprung from broken stitches in the bags, rust ringed the iron bars, and there were cracks in the edges of mirrors. August wandered around the room and scanned the scores of martial arts posters on the walls, assessing only he knew what and occasionally busying himself with his phone, while Graham watched us both with his oddly serene expression.

'Are you a mixed martial artist yourself?' I asked our host, only for conversation's sake. As I suspected, Graham Powers found this suggestion highly amusing. 'I'm afraid not,' he said, restraining his mirth. 'I am, however, a trainer, and guru, of sorts. I practise something rather more *epi-traditional* than the brawling styles your friend and his soon-to-be opponent are involved in.' Hearing this, August crossed the gym in a sudden excitement, snatching up a pair of gloves and pads from a crate by the boxing ring. 'You're a trainer?' August asked. Graham bowed his head slowly in modest assent, and August held the gloves and pads up and asked if he'd care to do some sparring, to trade some wisdom. This suggestion also brought a great peel of laughter from our egg-white guru, who said he'd be happy to spar with either or both of us, on the provision that we were open to engaging with some unconventional ideas about the nature of combat. These radical ideas, it soon became obvious, were centred around Graham's steadfast belief that he had acquired an ability to overcome his opponents without engaging in any actual physical contact. August showed no interest in these ideas, and he soon wandered away, tossing his gloves at the floor in disgust and returning his full attention to his phone. Rather than being disheartened, Graham simply turned his full attention to me, as though I had been the budding pupil all along – and perhaps in this man's complex metaphysical understanding of the situation, this was true. Being naturally more agreeable than August, I found it necessary to affect a certain degree of credulity as Graham detailed the many practical applications of focused air, agitated breath, vital energy and vapour cultivation, all of which enabled him to render people unconscious with nothing more than a targeted scream and a little hand waving. So numerous were the details of this special technique of his that I began to feel overwhelmed, listening to the various qualities and effects of his art. As he spoke, he moved his hands in a ludicrously fluid fashion, imitating the swimming of a fish now, next a dolphin leaping, and then the graceful flapping of an owl, like someone making shadow puppets on a wall with his long white fingers, and I began to feel light on my feet simply from watching the constant motions of his exposition. Lulled into a kind of sluggishness by this monologue, I was quite alarmed when he reached out and took my wrist, and pressed on it at two arterial points, as though there were hidden buttons under the skin, an action I found profoundly and irrationally irritating, to the point that I experienced a blinding rush of rage. 'That is an important area for the release of emotion,' Graham was saying, snaking his fingers up the soft skin of my forearm, looking for fresh buttons to push. 'Take your hands off me, you bald sonofabitch!' I hissed and snatched my arm back out of his hands, quite shocked at the degree of anger I felt towards his unsolicited touch. Graham beheld me strangely, blinking as though I'd slapped him. 'It appears you are overflowing with negative energies,' the spindly fraud remarked, as though talking to a recalcitrant battery. 'This release must be quite traumatic for you, you must have much suffering in your body.' His smile was gone, and now his browless expression was one of deep paternal concern. 'I'll give you traumatic negative energy!' I raged, coming at him with arms outstretched, and I grabbed him by the neck and slammed him up against the wall. Posters fell loose around us as Graham let out a high-pitched shriek. 'Balance yourself!' he begged, and suddenly August's long arms were around me, pulling me and the pseudo-shaman apart.

When August had separated the two of us, I couldn't help but plunge my head under his armpit, and in that comforting embrace, I began to sob, while August offered his apologies to Graham. 'This man has recently gone through a terrible heartbreak,' August explained with his arms around my head. 'He isn't himself, as the saying goes, and I'd be eternally grateful if you'd refrain from mentioning this outburst to anyone.' I heard Graham agree to silence, and when I pulled myself together enough to observe the man's disposition, I saw that despite a certain shock in his wide eyes, and a slight flush in his cheeks, he seemed to have recovered his affected serenity, nodding and bowing as we made our farewells and we walked out the door into the warm coastal noon. August hobbled me back down the drive with his arm over my shoulder. When we were out in the empty street at the end of the drive August slapped me across the cheek, and I looked at him, astonished at this action. He was smiling widely, and he placed his hands on both my shoulders. 'Now,' he said with a proud look in his eyes. 'That was a breakthrough, if ever there was one. Mark me, some deep unearthing went on in that gym. Must be some powerful technique that strange man possessed.' I begged August not to start legitimising the charlatan's vagaries, or going on about my so-called repressions, assuring him my outburst had nothing to do with any telekinetic martial arts, or underlying heartache, and he replied, 'I won't say a word, if only you'll do me a favour.' I assured him I'd do anything to avoid more discussion on the subject, and August gestured towards the car with his phone. 'Take over the driving.' I was happy to do so, if only to take my mind off my recent disgrace, but I should have realised something was afoot when August sat in the back seat, directly behind me, evidently texting someone madly. I set off, back to the caravan park, but when its blue-green sign came into view, August asked me to drive past it, towards the centre of town, past the luxury spas, retreats, hotels, and palm-treed resorts. 'Here's the thing,' he said at last. 'Cain Rivera isn't the only resident of Byron I've been in communication with of late.'

After this ominous throat clearing came the revelation that August had been messaging a woman named Vicki, an Irish expat who was staying at a motel in the middle of town and was desperately hoping for companions to accompany her to the fabled town of Nimbin. 'Congratulations,' I muttered, already painfully aware of his intentions. 'Not for my own sake, you understand,' he said, keeping his eyes on the passing Byron streets as he added, 'Besides, I'm in training for physical combat – I must keep clear of the opposing sex, lest I end up facing war on more than one front.' With an already sunken acceptance that the rest of the day was doomed to be a road trip and a surprise blind date rolled into one, with August as my mad chaperone and guide, I drove to the Water's Edge Motel, where a small woman with willowy blonde hair and a green backpack slung over her shoulder stood smiling and waving beneath a palm tree at our approach. 'Now, above all, be kind,' August intoned as this stranger swung open the passenger door and plonked down heavily with her bag held tight to her chest. 'You must be August!' she said, beaming to the large, tattooed figure sitting ominously in the back seat of the car. 'I am,' he replied, shaking Vicki's hand in a theatrical fashion. 'And this,' he said, tapping my shoulder, 'is the fellow I was telling you about.' Taking my cue from August, I shook Vicki's small firm hand, and we set off together for the hippie capital of the country.

August was uncharacteristically quiet as we headed out of town in Nimbin's direction, but as I conversed with Vicki, he watched me intently via the rear-view mirror, giving a running non-verbal commentary on my participation in the conversation – sternly shaking his head when he felt I was going astray, offering solemn nods when he approved of my chatter. My asking about Irish cuisine, for example, provoked vigorous shaking, but August nodded proudly when I turned the conversation towards my affection for Irish literature. Vicki claimed some scholarship on her people's love of letters. 'My dad could recite whole swathes of *Ulysses* when I was a girl,' she said with obvious delight. 'I could recite some myself, with his influence on me. A good man my dad. Better than most men. You know that's one thing that surprised me when I first came over – nobody seems to know much poetry here. I've been asking round and can't get so much as a whisper on the subject. It's sad, really. I grew up with all the Romantics. Yeats, Wordsworth, Shelley, you name it, and I'll spin you a bit of whatever you like. Simply can't get a conversation out of anyone on that subject around these parts.' August kicked the back of my seat, but I listened and agreed with Vicki that it was a lesser obsession in our fair country. Vicki seemed happy to carry the weight of conversation for the three of us, explaining her turn as a psych student at Limerick University. 'I started to lose all interest in study, after the first semester. I thought I'd take a break and travel about instead. And first place I set my sights on was Australia. Not a moment do I step one foot in the country, and they slam closed the borders, because of the pandemic.' She shrugged her shoulders and sighed as we passed a wide valley of lavender and thistle weed that stretched far into a hilly distance. 'I'm in love with the place now though,' she said. 'Dunno if I'll go back, when I can.' There was a silence for a moment, and I asked her what she loved about the country, a question which garnered no review from August, who seemed curious enough about her answer to have forgotten his critical duties. Vicki smiled and turned to look at the two of us, strands of her waxy blonde hair loose and dancing down about her cheeks. 'What's not to love about it?' she said, as she turned her playful smiling eyes back to the passing valleys. August gave a thumbs-up gesture in the mirror, and I determined not to look back at him for the rest of the drive.

The hilly plains around Nimbin were golden green and the roads snaked round them in disorienting curves. Spare signs of farms and estates emerged along the weedy fields, and occasional fences and windmills popped up near homesteads with barrelled water tanks and wire fences staked in the earth. A muddy creek ran alongside the road as we came close to town, flowing along a trench in the sloping hills, and mangroves and dead trees protruded from the murky water. The sight of blue mountains in the distance must have struck a note in Vicki, who stopped talking mid-sentence about the cities and towns of Ireland and recited, 'Into my heart, an air that kills, from yon far country blows. What are those blue remembered hills, what spires, what farms are those? That is the land of lost content, I see it shining plain. The happy highways where I went, and cannot come again.' These lines were a fine thing to hear in her sonorous accent as we passed along the merry country, and we thanked her for raising the tenor of our travels, which we agreed had suffered greatly from a general lack of lyricism. 'Keep it coming,' I begged, and Vicki smiled and assured us she would spout verse whenever it seemed appropriate to the occasion.

The first sign of the notorious town was an ordinary bowling club, a series of sensible barns, large vehicles with bumper bars and spotlights parked in driveways, and a plain-looking park with blue monkey bars and children's slides. The park was peculiar only in that several older men in leather hats and sleeveless shirts were sitting at a table together, under a weathered gazebo. 'Stop the car,' August said at the sight of these old gents, and I parked outside a store with an ochre rainbow mural painted on its awning, and flowing dresses of purples and blues and acid greens hanging from pegged displays out front. 'Now remember,' August announced as we stepped out of the Corolla. 'Our task here is to acquire consciousness-expanding substances at any cost, though we should try to do so without offending the locals.' Vicki made it clear that though she was willing to try whatever drugs we could scrounge, she'd much prefer not to be involved with any dealing. 'I'd rather have my fortune read. I think I'll see if I can find a gypsy.' We agreed to split up, for the now, to accomplish our separate aims. August waved me to follow along, and we headed into the park where the old bearded men were sitting around, minding their own business.

As we approached the sleeveless smokers, there was a terrific ratty smell of pot, and one of the old boys who had spied us coming called out, 'Hey brother! You looking for weed? We got that hyperspace weed! Get you flying like Scooby Dooby on a rocket-ship! We can get ya zipped like Dumbledore on LSD, boys!' The exclamatory man stood up as we approached, preening his grey beard, and the others eyed us with suspicious eyes under their leathery hats, like outback wizards with impassive grey expressions. 'How much you want?' the greyest of the bearded men asked, trenches of age running under all that clouded hair. Hearing our opening offer, they all waved at August and me and shook their heads. 'Nah, nah, boys. C'mon, now, be real. Can't do nothing that small around here, aye.' There was nothing to be done, we couldn't afford to get our hands on the space weed for sale under the gazebo, though the four wise men directed us towards a part of town where we'd likely have more luck, and we made our way there, passing a shack selling skirts with psychedelic spirit symbols painted above its old tin awning, an arts and craft gallery with rainbow banners waving from its doors, and an old backpacker hotel where the smell of beer and the sound of pool balls could be heard on the cool breeze blowing from its open bar.

The dealers the men in the park directed us towards were

assembled outside a store selling an impressive array of bongs, blankets, oil extracts and pungent amulets – a catalogue of goods particularly impressive when you considered the store itself claimed to be a political embassy, rather than a shop. The small gathering consisted of dozing people and sleeping dogs, all of whom looked as though they could increase the mineral content of ground soil simply by walking over it. It was impossible to tell the ages of the men and women, though even the youngest of their number could fairly be described as wizened. The palest, portliest, most Bilbo Baggins-esque of the embassy's overseers rose from his carpeted milk crate and asked, as if possessing mystic intuition, which edibles we were after. Perhaps taking his cue from the excitable old dealers in the park, August replied, 'We need that starship-strength shit – something that'll make us feel like Dumbledore on LSD, please.' The portly poet providore gave this specificity a seriousness I could hardly credit, nodding his head, scratching his chin, indeed taking out a pair of circular spectacles and looking at something in the far distance, where my own eyes could detect nothing but the wisp of passing clouds above a nest of hills and a receding flock of crows. 'Yes,' he said, affirming that he could supply us with just such an experience, if only we'd mind his spot until he returned. August took this request more literally than I felt was appropriate, sitting down on the man's crate, and even asking other tourists as they passed whether they were looking to score. I begged August to cease this false advertising immediately, encouraging him to observe the funny looks the real dealers were giving us. One of them, an ancient-looking woman seated beside August, who had a large brown bloodhound barely breathing at her feet, leaned towards us and said, 'My first car had BMW on the back.' I smiled and congratulated her. 'You know what BMW stood for?' she asked, with a twinkle in her eye and a smile on her wintery face. 'Bob Marley and the Wailers,' she said, and pointed at a poster hanging in the embassy display on which that famous Rastafarian was featured. The man with the promised supply was back quickly, returning with a snap-lock bag full of pale and crumbling biscuits in hand, for which we exchanged a fistful of fifties and much gratitude. 'Give it fifteen minutes between bites,' the bespectacled fellow said. 'And whatever you do, don't start eating until you've made it home.'

Having made our score, August and I proceeded down the potpourri splendour of Nimbin's main street, stopping only briefly to buy some sausage rolls from a bakery operated by a dark-haired woman and her four daughters. Shoving these into our mouths, we made our way towards the fortune teller, having taken direction from the baker, and soon came to the mystic's enclave, upon which were posters promising the power to read signs, palms, tea leaves and other arcana. We waited for Vicki on the bench outside, watching the passing parade of minivans and beat-up station wagons, inhaling the smell of musk and coffee wafting out of the rainbow café down the street. When Vicki emerged from the fortune teller, she was beaming. She put her pale arms over our shoulders as we headed towards the car park together, our aims in Nimbin satisfied by this short visit. I attempted to press Vicki on the revelations that had been made to her behind the darkness of the psychic's curtains, but she would not reveal what the tarot showed, except that she was pleased with the hand she had been dealt. When she asked in return how our scrounging had gone, she was surprised to find we'd been successful in acquiring edibles.

'Well show them to me!' she demanded, but I refused, the dealer's ominous warnings of forbearance echoing in my mind. 'I just want a little look!' she said incredulously, and so I took the bag of biscuits out and passed them to her.

No sooner had we passed the first of a series of sea-green hills covered in the tidy rows of fig trees and macadamia farms which line the rises and falls between Nimbin and civilisation than August, our brave conductor, snatched the bag from Vicki's hands and took his first nibble on a crumbling biscuit before handing the bag on to me. 'You shouldn't have done that!' I said. 'You got no idea what effect these things might have on you.' August scoffed, saying he knew precisely what effect the cookies would have, and had timed his slight partaking to sync perfectly with our safe arrival back in Byron. 'That means we should have some now too, then aye?' Vicki asked with her mischievous smile on me from the back seat. I swallowed down a chunk and handed the bag to her. We continued through the sweeping curves of the country, the green lustre of which reminded Vicki of her emerald island home, none of us feeling any effects whatsoever, all of us keeping close watch on our senses for signs of intoxication. Just to be sure the dose was adequate, we each took a second course of the biscuits, and then a third, discussing the differences between Vicki's native home and ours. It occurred to me that there was some Irish blood in my own ancestry, but when Vicki asked for particulars and I took a moment to consider, reflecting on my father, and his father, and the father before him, it seemed strangely laborious to do so, and I had to make use of fingers to aid my memory, and by the time I had arrived at the distant relative who had ventured from Ireland's shores to bring his lineage here, I'd forgotten why I'd begun in the first place, and simply watched the rolling hills and fields and meadows, the cows and goats, and the occasional gang of llamas, and a pair of dogs lying by a tyre swing, and a dismantled tractor engine here and there. I've heard it said that the inevitable sign a woman in labour is finally ready to birth her child into the world is when she declares, in pained tones, that she simply cannot do it. So too, it seems that the effect of edibles amongst uninitiated consumers invariably begins with someone declaring the edibles to be without effect. In this case, I was the one to utter that cliché, announcing that it was apparent we had been ripped off by that Bilbo-looking so-and-so and his reassuring demeanour. 'You can't taste anything but peanut butter in these things anyway,' I said.

The first indication that I had spoken too soon came when I turned around to observe Vicki, who had become deathly quiet in the back seat, and saw that her face had taken on a mild petrification, as if she had been awake for several days, with stark circles round her fearful eyes as she stared out the window with the solemnity of a soldier unable to return from the trauma of a battle. When I called her name, she was startled, as though encountering an apparition, and she whispered back at me so softly and eerily that all I could do was laugh in response, though I wasn't in the least sure why it was so amusing. In hindsight, these odd effects were obviously the earliest presentations of being under the influence, but being unlearned in the consumption of THC we continued to nibble away in turns at our crumbling supply. The point where even I became conscious that we were losing ourselves came with a two-fold realisation. The first was an awareness that for several minutes August had been speaking entirely in the character of the wizard Dumbledore, making such refrains as 'Harry, Hogwarts is in great danger!' and 'It is with a heavy heart I must subtract ten points from Gryffindor,' repeatedly. The second step in this process of realisation was that I myself, for time out of mind, had been responding to August's theatre with my own imitation of the character Dobby, from the same franchise, replying to August's refrains exclusively with such comments as 'Dobby has no master!' and 'Dobby is finally free!' When the strangeness of this theatre occurred to me, I was struck by the thought that August had ordered precisely this experience, requesting 'Dumbledore on LSD' weed from our dealer, and between strange fits of laughter, I tried desperately to draw his attention to the fact that this miracle was taking place. How slim was the chance we would actually get what we asked for? How unlikely the verisimilitude of our intoxication! But I could no more express my wonder than account for the phenomenon which had caused it, so I surrendered instead, covering my face in my hands and announcing continuously, 'Oh August, we're fucked! We're completely fucked, aren't we?' Though even this was hard to express. My lips seemed to stick together, and my tongue felt as heavy, hot and awkward as a porterhouse steak in my mouth.

Against a bombardment of spasmodic ripples erupting through my nervous system, I marshalled my remaining coordination and turned back to check on Vicki. God forgive us, that poor Irish lass whose pale skin had the sweet smell of powdered milk, and whose kind hazel eyes were as full of trust and innocence as might become a Disney princess, now looked as one who had beheld Medusa. The faint trace of colour Vicki's fair complexion possessed had fled from her, and she stared ahead as though stupefied, clutching her knees, rocking and rolling gently as we took the wide curves around the hills. It took a long time to turn back around, but when I did, I saw that we were close to Byron's city limits. 'Vicki's fucked, man!' August didn't respond, but I could see from the look in his eyes that operating the vehicle now needed his maximum attention, and so I trusted that my message had sunk through somehow, and that he would know what to do. But the further we went into Byron town the more my despair began to swell. The distance to Vicki's motel seemed interminably long, the road went on forever. We passed a four-star holiday resort surrounded by fig trees and I saw a family of five glaring at us as we rolled by, an old man stopped under a TAB sign outside a golf club scowling with owl-like eyes, and a storm of black currawongs that streamed out from a caravan park with sagging electric wires reaching out like a trembling web for some gargantuan spider. 'You went past Vicki's hotel, man!' I said to August, once, twice, three times, increasing in volume and exclamation until I felt myself in a panic, to the point that the urge to unbuckle my belt and unlock my door became difficult to resist. At this speed the impact would likely kill me, but it would be better to die a free man than to be trapped in this endless road of motels and strangers. We went by a roadhouse where a yellow kombi van of surfers was laughing at us, and I felt the urge to leap from the car growing irresistibly, but we came then upon a more residential part of town, with neat lawns and clean white picket fences, with tropical trees looming over the yards, and I felt that we'd become anonymous again. Soon enough, in this more subdued part of the town, we arrived outside Vicki's motel, but there we encountered a new problem. Both August and I were equally unfit for the task of helping Vicki to her hotel room, so, like two benevolent captors encouraging a rehabilitated animal back to the wild, we simply opened Vicki's door, gave her some encouraging words and hoped she would figure the rest out for herself. Muttering a vague and distant assurance of being okay, and having had a great time, and looking forward to catching up again and so on, Vicki managed to free herself from her seatbelt, left the vehicle and, operating on sheer instinct, wandered up the stairs, opened the door to her room, and disappeared behind it. What would become of her behind closed doors, August said, was between fate and the angels. And so, unburdened by our Irish Rose, we were free to do whatever we wished – and what we wished was to be back at the caravan park, sitting very still.

Despite some small difficulties inputting the passcode into the caravan park's boom gate, we soon attained our desires, and found ourselves sitting outside our cabin under an awning, watching surges of white cloud pass over the afternoon sky above Byron's outer limits, my body trembling with nerves. 'We were fools not to take that old drug dealer's advice,' I said to August, but he waved that away, saying it had all turned out for the best. We were stoned in Byron, on numbing weed, a pair of good old-fashioned tourists doing what they thought the locals would do. 'Well, what do we do now?' I asked him, and we drank a few beers, still discombobulated with the effects of our magical biscuits. Sitting there in folding chairs watching the clouds passing overhead, trembling beneath the cabin awning with our beers in our hands, we both agreed it would be a mistake to take more of the edibles, whose potency we could no longer doubt. Then we got the bag of biscuits out and ate a bunch more of them anyway. As it would soon turn out, it was a mistake to repeat that first mistake.

The second dose of baked goods struck us within minutes, and the effect was a brief reprise of August's performance of Dumbledore, in which he began regaling me with new scenarios in which Hogwarts was again in 'great danger' from 'dark and mysterious forces'. All I could do was stare in amazement, as August next went into the opening of a verbal symphony that pushed me to the edge of madness, improvising a dialogue between an invented fictional father and son. 'Son,' he began by saying. 'You must take yourself out into the world, you must be strong, and face every danger. You must climb every mountain, my son. You must fight the unbeatable foe! For it is in facing the chaos of the world that one remakes it in the noble image of the divine!' He said this to the air, and then replied to himself in the character of the imaginary son, saying, 'But Dad, what if I'm not ready? How will I know how to encounter the multiplicity of chaos as I emerge into the world?' Then shaking his head at his own speech, he replied, 'Son, have you not heard a word I've said? You face your fears even in the throes of indecision! You must make your mark upon this world even in your deepest doubt!' He lurched forward in his folding chair, his eyes bulging with sincerity as he pleaded, 'But Dad, what if I fail? How will I know how to begin? What is there in the world which wants me to succeed?' Again, August shook his head in disappointment at his own words. 'Son, there is nothing more I can teach you here, you must take on board all that I have taught you! You must sow your peppertree seeds in the verdant valleys beyond this place.' August lurched again, almost falling out of his folding chair. 'But Dad, how will I know my training is enough to prepare me for this transition into the world of the plenipotential!' And so on, and so on. This circuitous dialogue continued interminably, until the theatre August was spewing out in his strange gesticular fashion began to swallow me whole. Each time he spoke as the father, I could see him becoming older, more ancient and eternal, and each time he lurched forward and spoke as the son, I saw him become much younger and innocent. This mummery began to feel more real to me than my own existence, and the puny little drama of my actual life began to pale in significance to the characters of August's invention, and for a moment I feared that I would be utterly lost in this fiction of his creation, and so had to hold my hands over my ears to keep his Socratic banter out of my head. For a while I steadied by focusing all my attention on a blue tent across from our cabin, and the way three magpies were hopping about on the bright grass, digging for bugs and worms and whatever magpies eat. A strict focus on this ordinary scene helped to keep August's chanting at bay, though I could see him peripherally, hunched into himself, his head bouncing up and down. I knew that when he was bent double, he was doing the voice of the father, when he lifted his head and lurched forward, he was doing the voice of the son, and he bopped up and down like this, wide-eyed, waving his arms and doing little dances with his feet, as he unfolded more of this paternal hero's journey nonsense. I held my hands tight to keep his constant rambling out, muttering very quietly for him to stop talking, focusing all my attention on that blue tent, and now on some cockatoos in the limbs of a gum tree, shitting occasionally on the lawn near the park's fence. Time out of mind passed this way, holding August's voice at bay, watching the birds, my body trembling terribly in my seat. The afternoon shadows grew long, and a purple sky began to grow over the distance, and I became complacent, releasing my ears and reclining lazily into my chair. For how long I sat there I could not say, but slowly I became aware of something incredibly disturbing, shocking, terrifying. I looked directly upon August, who was now bobbing brutally in his chair, like a man violently fellating himself, and realised that for at least the last hour he had uttered only a single abbreviation, over and over, with a breathless rapidity. Bouncing up and down in his chair, holding himself in the poise of a loony in a straightjacket, he was repeating continuously, 'bro, bro, bro, bro, bro,' so that all I could hear, bouncing around the shelter was a bombardment of 'bro, bro, bro,' and it triggered in me a profound paranoia. Surely anyone who saw or heard this bizarre spectacle would conclude that something was seriously wrong and would call the cops on us immediately. Loudly, I asked August to stop. I demanded his immediate silence, but he seemed unwilling or unable to hear, and I was afraid to get too close to his 'bros' to restrain him. Instead, I stepped around him like one might do on encountering a tiger distracted in the act of grooming itself, hustled myself through the cabin door, locked it at once, and shut up all the windows so that his everlasting 'bro, bro, bro-ing' would not so easily get in.

To calm my nerves I went to get a beer from the little fridge, but there were 'bros' bouncing around in the chamber of the fridge, so I slammed it shut. I tried to crawl under the blankets of the bunk bed, but there were 'bros' rolling about in the bedsheets too, they were coming in through the vents – and so I fled into the bathroom to cover my ears in the water jets of the shower. But they were coming up from the sink, and there was a definite 'bro' in the leaking toothpaste tube, and 'bro' on each ant coming up from the drain in the floor, and climbing up into the shower recess. I had a peek outside the tiny bathroom window at the evening's descent, and no one seemed to be alarmed at August's evermore vigorous chanting. I slumped down in the cramped shower and though I could still hear the bro-ing, coming in through the thin walls of the cabin, my own thoughts were loud enough in that tight capsule to keep me sane, and with my eyes screwed shut, I could almost keep out the madness of the world, and great startling flashes of complex patterns and colours rained down upon my inner eye with an inexplicable feeling of interconnectivity raging rampant through my senses. I saw that man was simply part of an enormous self-defining universe, each of us amounting to a small node of consciousness spreading out into an enveloping web of universal sensation and profound cosmological silence. Sound and longing, self and assemblage. How many hours I passed prone on the slick shower floor in this mediation I cannot tell, only the realisation slowly came that all 'bros' had ceased, and the sun had set, and upon me I wore a suit of ants. I took the pillow off my head, washed away the insects, retrieved an unconscious August and stewarded him on to the bottom bunk. He lay there, restful as a babe, and I climbed up top and said a heartfelt prayer to Jesus, apologising for entertaining the blasphemous clichés and pseudo-profundities that the cookies had cast upon me.

I awoke to a world unintelligible, astonished at the state of my surroundings. An ecstatic richness of sunlight beamed through the curtains of the little cabin and revealed the interior's frightful unfamiliarity to my uncomprehending eyes. To orient myself, I tried to remember what events had led me to sleep, but the effort was beyond mental reach, so that even a general awareness of the day prior was like reading a clue in a cryptic crossword several times only to confront the terrifying possibility of finding one's comprehension in a cul-de-sac of confusion. Empty beer bottles were scattered over the cabin's small circular table, with the strangely perfect chaotic symmetry you might expect from a still-life arrangement. Clothing of all kinds was discarded along the patterned lino, and a wet snoring was coming from the bunk beneath me. In the distance, whipbirds and magpies were whistling to one another, while country music played on a radio somewhere just outside the walls. All this sensorial information spun in my nauseated head with a vagueness that lasted several moments, until I looked down and spied a tattooed leg hanging over the side of the bunk below, its foot wearing an Adidas sock. The sight of August's long limb recalled my present predicament, and all the strange associations of our brief trip together came rushing back upon me like a hastily reconstructed theatre set. 'August,' I called out to the leg protruding over the lower bunk. 'What time is it?' He didn't answer, but a tattooed arm slung itself over the edge to greet the lonely leg, and this seemed a satisfactory sign that all was well with the world.

August's first act on awakening was to contact Vicki and make sure she'd recovered from her taste of the cookies without much trouble. While he spoke on the phone, I sat on my bed swaying slightly and watching a family cook sausages on a barbecue by an old-fashioned tent through the cabin's sliding glass door. The two kids, a brother and sister, were running around each other, swinging sticks like swords in the sun, and a pregnant woman was lazing in a hammock between two trees close to the park's fence. Their father was shirtless, and his belly hung down in a pale pouch, not unlike a pregnancy of his own, and sweat was dripping from his brow and catching in his eyes. 'God help us,' I said aloud in the little cabin, a terrible feeling of dread growling up inside my mind at the sight of that ordinary family and the sound of their play. All thought of the scene was trampled by August's return to the cabin, and he sauntered in announcing that Vicki felt fine but for a little dizziness, and she would join us in the evening after 'our excursion'. I didn't bother asking August what he meant by that phrase, but when I'd showered and washed off the swelter of the cabin's close quarters, and the uneasy feeling I'd had watching the barbecue going on outside, he told me it would be good to dress for a hike, since he had plans to lead us on an expedition through a nearby forest. 'To say that's the last thing I want to hear at this moment overworks understatement,' I told him. He chastised me for using clichés, and I dressed appropriately for what I assumed would be a long day lost in the woods.

We set out with a few bottles of tap water and August resumed the duties of driver and spiritual guide. 'The mistake most people make, after expanding their horizons by use of psychotropics, is they don't bother restricting them again. As the mildest elementary examination of the situation ought to make apparent to anyone interested in psychological engineering, expansion is fine, but without constraint there can be no structure, and without structure and form a mind is no better for thinking than a cloud is for heavy lifting.' It was too early to start fishing around for the flask that was still stashed somewhere in the car, but I felt a growing thirst at hearing these sentiments. 'I'm taking you on a hike,' he said, 'into the heart of nature – for my own benefit too – since it's obvious we overdid it with those edibles yesterday, and I can't go into my fight tomorrow with a mellowed frame of mind. And what better way to undo a hippy high than some vigorous physical exertion out in the rigours of nature's merciless excess.' I suggested we try bacon and eggs instead, and he permitted us the luxury of stopping for breakfast at a café close to the caravan park, where I sat on a plastic chair and ate very slowly in the intense Byron morning with my swollen eyes closed against the glare, listening to two surfers talking about the promise of the day's conditions.

After this brief repast, we drove for about an hour out of town, and wound our way up to a lookout which revealed a distant green valley, crowned by pale scribbly gums whose branches shone with a golden hue when the sun pierced through the grey clouds, illuminating the steep plunge of the valley's mouth. Opposite our position was a cliff-face from which three heavy river streams cascaded down in an immense spray of white rain. Never in my life had I seen such a view, and the waterfall flowing down into the valley's void was more powerful than any flow of water known to me. 'We'll take the trail down to the gorge,' August said. 'We should be standing under the waterfall by midday, so try to keep the pace,' he said, and he marched into a trail lined with waving ferns without another word.

We proceeded along the trail without much conversation, both of us trying to find a pace that suited the muddy, obstacle-strewn conditions of the descent down the mountain. 'Tell me, August, why are you going to fight Cain Rivera? Surely there's nothing to be gained in this whole avenging business?' I asked. 'It's a mistake,' he replied, brushing a low-hanging branch away from his face, 'to go looking for hidden motivations when the overt and stated is sufficient. You're always making that mistake. You're always surprised to find people and things are what they seem to be. You expect the obvious to be all surface matter, but sometimes the surface is more than deep enough. We are all making meaning where we can in this world, and what seems absurd may have some deeper significance. Not hidden, not disguised, not some repressed unconscious dimension, but a meaning one keeps alive in themselves. It's true that beneath all our actions there is some distant echo of a feeling that calls to us out of the dark, a little voice of hope springing eternal out of dreams and a half-forgotten innocence, a sweet song-like voice so close to fading away, and we cannot see its source in the emptiness, we cannot know the path it's calling us on, only that there is a brightness and a light it gives to our outstretched arms, a tingling in the calloused nerves of hands held up, as we stumble forward and make ourselves who we are in the numb becoming of life, and if we lose that touch, we know then that we are forever lost. And yet, we pretend not to notice our loss when it is final, we tell ourselves we never knew the voice, the feeling that called us forward. We lie to ourselves and say, there is no sense in our surroundings, our actions – there is no meaning but that which the parts of the whole disguise to reason.' It was becoming difficult to listen to August as we marched on through the trees and the mud, and his voice called back to me over his shoulder at a greater and greater distance, and I felt my breathing growing heavy. 'Did I ever tell you about my trip to Vegas?' he asked, as if this would more easily explain his proposition. 'I'll tell you about it.'

'It was a cousin of mine, Vincent, who was to be married, and wanted us to celebrate with him in Las Vegas. And such was his generosity that he arranged each of us – there were at least a dozen guests invited – to stay in a luxurious Las Vegas hotel for a week in the Christmas holidays of that year. When the invite came through, I accepted in an instant, never having been there before, though always strangely drawn to that city's flashing colours and baser seductions, its carnivalesque promises of a world where the ordinary rules, if not quite inverted, are tugged a little to one side. The hotel he paid for us to stay in was a glittering beast, a palace by day, and a funhouse by night, with Rolls-Royces and Mercedes-Benzes rolling up to valets in red coats, and green Ferraris and blue Lamborghinis arriving by the hour, and handsome men in tanned suits and glimmering gold chains coming through the doors like an army of male models on the march, and by their sides were countless women more beautiful than any I'd ever seen.' August's voice was trailing further ahead, as my feet sank into a soft goop of black clay hidden by a slush of decomposing leaves, soaking my socks in the wet earth. 'Two nights we spent drinking and dancing and gambling. Surrounded by the people whose beauty and hunger were beyond imagination, women in red dresses with eyes like panthers, men in cowboy hats and snakeskin boots, old ladies who sat still as gargoyles for days on end at a single machine, not moving except to suck down free vodka martinis, and the sound of machines running and buzzing was in my ears, and the soft carpet beneath my feet, while the dark desert sky surrounded us in every direction outside the golden windows of the casino. And the food! Short-rib grills the size of cinder blocks, dripping with three kinds of cheese and a pound of pork belly, bottomless buckets of sweet-and-sour buffalo wings which dribbled their sauces down your arms, bison burgers with bone marrow relish and ghost-pepper butter, spice-rub slabs of charred smoked brisket served in baskets crusted with onion ring walls, with dipping-sauce-fondant fountains free at the bistro tables, all that served with castles of cornbread and bins of collard greens and washed down with all the bourbon and whisky and rum and coke you can swallow. I wandered around in that artifice of excess, drunk and full and slushed and gassy as a compost tumbler spinning in the sun. On the third day of this abundance, I found myself sitting alone at a long empty table amidst the bleeping and the blearing, in the very heart of the casino, watching the whole parade mobilising around me in its bacchanalian order, my eyes bleary and my belly heavy. I sat there, and my cousin caught my eye from across the frenzy of the room. When he came upon me, I was sitting there frowning and smouldering like a dying fire, and he was wild with frustration. "What is the matter with you?" he said. "Haven't I favoured you, August? Haven't I brought you to the centre of universal pleasure? Provided your flights to carry you, your bed to sleep on, the wide vantage from your windows to look down upon the world, your feasting, your liquor? And what do I ask in return? Only that having spread my joy at your feet, I ask you not to tread upon it in contempt, I ask you not to trample my joy with your refusal? All I wanted," he said to me, "was three nights of pleasure to share with my family. That's all!"

'What could I say to my cousin, that despite all he'd given to me, I couldn't be happy? How could I explain to him my overwhelming feeling, that no matter how the roulette wheel spun, or what hand was dealt to me – no matter the machine I played, or with which lucky dice I rolled, that the result would never undo my sealed fate? I knew that no matter how much I ate, or drank, no matter how much I wasted in the slots, or on the craps, whatever I did, I would still be heading home to a life of ordinary hours, standing in the deli section of the supermarket, wiping my hands on an apron amidst the cold meats and stuffed olives, wrapping orders in sheets of paper for people who will never know my name. My cousin walked away from me, in disgust, and I sat in silence at my table, rolling the balls of ice in my drink, with the calamity of the casino ringing and squealing around me. I stared into the light bending in my glass and felt the urge to scream and smash it all to pieces. I wanted to upend my table and smash myself apart like a statue of ice tossed from the ceiling. And then, from nowhere, like a visitation from the heavens, the most elegant woman I have ever seen placed a hand on a stool at my table and asked if she might sit down with me. She was black of hair and her eyes were green. There were gleaming rings on her fine fingers, and her purple-painted lips made such a kind smile that I couldn't help but smile back despite my inner turmoil. She asked my name, and I told her, and hearing my accent she gave a gasp of delight. "August from Australia!" she exclaimed, and she clapped her jewelled hands and flicked her hair over her bare shoulder. She had the smallest round ears, and tiny diamond piercings. I bought us both drinks, and we sat and chatted for a while. Her name was Amber, from Alabama, she said, and I tried my best Deep South impression, and she laughed and took my hand in hers. She turned it over, ran a finger gently across my palm, over the callouses and scars, then asked if she could read my future in the cracks and lines. I said she could, and she traced the markings of my skin, just so, holding my palm close to her curious eyes. "You're fated to live a long and lovely life, August," she said, still holding onto my hand. She turned it around and pressed her lips just above my knuckles, like a gentleman in some old movie. Then she rose out of her seat, smiling, and said, "Between the beginning and the end, life is but a little music in the middle." Then with a tiny wave, she disappeared into the crowd. I sat there for a while, and I finished my drink, the faint wetness where her lips had touched me tingling like a cooling burn upon my skin, and I could have laughed. I realised, sitting in the deepest heart of this great temple of hedonistic masochism, that this one moment's intimacy with a stranger – this one moment of human connection – was worth more than all the glittering lights and flashing riches of the earth combined. One moment of being seen, the touch of a single finger, the sound of one smiling word, had outweighed it all. That one moment of humanity was the entirety of my time in Las Vegas. You see what I'm saying to you?' August asked me. In the excitement of telling this tale, August had outpaced me considerably, and so I had to cry out to reach him with my reply, saying, 'You realise she was looking for work, yeah?' He made no direct response, other than to quicken his pace even more dramatically, so that he slowly disappeared around another curve in the declining path down the mountainside.

I increased my trot to try and reach my companion but stepping round muddy pools and sodden tracks along the trail was difficult going, and soon not even the sound of August marching ahead of me was to be heard. On and on, I kept the best pace my blood-shod body could manage, climbing over the moss pelts of fallen trees, and boulders half-buried in wet slips of earth, and roots reaching across the winding way between the gums. The sun broke free from the silver clouds that had swept over the sky, and it glared through the trembling limbs of the trees with a terrible heat, and fresh sweat flattened my hair and spilled into my mouth as I pushed on. Soon I was reduced to a heavy, haggard breathing, and coming upon a sudden flight of wood-block stairs leading down by the hundreds, deeper and deeper into the valley, I stopped for a while to catch some air, with the lizards darting invisibly in the undergrowth around me. For a moment I considered turning around and heading back up the way, but that would have hardly been an easier task, so I stomped on downward, holding onto branches and scattered fence posts staked in the trail to spare my legs and lungs a little effort. The air itself was rich with the damp lineament scent of eucalyptus, and a citrus scent caught my attention as I passed bogs of wild plants with yellow flowers buzzing with tiny insects. Nearby a monitor lizard clung to the bulb of an enormous trunk by a wide patch on the trail, surrounded by the formidable spikes of palms and their fallen fronds, which made an armoured ring around them in the mud. Just beyond this odd clearing was the sound of flowing water, and I emerged at the bend of a rapid stream, where the only way to proceed was by hugging three slick boulders. On these rocks were several young couples in bathers, lying in each other's arms and talking in whispers under the rush of the heavy waters. On the other side of the stream, I could see August, turning to the east at a fork in the trail. I took a moment to study the movements of the water, which must have come forging down from the falls, and I knew that this meant I'd reached the bottom of my descent. The wet boulders were slippery and crowded with couples, and I was reduced to crawling past them awkwardly rather than taking the more elegant passage of leaping adroitly from the rocks. The young couples took a giggling amusement at my undignified progress, my soaked shirt and sweat-slimed hair lending a little theatre to my reptilian approach to the crossing, and the youngsters clapped and cheered for me once I was on the other side. My right foot slipped into the river water for a moment, and it emerged bejewelled with a host of shining leeches.

August had long since disappeared around an ascension crowned by more mossy boulders. I plucked the bloody leeches off and followed the trail he had taken, the colossal surge of the fall's increasing proximity was becoming a deafening enormity of sound, and the air around me was soaked with the spray coming from their cascade ahead. The pathway towards the falls and its rocky outcrop was saturated, and the spray was more like heavy rain than mist, making the rocks so treacherous to climb that I had to slide up on my belly, the mud smearing over my clothes and skin so that I began to feel like a kind of worm crawling through the muck. Squinting into the intense spray ahead, I spied two bare-chested men coming down the rocky rise, both drenched and panting, one limping in obvious distress as he went along. The limping man paused to look at me, his round frame laid against a cold rock for a moment between his laboured exhalations. 'Be warned,' he said to me, his chest heaving between each word. 'Everything is so slippery ahead – so frightening to climb. I almost broke my leg and might have done my neck in too, if not for my friend here,' he said, indicating his more capable companion, who was already halfway down to the level ground below. The two of us, wet-bodied and abused, passed each other then, exchanging meagre purchase in opposite directions, so tired and drenched we paid no heed to the uncomfortable closeness of our shared breath and space as we went by one another. Inch after inch I went on, over wet rock and sludge, until at last, over the next rise, I saw the falling water.

Beyond the slick rocky outcrop the full force of the water cascading over the cliff spilled continually in an astonishing free fall, and the spray rained down over the entire plunge pool at its base, the churning white froth exploding against the rocks, and the air was so thick in the blasting excess that it was as though a storm had been trapped in this idyll and could not get back into the air. Clambering up over the last of the boulders between myself and the clearing, and shielding my eyes against the intensity, I dropped down to the shore of the pool, half-blind and deafened by the raging waters. There was a small clearing sheltered beneath the outcrop and it was possible there to get my bearings. 'You've made it down the mountainside,' August's voice came from behind me, and I turned to find him soaked and soiled with mud. 'Do yourself a favour,' he said with an exhausted expression, 'and peek behind that last rock there, on the edge of the waters.' I forged back into the maelstrom of the fall's sheeting spray, and crept slowly round the side of the rock August had pointed me towards, and on its far side, four pale women were huddled together before the plunge pool, naked under the pressure of the falling water's collapse, their exposure hidden in the shade of the rock. They were swirling their bare legs in the waters of the pool, like mermaids straight from a fairy tale, whipping their long hair about with closed eyes against the hard rain. The water blinded me for a moment, and I wiped my face and looked back at August, leaning against the stony walls, a great glimmering smile on his face. 'What did I tell you?' he yelled to me. 'I told you you'd learn to love again,' he laughed. I made my way back to him, blasted with water and almost dizzied from exhaustion, and slapped his shoulder. 'How far distant do all my troubles seem,' he said to me, closing his own eyes. 'And suffering is but a fading whisper, and all ill moments, whose vast shadows descend over my worried mind at midnight hours, are so brightly washed away in this moment, that I am willing to believe they will not return to master me.' And he threw his long, tattooed arms around me, laughing and gesturing up at the great stone cliff with its endless supply of surging water. 'But bless us and keep us,' he said then, with a joyful expression in his face. 'We're still among the living, aren't we? And the living world happens in a stream, not in the stillness.' He grabbed my wet shoulders with saturated hands and shook me like a ragdoll, saying, 'Come on now, that's all the praise of nature a man can abide. Let's get out from under this ostentation.' And we began the torturous ascent back up the cliff.

The climb up was a grunting, gasping effort of mind-numbing repetitions, and by the time we returned to the Corolla neither of us had a word to say to the other. We drove directly back to the caravan park and washed all trace of the trek off us in the shower's weak warm water and bummed about the cabin waiting for the motivation to move again. Had Vicki not made plans with August to meet us in town, it's likely we would have sat there in the cabin dozing off till the crack of doom, but the meeting had been arranged and we followed through. We met Vicki at a bright Thai restaurant in the middle of main street, clinking glasses of Bollinger at dusk over crispy salt-and-pepper squid with a rich chilli marinade, and then we topped that off by stopping at a pizza parlour for single slices, and bubble tea from a vendor in an alleyway, before we finished our feasting at an Italian joint with bowls of puttanesca and Tuscan wine. We bought tie-dyed shirts at a place called Scallyrags across from the Beach Hotel, and Vicki wore hers on the hotel stage, singing 'Hurdy Gurdy Man' in her discordant Irish lilt to the whistles and cheers of a crowded bar, and we took fresh bottles of wine across to the beach, and there August narrated the meaning of the night's waves, claiming to have learned to read the motions of the ocean from his uncle in Fiji. 'Ask yourself what it means,' he said, sucking on the bottle. 'To look into this eternal refrain of the sea.' And he indicated the size of his implications with outstretched arms, gesturing to the faintly foaming darkness along the horizon of the easternmost shore. 'They say the sea is cold,' Vicki recited. 'But it boils with the passion of the whales.' Yes, August agreed with her quotation, 'That is the foamy heat from whence comes Aphrodite, on her oystered clam and out of the briny black. All beauty floats out of the same bleak oblivion, emergent star prick of universal consciousness, our minds made of that same contradicting law which is the rule of all creation. That is why the dark sea still waves to us, it is our sorrowful mother, who birthed us.'

'Oh, enough of this!' Vicki said. 'Let's go dancing, lads.' So, we shoved our empty bottles into public bins and tracked down the unmistakeable throbbing pulse of a nearby nightclub, doing our best to appear sober as the bouncers out front with their little torches inspected our identities in a queue of barely dressed teenage revellers. Inside the place was pumping, as they say. As we passed, one pug-faced young man with stubby red arms asked sincerely, 'What are youse old cunts doing in here?' The three of us took up residence at a table nearest the dance floor, right beside the groaning speakers and shouted at each other for conversation. 'Go on, what are you waiting for?' Vicki said. 'Go on up there and show us your moves, August. Go on, look at that!' she said with a nod of her head to the gaggle of girls dancing wildly on the little floor. The young girls were shaking their bodies as if attempting to fling them apart at the seams in the flashing red lights of the club. August seemed momentarily sober, the dark whiskers on his face bristling, and I thought for a moment he might refuse the invitation. 'Look at that!' Vicki said again, clapping her hands and whistling. 'If you lads won't dance with that, then I'll take my chances!' August surrendered and followed Vicki onto the dance floor, into the flashing lights, and I saw him, enormous, black-bearded, tattooed limbs moving with the monstrous music's pulse, dancing towards the young girls like some totemic creation carried above the crowd, while Vicki waved her fine blonde hair and held her arms above her head in the pulsating thrum shaking through the speakers. Two girls, whose denim shorts were slipping up and disappearing between their cheeks, began rubbing themselves against August's thighs, and he closed his eyes in a kind of trance. Good for him, I thought, and went in search of the bar. With a shot of whisky and a schooner of beer, I wandered out to sit in the garden, where the harangue of the music was less barbarous in the chill night air, and I watched young couples, so like those lovers we'd seen on the rocks of the waterfall's stream, leaning into one another's necks, with the moon full and pale above the coastal town, and the dim stars emerging from behind the shifting passage of unseen clouds.

I stewed in my little spot in the garden, trying to feel invisible amidst the carnival of youth. 'Why did you take off?' I heard a voice, Vicki's voice, calling from behind. 'I was looking for you,' she said. 'I'm afraid I've never been much of a dancer,' I told her, swallowing my drink. 'A man who doesn't dance is an insult to the Holy Spirit,' she said. 'Besides, all the best lovers are dancers.' 'I never been much of that either,' I told her, and she patted my head like you might a pitiful child. 'Let's go sit,' she told me, and we sat by the garden wall, almost unseen in its slim shadows.

We sat together there with the long fronds of a potted plant curled round us like a thin snake wrapping around our shoulders. The pounding dance of the music was a pleasant wash at this distance, and the faint sound of the constant sea. Our legs were touching as we sat close, and Vicki said, 'You like the Irish writers then?' and her shagged blonde hair hung down around her flushed grinning face. 'A land of story and emerald green songs, a most charming people are you Irish.' She pinched my arm at this twaddle and told me to stop. 'I'm sorry,' I said. 'I'm too in the bag to answer you earnestly.' She took the schooner from my hand and set it hard on the seat beside me, took both my hands in hers and closed her eyes, and with a fine fluted intonation sang to me softly,

'If you ever go to Dublin town
In a hundred years or so
Inquire for me in Baggot Street
And what I was like to know
O he was the queer one
Fol dol the di do
He was a queer one
And I tell you.
On Pembroke Road look out for me ghost,
Dishevelled with shoes untied,
Playing through the railings with little children
Whose children have long since died.
O he was a nice man,
Fol dol the di do,
He was a nice man,
And I tell you.'

Vicki's lips pressed softly against my own, and I kept my eyes shut as we kissed. The moment was broken by a shout erupting from beyond the garden, and the sound of a glass breaking, and I heard a familiar voice bellowing over the din of the night in a tone of indignation. I leapt up on the bench to see over the garden wall at the kerfuffle kicking off at the club's entry. Three guards, large grey uniformed men with gloves and earpieces had formed a row around the entrance, all facing August as he held his arms up in confusion, repeating over and over his dumbfounded frustration at the unfolding situation. 'I'm only asking you gentlemen to set me straight!' he kept requesting. 'It's apparent that I am drunk, so I'll not deny it, but with all earnestness, were you gentlemen to toss every intoxicated patron out, the street would be crawling with them till dawn.' Managing to climb out over the garden wall and leap down into the street with a minimum of collapse, I gathered myself up and demanded to know what these enforcers were doing manhandling my friend, an insistence the saccos paid no heed to whatsoever. 'We've had a couple of complaints about you, mate,' said the chief of the guards, a shovel-jawed ogre of a man whose bald head was lined with wriggling trenches, as if the grooves of his brain were sucking down on the skull around it. I began to explain that it was I who had made all the complaints they'd received about August, and having thought it over, had decided to withdraw them. 'Piss off dickhead,' replied another guard with flames tattooed along his folded arms, adding, 'You and your mate are all ass, no class.' Just at that moment Vicki appeared at the doorway, and rained down upon the scene such a medley of abuse, slander, and derision as I'd never heard in all my years. 'You fecking gobshites! What gutless eejits you lot of fannies are! And the head on this one could embarrass shite!' she said, rounding on the flabbier of the guards, a portly, red-freckled chap with a sheen of oily sweat running down from his receding hairline. 'I'm just asking you to explain your first principles here,' August was saying to the chief guard, ambling up towards him with his arms still out in confusion. 'Am I really the only pisspot on the premises? And who was it, I wonder who had a problem with my behaviour? Another drunk who's envious of my perseverance? All I'm doing is dancing, is that not what this premises was established to cater for?' The guard with the fiery arms held them out, barring August's approach, as Vicki continued to spray all the men with a stream of undying contempt. 'And this geebag,' she said, pointing at the guard with the dimpled scalp at the centre of their formation, 'the tide itself wouldn't take this bastard out, like a hot bucket of smashed crabs.' The fervour of her abuse redoubled as its coherence began to crumble. 'I'm just asking you for an explanation!' August was now roaring, as the man with the flames shoved him backwards. 'Put your hands on him by fuck!' Vicki screamed, and she flung herself at the guards in a tumult of kicking and thrashing. They retreated from the tiny fury, and I grabbed hold of August and tried to restrain him as he attempted to barrel forward at the receding enemy. By now a crowd had assembled, and patrons stood around the club's doors, jeering and calling out in support for one side or the other. 'You're a bunch of fucking racists, you all are,' Vicki hollered at last, and the guards moved back to a position further inside the venue, as it seemed August had lost his will to continue any direct resistance. 'It's not right!' he began saying to me, and I patted his back and said, 'Oh well, let's move along now to the next place, shall we?' But August didn't move, he stood as though rooted, then turned away from the club and stumbled over to a dim streetlight across the road, which he leant upon with his full weight. From August came a horrendous expression, a look twisted up and wrought in a fashion I'd never seen on my dear friend before. 'It's not right!' he said again with gritted teeth. 'There's nothing I can do!' he shouted up at the light above him, and Vicki moved over to stand beside him, and she held him tight with her cheek pressed up against his bent back, patting and soothing him like a mother to her child, and soon she was joined by another woman with a pierced septum and bright green hair, whose bracelets jangled when she embraced my distraught friend, and she too began talking softly, assuring that all would be well. 'You're loved,' another woman with a trucker's cap and red high heels said. 'You're loved, and you're beautiful.' Soon it seemed that half the population of the Byron night was encircled around August, holding him tenderly and whispering sweet succour into his ears, mothering women with empathic eyes and comforting arms. 'August's crying?' I asked myself, still unable to process what I was seeing. 'August crying?' I said to someone standing nearby, a man with long greasy hair and bony arms, who threw me a strangely disapproving scowl at the question. When the hugging under the lamplight was done, August's tears were gone, though his eyes were red and swollen as he swayed in the street, his cultivated well-wishers melting into the night with waves and blown kisses. 'Let's get you boys home,' Vicki said, when the three of us were alone again, as she flagged down a taxi, planted a last kiss on my cheek and said, 'You're a queer lad, you are. A good man you are,' with bright smiling eyes. 'It was lovely to meet you,' I said, too drunk and worn out for anything else. Vicki shut the taxi door with a wave of her fingers, and turned her back on us as we drove to the park, to sleep off our last night in Byron Bay.

In the morning I woke from a dream of a bridge over a serpentine river, where barefoot children with thin bodies were tossing coins over the edge, then leaping over the sides into the air with wild, wet hair whipping around them like halos. The eyes of one young boy were on me as I walked by, the excited chatter of children and the resonant splash of their bodies plunging into the deep waters of the channel flowing under the height of the bridge, a thoroughfare leading me to some mysterious new land. The sound of their confused chattering and splashing was replaced with the bubbly chug of August standing at the sink, sculling down a two-litre bottle of tap water while the morning light eked in through the stained yellow curtains of the cabin. He let out a large sigh of partly quenched thirst, droplets cascading from his chin, and turned to me with the pinched bewildered expression of a man still coming to terms with the extent of his hangover. 'What did I tell you about the opposing sex?' August said to me as he began to refill the empty plastic bottle. 'Casual proximity to them on the eve of battle was an uncalculated mistake. Observe me now, a house divided against itself.' Once more, he chugged throatily from the container, indifferent to the spillage running from his mouth.

'Of more concern to me,' I said, raising my own ringing skull tenderly from the bunk, 'what on earth are you going to do if you're hurt in this fight? You'll have to recover on the car ride home, without a cabin to crash in.' August gave me a sideways glance, and smiled, leaning heavily on the edge of the sink. 'Now that,' he said, raising a long index finger like a conductor's baton, 'there was method there, my friend. In a hypothetical world in which it is possible for me to lose this contest with Cain, a heavy loss would be akin to catastrophe. The way I have arranged events, I must not only win, but win well, and drive off into the sunset under my own power, never to look back with ego or doubt. Were I to do less, well, a slow death would be my preference.' He said this hastily with shortened breath, and doused himself with the remaining water, though I could already see his back was straightening, and the formidable stature, that came to him so naturally, was regaining its full majesty.

The sun was already beating down, but a cool coastal breeze was blowing when we left the cabin for the last time and set out for the confrontation August had arranged for us both. We stopped for a time at the beach beneath Byron's lighthouse, where the water was so clear and blue we could see the bare legs of a pair of long-legged bathers wandering out into the sea, splashing each other and laughing in the saturation of the day's light, and we sat on the grassy hill before the beach with the cleansing salt air in our lungs. By the time we were ready for the drive to the gym, the sky was beginning to cover over with waxen grey cloud. We took in the movements of the orange gumtrees leaning out of the hills around the beach, and a restaurant with white sails where couples in soft white linen sat eating fruit platters and drinking champagne by a steep road coming down the hillside, and the yellowed bough grass around the restaurant's lawn bobbed and trembled in a breeze that threatened the arrival of rain.

August insisted on driving us to his confrontation with Cain, claiming that he must arrive and depart under his own energies to meet his private conditions for triumph over his old adversary. We parked some distance from the gym, and on seeing that sheet-metal barn behind the shabby house, where I had so recently suffered a momentary loss of control, I felt a disquieting shame. This feeling was expunged immediately upon the arrival of a green ute, which came to a stop near the stony driveway leading up the gym. 'That must be him,' I said, stating the obvious in my excitement. A tall, broad man with long dreadlocks neatly captured by a red bandana emerged from the ute, a sports bag in one hand and a towel draped over a grey singlet. There was no doubt at all, the man was Cain Rivera. I glanced at August, and it occurred to me that having known someone long enough, you are able to read the subtleties that are barely present in their expressions, their body language, their eyes, almost the nerves under the skin, become a kind of index of their inner world. Looking upon August's face as his nemesis hobbled up the gym's car park, limping slightly, more rotund and hunched than either of us could possibly have imagined him to be, I saw precisely what August was thinking, and sensing that he might be hesitant to speak his thoughts aloud, I articulated them for him. 'August, I can see your thoughts written right across your face. You're thinking that, though it would seem a madness to come all this way and walk away from the chance to fight this man, after the distance that we've covered and the strangeness we have seen, as you look at the large and overburdened body of your enemy, you recognise that sometimes the best revenge is simply to see the sorry state of others, and to acknowledge that no beating you could serve out upon this man could raise you up and put him down. I think it's time we got back on the road, and headed for home.' I put my hand on his shoulder. 'Truly, to live well is the best revenge,' I said. August looked into my eyes for a moment, drinking in the truth that I had spoken. Then he shook his head and told me that I couldn't be more wrong. He assured me that the sight of Cain's swollen gut and pathetic limp had only redoubled his desire to batter the man senseless.

August changed into his gear in the car, tossed the clothes he'd been wearing in a pile on the back seat while I stood outside leaning on the boot in the growing heat of the Byron day. Two more cars arrived while I waited, with a large bodybuilder exiting from one and a bald-headed, bow-legged man in his late fifties from the other. They shook hands and crunched up the driveway without paying me any heed, and then August emerged in his fighting gear, plain red-blue shorts and a black top, his trusty bottle of water clutched in one hand, and his bag of gear in the other. It occurred to me, that apart from his attack on me back at the house, I'd yet to see evidence that August had any idea how to perform in a combat situation, and it suddenly seemed very suspicious that he had not even mentioned training or preparation during our time together. 'Are you sure you're ready for this?' I said, sounding more doubtful than I intended. He smiled at me, made some vaguely convincing stretching motions, and crossed the road towards his moment of truth.

Inside the gym, an alarming transformation had taken place. Where previously the interior seemed like any ordinary combat gymnasium, the walls were now covered in billowing crimson banners, reminiscent of a fascist rally, and an enormous poster bearing Cain's face, mean-mugging for the camera like a dictator, was displayed on the far wall behind a crowd of a dozen witnesses assembled on folding chairs around the boxing ring. Sitting in the front row of this audience was the unmistakably sardonic serenity of our former host, Graham Powers, who had not only swapped his green robes for a new blood-red gown, but had also dyed his bald scalp in a matching hue, so that he looked like a fire priest from a neo-druidic cult. I did all I could to ignore his terrifying presence, taking my seat at the back of the audience, while August chatted with the bow-legged man who had introduced himself as the gym's owner, and was busily explaining that he would serve as the officiator for the day's bout. There was much chatter amongst the crowd, and a few families with young children, including a dark-haired woman I took to be Cain's wife, who was bouncing a chubby boy in blue overalls on one bare knee while Cain, yellow-eyed, danced about inside the ring, his red leotard matching the gloves he wore, the banners on the walls, and the circular stain on Graham's head. From time to time, certain members of the audience would call out in support of the local, and August kept his distance, warming up lightly as the bow-legged proprietor talked him through the expectations of the event. At last, the preliminaries were concluded, and August followed the shambling owner into the ring. There was a look of stark uncertainty on both combatants' faces. They touched gloves, a bell sounded and the small crowd roared into life.

As the two men circled one another in the ring, I rose to my feet, cheering and ventriloquising my desire for August's success with wild swings and spit-heavy screams against the consensus of the crowd. In those first few moments before the pair found their range, I recalled something August had said to me on the first day of our trip. As we'd rolled past the hillsides and plains of the state's north coast, I'd asked if my friend had a plan, once he found himself in the ring. He'd thought for a while, concentrating on the passing traffic, chewing on his lip as we overtook a learner driver in a minivan, and then he'd said, 'When I'm done with the man, he'll piss blood for a month.' I'd taken this as an uncharacteristically crass attempt at rhetorical self-inflation, but in the next few moments of this fight, I saw how serious August was about this intention. In the opening round, August attempted continuously to strike illegally at Cain's testicles, hitting them several times with front kicks and wild lunging punches, so that I had to cross my legs in sympathy as I watched, and wondered with astonishment that the bandy-legged referee refused to put an immediate stop to it. The two men soon abandoned the natural grace of martial combat and took to mindless brawling techniques, battering one another with such inelegance of form that it was difficult to tell at times which of them was covering the other in blood. August tackled Cain to the floor, against the howls and gesticulations of the crowd, who, with the sole exception of the zen-like stillness exhibited by the fraud in the red frock, were all on their feet, screaming and flailing in the air with theatrical punches and kicks of their own. 'C'mon, babe!' the dark-haired woman bellowed with her overalled kid hanging perpendicular from her hip. Watching the fighters struggling on the floor of the ring, I was reminded of a scene from my youth, when my family had attended a lion safari on the outskirts of Penrith. On that occasion, I'd witnessed the strange sight of two lions engaging in a congress with each other that I was too innocent to understand, and I had turned to my parents to ask what the larger, bearded lion was doing to the smaller lady lion. My mother, hoping to evade the reality of the situation, explained that the large lion thought the other looked a little flat, and he was 'trying to pump the little one up a bit'. It was impossible to say what precisely about the fight taking place reminded me of this zoological experience, and so I watched in bewilderment as the two large long-limbed men pressed their bodies into one another, heaving and grunting in a mess of tattooed arms and gasping expressions until eventually, Cain Rivera gave a horrible screech, grabbing at his elbow, and the referee waved August Saint Augustine to a bloody triumph.

An eerie silence descended on the gym when the match ended. Both combatants lay breathlessly in the centre of the ring, Cain on his back with a blood-rinsed look of despair, his round gut rising and falling with a hysterical urgency. August rose to his feet, a large lump swelling above his left eye as he grasped at the ropes of the ring for support. The woman I took to be Cain's wife and baby-mother put her crying child in the arms of someone nearby, and rushed over to the ring to run her hands over Cain's prone body, her distress chilling to behold. August shook hands with the proprietor-cum-referee, and a singlet-wearing gym rat tossed a towel up from the floor. He ran the towel over his face, and much of the blood he wore was transferred onto it. Cain soon regained his composure, and the owner began applying an ointment of sorts to his smashed and swollen face. I overheard them implore August not to leave town, but to stick around at one of their places for the night, so that we could all celebrate a clean and brutal bit of biff with a few drinks and laughs, but he was unmoved by their pleading, and simply repeated strange sayings such as, 'To arrive where you are, to get from where you are not, you must go by ways wherein there is no ecstasy.' I made every effort then to avoid catching sight of the red-headed Graham, who no doubt would be doing his best to appear undaunted by the defeat of the local champion, but I could feel his presence, standing in the doorway behind us, when

I helped August limp out of the gym onto the stony path. As we came close to the Corolla, August leant more of his weight upon me, and then rested on the car for a while, looking up at the grey over the afternoon sun. I stood beside him with an arm on his shoulder, listening to his breath and feeling the movements of my friend's exhaustion pulsing through him as two vans with yellow surfboards passed us on that ordinary street. 'Let's get out of this place,' he said to me at last, and, once again, he insisted that he should be the one to drive.

For a long time, as August drove through the wild winding passage of Broken Head Road, past tall pale gums groaning high above the engorged mounds of land on either side, I sat silent and glanced occasionally with a kind of tender pity at the swell of trauma above my companion's left eye. The road was bereft of travellers, and we raced alone between the leering trees and quiet farms as the sun emerged from behind the clouds and the tall bodies of the gums were black with shimmering gold leaves against the late afternoon light. 'Tell me, August,' I said, as we hurtled through the surrounding green, 'How does it feel, to reach satisfaction, after all?' August took one arm off the wheel, reaching into the back seat to search around for something under the clothes he had tossed there before the fight. What he found there was my flask, and he handed it to me, saying these words, 'Oh, you know. The usual.' I took a long drink, and considered his remark, wondering if there was some secret meaning, or if perhaps it was only a misfired response caused by the calamitous effects of serious frontal lobe damage. Whatever he meant, it made me smile to think of him, this strange prototype of man.

All remembrance of this time past faded out of mind, and I found my consciousness returned to its place under the awning of Darren's patio bar, listening to the drone of the tattoo gun make the final incisions in Jason's dark fleshy thigh. Darren was squatting down over his work, and wiped at it with a stained rag, as he announced, 'There she is, mate! All done, princess.' Jason took a picture of his bleeding new adornment, posted it to social media while the artwork still wept blood, running down his shin in twin rivulets. One of Darren's dogs waddled over to sniff and lick at the injury, wagging his tail in an excitation of sympathy. From where I was sitting, with the scene dimly lit against a clear night where the only sign of life beyond the electric lights was an insect choir chirping insistently around us, and the restless tossing of dry leaves in the surrounding darkness, Darren's handiwork looked less like a penguin wearing a sailor's hat than it did a mouse riding a baked potato, but you get what you pay for, as my mother used to say. 'Alright you bastard,' Darren said, turning to me with the dripping instrument raised in the bony bulk of his smudged hand. 'You ready to have me jab something into you?'

I'd thought of something to wear on my skin, all right. I thought of August, standing in my driveway at the outset of our mutual adventure, solemn and renewed as a man could ever hope to be, covered in the tattooed images of angels and saints and spiders and snakes, his hands on his hips, proud and prepared for the strange road set out before us – a road leading through the tropics of northern New South Wales, where August carried his peculiar visions of a giant banana with him like an innocent, overflowing all the while with inchoate theories that he'd conceived while standing behind a stack of cold meats and assorted olives, sun-dried tomatoes and feta cheeses. I wondered where August might be that very moment; the man who conquered time, the man who rewrote the story of his life in his middle age, and I hoped he was sleeping somewhere soundly, snoring lightly under the starry skies of the west, his head full of the shocks and flashes that kept him sane, and the memory of us on that northern beach, with Vicki, the Irish lass, listening to some faraway beach blessing its children in the roar of constant breaks. I knew precisely what I wanted tattooed on my body. 'Give me the usual,' I said to Darren. He looked at me for a moment, eyes flashing in the shadowy light, as though trying to read some meaning in the nonsense of life, and then shrugging his wide shoulders, he muttered, '*caveat emptor*,' and he came at me with his whirring needle, a dribble of ink drooling from the pulsing tip's tiny eye.

A Woman to Her Lover Clings

'When I was at university, every straight-white-so-and-so wanted to be Raymond Carver,' Justin claimed when they first met. 'I was the only mug who had a hope. Honestly, I could maybe have made a name that way. But then it came to me – all at once, like a kick in the head – does the world really need more pseudo-American mediocrities? As Matthew Arnold framed it, there are only three questions to be answered by art. First, the question of intent. Then, the question of quality. And finally, this one question remains – was it worth doing? No matter how much success I made of the first two points with my work, I couldn't make anything of the third and final question in the mode of Carver-esque. So, sweet sorrows, I parted ways with prose and descended into poetry. And the rest, as they say, is mystery.'

So went the tale of Justin's progression, and he recounted to Alice, on more than one occasion, that his next career move would be to skip assiduously over the more fashionable forms of poetry and race headlong into avant-garde obscurity, embracing epigrammatical eco-poetry with all his energies. Justin would make his living in that tradition, he swore it, and would do so with a clean conscience – refusing to monetise his art in the mendacious late-capitalist style – or would die trying. 'Dying in the process of mishandling poetic aspiration is a fine antipodean tradition,' Justin said, and he littered their evenings with these proclamations whenever new people turned up to their parties, or when a stray thunderbolt of excitation struck him, or when the usual crew arrived at a virgin location. These facts he spoke with a certain robotic solemnity, as one reciting antique verse learned by rote. The get-togethers and soirées at the homes of their many friends and lovers ran riot with all sorts of idle distractions. Musical interludes performed on mandolin by suspendered men with wild bushranger beards, and caped women with tattoos on their bared chests displaying amateur acrobatics on shuddering tightropes stretched between backyard trees infested with protesting bats. There were budding folk bands made up of assortments of black-clad strangers, all suffering from an involution of the legs displayed proudly by means of the skinniest jeans, and they would sing lyrics like: 'Christopher Robin, what exactly is doing nothing? Well, I'll tell you what it means. Going along, listening to all the things you can't hear, and not bothering.' Amidst these carnival affairs, Justin often got up on the verandas and read his short prose poems between the acts, or raved about in drunken abandon, or else sat stoned and quiet on the couches, gazing into infinity with his motoring mouth uttering strangled-sounding soliloquies.

One night, Alice crossed herself and leaned back from the civilised revelry of a friend's winter-warming party, like someone grasping for cleaner air, and shifted her gaze greedily over to Justin's private conversation. His pouty lips were exuding a wetness close to drooling while he disinterred his busy thoughts at Silly Nick – a quiet political-science major down from Newcastle who was a thin, sour and bobble-headed young man. 'Justin can never repeat himself enough,' Alice marvelled with eager eyes. 'If it's worth saying, it's worth it again, a thousand times over. *More, always*, is his maxim.' Soon enough, the two young men were sunk in the cushions of the old couch, pressing shoulders, and Justin's bloodshot eyes seemed to be rolling as he declared that, 'Every art, from classical opera sung in the Utzon Room, to the contemporary novels stacked up for the Miles Franklin committees, is under the thumb of a cabal of secret leather-freaks. A clandestine tribe of leather-jocks and bondage-maidens are out there right this minute, all of them with an endless, insatiable appetite for psychosexual discipline, and that perverse hunger predicates all facets of our cultural life as a direct result of their...devious strangulations.' As he spoke the word 'devious', he scowled and spat a little in his companion's direction. Alice couldn't see Silly Nick's expression, but she could surmise from the tight maintenance of his turned neck that he seemed to drink in Justin's wet reportage without distress. 'Mark my words,' Justin warned with a sudden finger up in the air. 'There's an arts mafia in this country, my man, and its face, if you can call it a face, is like a grinning gimp, with pale, oystered eyes.' Justin's own eyes moistened and glazed with a melancholic light as he offered this ominous threat, and then he appeared completely spent, like a scarecrow who had dug his stuffing out and tossed it into the air, and had become a puddle of old empty rags. Even in the moment, Alice could admit to a certain fascination with Justin's unsavoury disquisitions, feeling suddenly disappointed that this particular soliloquy had come to a premature end, without the usual paratactic imagery of obese impresarios squirming into leathers on weekend nights, gleefully crushing each other's testicles under their black heels, or greedily lashing clamped nipples raw and bloody with whips in the club's exclusive, sweaty dungeons – and other such assorted pornography which Justin's paranoid accounts lent to her imaginings.

Later that night, in the total silence after the celebrations, Alice helped Justin find his way to the backyard in the morning gloom. She heard him stumbling down the hallway, belching and bumping into walls like an old blind king. Alice tossed the covers from her mattress, lay listening to her own heart beating, and then emerged into the hall to discover Justin breathing heavily against the wall in the cataract-blur of sleep-blinded sight. She took his hand and determined by some half-conscious communication that he wanted to be led outside. She helped him through the sliding door, and the pair slipped out onto the wet grass, under the branches of a poplar tree and a swinging orb-weaver spider's web. Alice watched him slowly bend and slide his pants to his ankles, the haunches of his furry backside pale as creamy moonlight, then despoil the ground behind the patio where they stood. She hissed, 'Justin! What are you doing?' as he performed the musty act, and when he'd finished, she helped his stretching pants back to his waist and took him to his bed like a nursemaid, feeling strangely overcome by the thought of a shared secret crime as she eased him, mumbling, between the sheets. When he was safely pliant in the dark, she left him alone to slip back outside and hose away the dark mess he'd left behind, the starry coastal air brutally gored by the rattle of possums hidden above the house.

'I couldn't be happier for you both!' Alice's mother proclaimed over steaming teacups when the news of their romance was let slip on a visit home, and the two quickly became what Alice believed to be a couple like most others of their age, though she couldn't be sure. Alice's parents had moved to the Central Coast in their retirement and were of no use at all. They were old, had borne her late, and cursed her with being 'out of step'. Swearing in their presence was impossible, for instance, long after they'd stopped censoring themselves for their daughter's sake. 'You should have kept one of the other ones. The surfer with the drums,' was all her father would say on the subject, his imperious gaze out on the rushing waters of the channel near their unit, watching, Alice knew, for signs the blackfish might be in – and since her mother had long ago given up contradicting her husband, there was no help from her on the subject. Diana, the elder sister who lived back at home, didn't talk much anymore in the sober daylight hours, and kept her attentions on the television's morning shows.

Justin's family was unhappy in its own way, and Alice discovered that despite all appearances, Justin had grown up wealthy, in a home he'd left back in Adelaide after his twin sister put an end to herself in the double garage between the rotting boats and the dusty pool equipment. He left the wreckage of her death behind and settled in Sydney-town, starting from scratch like a refugee. If Justin had mentioned his early years to Alice since they'd met, she could not bring more than a dozen of his words on the subject to mind, although he once claimed his father could name the succession of all the English kings and queens going back to somebody or other the Great, and his mother had rumoured blueblood in her veins, connected to the Crown, or something French, Huguenots she thought he might have said.

With all differences aside, the couple ambled through their post-graduate degrees in the discipline of arts, and Justin declared he was ready to become a poet proper now that his studies were at an end. He'd be able to pay the bills, he said, once he made his name as a serious poet and had won some respected awards, and he helped this enterprise along by selling the weed he didn't smoke to other poets and artists from their first unit in Concord. The poems, if anyone asked, began to explore a series of dynastic intrigues amongst a kingdom of crab-clans on an island off the eastern coast of Australia. The ten-legged citizens of those isles, beleaguered by the effects of climate change, became Justin's major obsession. 'Crabs carry their own redoubts about them. They're more secure than we are – born in carapace, marching forth from birth, charging the sea's caprice in loose formation,' he said, perhaps quoting a line from one of his works. 'I'm basing the anthropomorphic allegories on J.S. Harry's *Peter Henry Lepus* series.' The first real eco-poet in Australia, Justin would explain, if anyone inquired further about this influence. He was often heard to say that Australian poetry was obsessed with landscape, being a nation built on stolen territories, and Alice asked no questions, read the poems when induced to, and found her opinions on his efforts blessedly unnecessary.

In the next house they rented, an old unit out in Ashfield with rising damp, there was a map of the various crab kingdoms within Greater Crustacea spread out on the desk in their study, its major counties and regions labelled, and journals full of notes on the affairs and outrages of those nations and their crabby populations accumulated in the drawers. All this crab talk in the poems was disturbing – highly arch and ironic, Alice saw that much – but being aware of the intended tone didn't help her understand the obsession or the verse, and she suspected there was nothing of substance happening in the lines Justin spent his Sundays transcribing from the battered journals into endless documents saved on their laptop. Each file he named after the date it had been transcribed, and the long lists of dates proliferated, as did the physical journals strewn about the house, like some private joke gotten out of hand. Alice thought of the houses she sometimes saw, with legions of gnomes stacked on the front lawns, a madness of imaginary excess accruing on neat even lawns without rhyme or reason.

Justin may have been born into a background of money, but the source of the income keeping them solvent was Alice teaching various units to undergrads at the local university. Teaching 'media' meant that whatever subject the students were supposed to be learning, there'd be a slide on Maslow's 'Hierarchy of Needs' somewhere in the lectures. 'Self-actualisation' was at the top of the pyramid, 'food, water, warmth' on the bottom. 'I should add some needs of my own to this thing,' Alice joked to her colleagues in the casual staffroom, a very old lady with long grey fingers, and an obese man with thinning hair who used his guest lecture in Alice's unit to point out that the word giraffe had two giraffes hidden inside it, disguised as the letter 'f'. There was a word for that sort of thing, words with their things hidden inside them, and it gave Alice a strange thrill to make the effort needed to avoid retaining this frustratingly stupid information.

The permanent staff liked Alice. She was conscientious, and quiet, and took care with the brittle egotism the academy afforded them, though the students wore her out with their perpetual youth, coming on like waves, beating at her, endlessly, year after year, with the same optimistic faces and wide-eyed sense of promise, always demanding such vital sacrifices. Four years into this casual occupation, just when the thought of other career options – supermarket stacker, designer-drug guinea pig – began to take root in her daydreams, the head professor talked Alice into taking on a full-time lectureship, an offer as irresistible as divine intervention. She posted the news and received a great deal of applause from friends and colleagues, little smiling emojis sparkling on her social feeds. The head professor was an older man, bearded, of course – an animated chunk of bristling mothballs in a stumpy leather jacket, with an unmentioned marriage to an invisible wife, and a curled bonsai on the sealed window of his office, with photographs from his tour of South American universities displayed on the desk, showing his arm slung over the slender shoulders of a postgraduate student he'd plucked from obscurity to raise into the full-time academy. He was a genial little man – authorial and beneficent – and he waddled about the campus in his thick black jeans like an aide-de-camp in a time of imperial discontent.

Alice shared affection for this professor with her colleagues, and his benevolent marshalling of the school's command, though she came to believe he considered her an *incurious flake*. Alice had heard him say the words to someone over the phone when she was coming up to his office from the casual staffroom, carrying the signed employment contract for his approval, like a page-bearer toddling about with a ringed-cushion. 'Yes, what else does she bring in though, she's an *incurious flake* once you get past the crust.' Alice heard the words come from his open office door, and she turned back to the nearby refuge of the photocopy room to settle her distress, not sure what she had done to have earned this gutting autopsy. The photocopy room was two doors down the hall from the head professor's office, not much bigger than a walk-in closet. Alice stood in that windowless space, under a blinking fluorescence, staring at the thin red light flashing on the humming machine, indicating it was out of toner until the hot flush of shame evaporated through her cheeks, burning them to a bruised shade of puce on its wriggling passage out of her body.

Justin was thrilled at Alice's new full-time position, and

bought a ring the following Friday from a jeweller in Newtown for one hundred and twelve dollars, and hollowed out a second-hand Clarice Lispector novel, *Near to the Wild Heart*, with which to present his ring to her. Alice was exalted to discover there was nothing crab-themed about the ring when she opened the mutilated book. Neither party believed in marriage, not while it remained an arrangement excluding those outside the narrowness of heteronormativity, but there was no harm in a honeymoon, and a party at a South Coast holiday house to celebrate the union, where the families came together and stared bemused at one another across a large table covered in leftover Christmas decorations. Justin's parents, who had come all the way from Adelaide, got drunk and bickered until everyone excused themselves to avoid their odd expletives, except Alice's older sister, who passed out drunk on the couch before anyone missed her presence, and managed by that sly stratagem to stay the night with the lucky couple, unnoticed until late next morning, snoring passionately into the couch's cushions.

Alice dreamed of holidaying in Argentina to celebrate the promises they'd made to one another in exchanging rings, and eventually Justin agreed to go along if she paid for the flights and accommodation, though he insisted on cursing the trip in the taxi on the way to the airport, elaborating on his anxieties about flying, and saying the whole distraction would ruin his chances of finding a publisher, with much of what he'd written suddenly being highly relevant to the politics of the now – a status of cultural relevance which could change at any minute, and Alice would do well to remember that what seemed avant-garde one minute might be beyond the pale the next. 'Poets,' he reminded her, 'are the uncredited legislators – we must strike when the thunder is overhead or forever hold our infamy.'

On the twelve-hour flight, Alice learned to say, 'I love you very much' in Spanish, and 'Where is the pharmacy, please,' while Justin played with her under the blankets and pleasured himself in the bathroom when the excitement built to a pitch. In the middle of the night, while the dull calamity of the jet's engines perpetuated their droning hum, Alice opened the blind a crack to watch illusions of distant light moving above an inky void, as Justin slept and snored in whispers, tiny bubbles collecting on his lips. This was Alice's first time in a country where it wasn't possible to rely on English, and the risk struck her most fully as they stepped into the hotel transport she'd arranged over the internet – a van, driven by two dark-haired men wearing suits and ties who punctuated their accented Spanish with single recognisable words like 'welcome', 'hotel', 'traffic', and 'kangaroo'. The only trouble was a fake note in the change they received, but they didn't notice for several days, until a newsagent down the street from the hotel explained that the van drivers often dealt in forged currency. They stayed at the Elefanti Rosa in Mar del Plata, and Justin entered their room with a terrible virus and stayed in bed for days, cursing and sweating. While he was laid-up of an afternoon, with the bronze summer light coming through the window, it was obvious the years of drinking had taken their toll on the rapscallion looks Alice believed he had once possessed, and his face was swollen and pale, but when the sun went down and he was asleep in the dim reading light of the late evening, the sweetness returned to his face, slick and sticky with fever, and the soft wet skin of his eyelids like little pale petals, and the wispy trace of a moustache above his lip was so patched and twisted in a mess of directions that Alice had to fight the urge to run her fingertips along the tickling hairs.

When the morning light broke through the curtains the next day, Alice was out on the balcony watching the surfers in the long white breaks of the sea, their movements thick with foam that caught the sun. Their boards made sharp incisions in the waves, flashes of silver bursting around them in the water like mirrored scales catching the light, and even the clouds moving over the morning distance, faint and grey on the horizon, seemed an extension of the urging sea. 'What are you thinking?' Justin said, stepping out onto the warm balcony tiles. 'Thought? Oh, I'm not really,' Alice said, looking out at one surfer in particular, long-haired and blonde as the sun, the sea spray in her hair like wind plying sails, her board tracing across a solid wave she was riding with such serenity in her balance that Alice recalled a line she'd heard from a poet long ago, back when the sweet romance of the world was still inside her like a heartbeat in a womb. 'Grace is an escape chute,' she recited under her breath. 'And upon its immutable rhythms we can ride the chaos surrounding us unassailed.'

Justin wanted coffee now that he was up, and he sat on the balcony tearing into a croissant that he dipped in jam and butter, waiting for Alice to deliver as he ate. 'I feel great,' he told her when she stepped out in her hotel gown, with the mugs steaming in her hands. 'It's so good to get out of bed and feel the sun! Can you believe how bright the daylight is? Look at us now, babe, this is it for us, true romance in living colour.' And that night, after oily meals of skewered meats and baked pockets of rice and beans, they travelled to a grand hotel designed by a renowned architect Justin had read about on the internet. Hallways, long and narrow, formed laneways of gold-panelled mirror and silverplated doors, punctuated at intervals by men in red-sashed uniforms standing like mannequins holding up trays with their white-gloved hands. On each tray was a legend, in several languages, indicating which door in the vast gilded hallway led to what chamber of the grand hotel. By following this signage Justin determined that access to the exclusive tango exhibition they had come to see required them to pass through a mirrored door to their left and into a dark room with broad red furnishings and pommelled golden rails, which traced a declivity around the room's perimeter, guiding its guests under a ceiling of glittering argentum mirrors, past curtains hanging down near the stage framed with thick velvet ropes hung from hooks like butchered pythons.

They were the last of the audience to make their way into the dim crimson heart of the room and they sat at a table in the centre, while other patrons watched them arrive from the crepuscular fringes of the cocktail lounge. Alice affected a stately poise to counter her nervousness at their visibility before the stage. A slight ruffling of the curtain's skirt directed each eye in the audience to a lithe dancer, emerging into the slim stage-light with a tantric deliberation. In an astonishing trick of the light she revealed a bearded companion dressed in an immaculate three-piece suit, trailing along at arm's length, who replied to the dancer's summons by such sudden and supple command of his own momentum that his bold advance towards his partner caused Alice to exhale at its execution. The saturating light on the stage showed the muscles in the dancer's legs tight and powerful as coiled roots, and when she lifted a bare thigh, the largess of the muscle was alarming in its definition. Her raised limb held in the air and then swept down her partner's chest, as she arched backwards to the floor in the crook of his arm, and there was so much sweeping movement on the little stage that the dancers seemed intertwined together, only to spin away from one another at the next moment, while distracting glasses of champagne were brought serenely to the table by silent waiters in white gloves. Justin leaned across and in Alice's ear he whispered, 'How these human marionettes can move on the stage! Truly their master must be an unseen angel, articulating the intentions of these minor cherubim in a hypnotism of intimacy, all to the refrains of an acoustic instrument played somewhere in the darkness behind the red curtains.' His words were moist and loud, and Alice strained to screen them out and keep her focus on the dancers' movements. There was a red flower tied into the woman's black hair, and her partner was dressed to match this thematic darkness, and they danced so close in embrace they must have felt each other's pumping exertions. The dancer's thigh ran up again against her partner's chest again and waited there, like a wing buoyed on a warm current of air, so that there was a flash of the snowy silk revealed under her black dress, and her companion lifted her responding body up onto the carriage of his chest, pivoting twice more, so as to swirl her trailing black hair down about his arms, and they moved cheek-to-cheek and then leapt apart, and spun a centrifugal motion with the urging guitars like flashing spirits in a storm's commanding drama.

Alice made a subtle survey of the audience around them in the confines of the theatrette. There were only enough tables to seat twelve people in all. From what she could see of her fellow attendees in the gloomy light, all were dressed either in long gowns or smart suits, all excepting Alice and Justin. It was strange the way they seemed to watch so quietly, not one person in the crowd made a sound throughout the performance, not even to applaud a particularly dazzling routine. Not once did Alice notice an interrupting cough, or the sound of a glass clinking, or a chair sliding along the floor, or a murmur between couples in the dark – not until the dancers had finished spinning on the stage, and stood holding each other, enveloped in the other's body like two petals of a closing flower in the red darkness around the stage. The lights fled from the stage, and there was a general applause. 'The most perfect dancers I've ever seen,' Alice said as they made their way out of the hotel once the curtains had come down, and the secretive audience around them had dispersed into the muted quiet of the gold, glass and velvet hall. Arm in arm they walked out into the streets, Alice looking into Justin's eyes with a hopeful longing. She'd noticed during the show, as they'd been sitting at their table, breathing softly, a crimson shimmer of light caught in Justin's dark eyes that seemed something bright and unaffected. She'd never seen that light before. Out in the street, she wanted to see that it had stayed in his eyes, though perhaps it was just the champagne and the wild movements of the dancers possessing her thoughts. Justin had explained to her, 'It's the opulence that enhances the effect, you see. The excessive and self-aware ornamentation of an atmospheric sensorial experience,' as he turned to look back one last time at the mirrored hallway, with its silent waiters and soft, red-carpeted floors, still visible through the hotel's opened doors from the darkened street. 'I'll let you in on a secret,' he said, smiling at her hopeful expression. 'If you're in the mood to hear a scandalous admission. My secret is – I was born for splendour. Born to it,' he said, as they marched past other strangers in the Argentine night. 'Born to suck the juice out of all this world's golden fruits,' he howled up at the smoky stars. 'I will taste its jouissance, in noble throes of passion!' The hairs on his upper lip, as he looked down to Alice with the night's fierce clamour of light and smoke in his wide eyes, were stretching up as if to meet some private inclination.

An alarm clock rang in the little room of their hotel, but Justin shut it down by swinging wildly in its direction, the pink elephants slowly appearing on the wallpaper, and the curtains hanging soft as folded crepe. From the bed, blinking in the parallax shadows of the room and the light of the open window, Alice saw the room inverted on the mirrors of a French armoire with a key sticking from its lock. Through the open window a peregrine falcon pulled at the grey expanse of day. High above the ocean it bobbed and dived, and the faint taste of salt was in the breeze blowing through their room. At moments the kite trembled in the rough air, as if in distress, and then it swung down out of sight only to shoot back into view a moment later. An urgent wind tore into the room with a great and sudden violence, shaking the bevelled doors leading out to the balcony so loudly that Alice jolted upright in the sheets, her panic stirring Justin. He rolled facedown into the pillows, his hair wildly pronounced like something snatched from the ocean floor, and his expression pinched and dark as he turned away from her sight. 'Wake up,' she said, shaking his shoulder. The hair on his back was spare and soft. There was nothing childlike about him as he lay heavy in that moment, his shoulders bunched and brawny, and Alice had a terrible fear some stranger was in the bed with her. She pulled ridiculously at his arms to try and awaken the imposter.

They broke their fast at a café across the park outside the hotel, having already missed their flight that morning, too far from home to take in the full consequence of this lapse of judgement. They sat gingerly at the table, Alice resting her head in her palm, not speaking at all, until a Marcel Marceau impersonator rode a unicycle up to great them. The performer bowed and doffed his black hat, offered the couple a long-stemmed rose, bowing again in gratitude, and rode away, turning back to wave farewell as he peddled uphill along a serpentine path between the park's buoying palms. 'This morning is the very definition of romance,' Justin beamed, his face still swollen from the night's excess, and Alice pressed the petals of the rose over her lips to take in its plastic perfume. 'Look at you snuggle-tigers!' the waitress said, arriving at their table, her English only slightly accented, and they straightened their backs and made space for the coffee cups placed between them. Alice wrapped her cold hands around the hot bowl, and the coastal air swirled through the café's open door with a faint moan.

'You were too good to me, in the beginning.' Justin said, licking the foam away from the bristling hairs under his nose. 'You had every worldly reason not to trust me, and I was a weak man with my appetites. I know that.' He smiled at his concession. 'You gave me time to get my act together, and I'll always be grateful to you. I'll carry it in my heart like a pearl locked inside a shell.' He said this with secretive eyes, as though what he spoke was meant to reckon with thoughts Alice herself had harboured deeply. Another uptake of the coastal wind whirling through the doors sent dried leaves scuttling across the chequer-tiled floor, like little crisp shells crackling sideways between the legs of tables and chairs. Menus slipped from tabletops and napkins escaped out from under heavy cutlery. The mug in Alice's hands was too hot to go on holding, and her palms began to sweat. Their waitress was at another table now, speaking in Spanish to a couple behind them, an elderly couple wearing matching broad-brim hats. It was impossible to know what the waitress might be saying to them. The sounds of their words didn't seem to possess a shape of any sort – she spoke in one long stream of unnatural noise, not like human speech at all, not like anything Alice had heard before. It occurred to Alice, that if she spent her entire life sitting and listening to that stream of expression coming from the waitress, sitting still with the deepest attention, it would all amount to an eternal nonsense, an alien and mysterious river of sound, foreign in its rhythms and patterns for all time. Alice – she admitted it – was an *incurious* woman – that was certainly the quintessential word for her fault. A profound malignancy appeared to her, spiralling up into her lungs with the steam rising from the cup of coffee. 'It is as though I am standing on a stage, in a fulmination of light, and simultaneously sitting in the darkness beyond the stage, watching myself perform like some internal anthropologist,' she thought. 'This moment would make for a great epiphany,' she teased herself with the idea, 'if I were in therapy, it's *this* that we'd discover – my therapist and I.' She wanted to get up and step out of her chair, it was so cold, she wanted to stand up, to ask the waitress with the most tender politeness what it was she was saying to the old couple in the matching ribboned hats, to shake hands with every stranger sitting around her in the café, and announce to them the charming news – they were meeting a *truly incurious woman*, and she would caution them to keep this flaw in their minds for the rest of their lives, to tell their children if they decided to have them. She could supply signatures and photographs, and an email address and a post-office box and no less than three references from senior-level academics at the university who could provide written testimonials on official letterhead signed by the vice-chancellor, stating unequivocally, that whomsoever was named above was certified to have run afoul of an *utterly incurious flake*.

'What do you mean?' Alice said. 'I don't know what you're talking about in the slightest!' Justin leant forward, his hand patting at her knee like a dog's rough pawing. 'Don't!' he said in a harsh whisper. 'Please, Alice, before you say anything more. I want to tell you what I'm thinking now, right this moment. It was that I saw the way you turned to look after that painted clown on the bike with the flower, and I saw the sun coming through the clouds just behind you – you couldn't have seen it – the way it broke over the top of that chapel back there, the cross above the steeple was like a spearhead in the sunlight, and that same bronze hue was caught in your eyes, and then you turned back to look at me with a full fathom of joy that almost knocked me from this chair! I want us, always, to come back to this already too perfect moment, like an unadulterated experience of a summer everlasting. Let this moment be as our true north. I want the two of us to pin this morning against the walls of our very being, as one slim filament of memory with which to orient ourselves through the vast surrounding mysteries of life, forever stitched together by a fragment of consciousness, unified in a singular space and time.'

Alice's mother once said, 'It's caffeine on an empty stomach, that's all it is! Gets the emotions in a mess!' Her loving mother had made the comment at the family dining table when her sister Di had cried, spontaneously, the first Christmas after her accident, with a wicked noose of stitches protruding from the skin tracing from her cheek down to her chest. Alice had bit her lip to keep from screeching – an absurd and insulting thing to say at a time like this! She'd wanted to get up and slap her mother across her pursed mouth, hard enough to wake her up, to get her eyes rattling around like marbles circling in a sink. Unreasonable urges are human nature, she reckoned, and intrusive thoughts thrust up from every angle. Alice knew there was no finesse in suppression, that to hold down one thing meant an adjoining impingement, and yes, all unhappy families are alike in their unhappiness, but isn't it simply unthinkable and unreasonable to go through life in a state of selective somnambulance, sleep-walking through the cosmos for sixty-six years, nodding and pottering about in the darkness of linen closets and crawling into kitchen cabinets looking for Tupperware and Pyrex, and sitting there at the dining table, frowning at the floral patterns on the teacups from here to eternity?

'Who ordered zucchini fritters?' the waitress said in her perfect English, and she delivered a plate to the centre of the table with a gummy smile flashing between her red lips.

The memory of their honeymoon, with its salted air and rose-scented hotel laundry, subsided out of mind, and ordinary life returned to a regular routine. The predictable business of 'the semester' – planning tutorial activities and writing lecture notes – consumed Alice's evenings, and the days became a procession of passing Justin in the house, occasional embraces, coffee trips alone on free weekdays, and bus rides out to the university where Alice would walk the aisle of the library with a white light of anxiety in her eyes, contemplating the walls of books still left unread. The status quo endured, until news came from abroad that Justin's grandfather had died in a curtained bed and left the family a proportion of his substantial wealth. There was no talk of attending a funeral, not even a date was mentioned, and sensing Alice's unease at this apparent insensitivity, Justin assured her that his grandfather, who'd moved to Fremantle in his retirement to make his own boats and drift on the calm waters alone with his thoughts, would not have wanted his only grandson travelling halfway across the country to put him in the grave. 'I have my memories of Pops. That's better than some ceremonial dirt-tossing, and the old man had no illusions of religion.' A video call to the parents in Adelaide was the sole acknowledgement of the old man's death, though there was little mention of the dead man during their conference, and Missy, the family terrier, barked so incessantly that she became the central subject of the conversation, her black face a furry mask flicking a thumb-sized tongue in panting excitation, until Justin disconnected, sat back in his chair and sighed, 'Thank God that's over.'

The inheritance permitted purchase of a tidy Chippendale joint, free from the ever-present damp of the previous unit, and Justin and his best mate Marco took whatever funds were left and devised the creation of an indie publishing company. 'Anyone whose soul is on fire,' Justin swore. 'Anyone who is so made that they cannot permit themselves to scrape and bow and submit to the lash of obtuse opinion-makers and gatekeepers incapable of thinking for sixty consecutive seconds, can now turn to this new player on the literary scene for their succour.' The publishing house was to be called 'Goonbag Press' and their maiden publication would be Justin's debut collection. 'Pops would be pleased indeed to know his endowment was going to this cause,' he assured Alice. 'With Marco as my Sancho Panza, I can reach for the rising stars and show all antipodean dreamers what can be done with a little bold advance.'

Justin and Marco spent hours one evening smoking pot on Alice's couch, scheming a book launch that would counterpoint the bourgeois banalities customary at such affairs, mulling over ingenuities unlimited as they played Leonard Cohen albums on Alice's antique turntable. Meanwhile, with a pen gritted between her teeth, Alice tried to grade undergrad assignments in the study. The papers were answering a question on 'The Dialectic Role of Private and Public Language in Contemporary Texts', and each began with some variation of 'This essay seeks to discuss the dialectic between the varying roles of both public and private forms of language in relation to the way contemporary texts are understood by their audiences.' The old worn needle cut up Leonard's lyrics, and Alice lost her traction each time the little silver wheel of a lighter crunched under a thumb in the lounge room. The muttered conversation of the two men outside on the couch flowed into her thoughts like leaking water from a puncture and a stink like ratty soil and burning rope wafted into the room as thick as billowing curtains.

Alice wondered if the smoke from the boys' session would cause a contact high, filling up the study with a fog of mind-numbing indolence, and she began to interpret her every misreading of the students' convoluted lines as an effect of intoxication, until she had talked herself into believing that nothing in any of the papers made the slightest sense. She tossed the papers aside and stared into the laptop on the desk. A spreadsheet opened on the computer screen waited patiently for each student's grade to be entered, and blinked as it remained unfilled, its empty slots stacked up in insurmountable profusion. There was nothing for it. Alice closed the spreadsheet and gave up her marking, and stared instead at the desktop's background screen – an enormous red crab holding its pincers up in warning. A folder on the desktop caught Alice's eye then, a folder containing all the histories of crustacea. There'd never been a reason for Alice to click it open before, but listening to the grand plans being traded outside gave her a curious impulse, one that made her underarms sweat. Alice opened the folder, beheld the enormity of file names – orderly titles created in relation to the dates of creation. All the files were inside inconspicuous folders that led to more and more files within simple folders containing a decade's worth of unenticing data, and beside these uninteresting items, the occasional saved image of a sea creature emerged – crabs, *of course*, and lobsters, too. Purpled crayfish, bugs, prawns, yabbies, yams, an albino whale sneezing black smoke, a Nubian mermaid with white molluscs sucking on her small breasts, a bivalve scallop in place of labia majora, a bloody heron with a frog in its mouth, a pelican whose beak overran with bream, a steaming bowl of shark-fin soup served with peppered pipis, periwinkles disrobing on the rocks, a sea slug used as a fleshlight, the cast of *Finding Nemo* naked at a Hollywood soiree, Salmon Rushdie catching a bass named Saul, choirs of Dickensian sea-urchins, and Ringo Starr wearing shades at an undersea tea-society gathering – all displayed in little thumbnail squares in the many folders within folders, lists made of innumerable dates, uninteresting documents *ad infinitum*.

Opening one of these dates Alice read the lines of a poem titled simply, 'Them'.

They click a tongue called Speak
all is Sound & towers of babble
collapse, in shadow over them
Like traps and barracuda jaw.
But the castles they build
are softer than the shells
of Blue Swimmer claw
or long-legged Reds
deep migrating
carapace.

Alice cycled through the folders, wondering at some point if she might have made a good detective, or a spy. Her mother had once mentioned wanting to become a private eye, was good at reading people, she said, and must have believed she could watch strangers for hours, could get lost in their comings and goings, become filled with endless questions about them which could never be answered, but Alice was not her mother, nor was meant to be. The thrill of finding nothing of interest was intensifying the search, Alice could feel it turning her stomach, and each file in every folder felt like it might contain some antithesis to the rule, a secret of the universe preserved under excess of the ordinary, until it too opened to unworthiness. At the far end of this search were the earliest files Justin had saved for his poems, and with an utter exhalation of satisfaction Alice saw that nothing in even these earliest folders varied much from the most recent years. There was nothing to find, and the exploration might now come to its natural end. It had been a thrill, but a passing one. Seek, the Lord said, and you shall surely find. Knock and you shall enter. Justin changed the album on the record player, it was that strange portly Daniel Johnston character he had once been obsessed with, singing, 'All my friends were Vam-pi-res, I didn't know they were Vam-pi-res, turns out I was a Vamp-ire myself, in the Devil-Town.' The boys were muttering outside, she could barely make out their receding talk, the smoke was hot in the room, and Alice turned off the laptop and politely made her way upstairs to bed.

The day of the launch brimmed with well-wishers who were unable to attend the official evening event coming and going with such frequency that Alice decided to leave the screen door unlocked. Their Chippendale house was on the corner of Wiley and Myrtle, and the courier coming from the distributor with the printed books was several hours late. Alice had foreseen that it was madness to have the books delivered only hours before the launch but seeing the watery signs of panic in her husband's eyes she felt no satisfaction at being proven right. Once the first box was safely delivered and plonked onto the dining-room table, Justin's face softened. Marco, in a neat lime-green suit, and his girlfriend Flipper, who wore matching lime earrings, posed with their arms around Justin while Alice photographed the unboxing. The knife in Justin's shaking hands sliced through the packing tape with such a flourish that styrofoam bullets sprang out into the air and rolled across the floor like confetti. There would be readings at the Boatman's brewery of course, and speeches which needed to be printed at the convenience store's internet café, and a bar tab organised, though they supposed this could be done when they arrived, and the live music was to be supplied by a friend's band that went by the name 'Call Me Ishmael', and their preparedness needed confirming by phone, and one of Justin's friends was to be DJ for the evening, and a playlist had been prepared for him. It fell naturally to Alice to ensure this playlist, saved on the laptop, was brought along for this purpose, and there were directions to be given on how to find the Boatman's for those not acquainted, and then there was transporting the books to be sold at the launch, and someone had to provide the petty cash for the sales, and these were only the things that sprang immediately to Alice's mind.

Justin, evidently, felt there was much drinking and smoking to do amidst the preparations, and as the ordinary hours turned towards the actual event, the house began to stink, and the poet's eyes were swollen red and wild with nerves. Justin tried to laugh out loud at Marco's every joke, with sweat beginning to run from his temples and soak into the collar of his shirt. Alice could see the collar scratching at his skin, and he kept trying to soothe the irritation with his hands, plying the hairs on the back of his neck as if they were to blame for all his discomforts. Marco was already too high to be much help, and Flipper too drunk to notice, having found good whisky secreted on a shelf in the pantry. Marco and Justin made several sweat-soaked runs to the Boatman's, hauling books and whatever else at Alice's instruction, and Flipper hung back at the house, trying her best not to lose purchase on her stool.

When it was at last time to leave the house and proceed to the launch proper, Justin began to swear to himself, pacing back and forth across the room, or smoking furiously in the street, nodding at his mates and shaking their hands without taking his red eyes from the road. Alice ran a hand up his soaking back. Dark clouds were moving fast over the eastern sky, but the sun was still out over the west, coating the narrow streets amber against the horizon. Justin stepped away from her touch, flashed at her with wild panicked eyes, and Alice took this as a cue to gather the laptop for the DJ's needs. The travel case was at the bottom of a drawer in the study, dusty with long disuse, and there was something weighty inside a zippered pocket. A portable hard drive with a long black cord. Justin's portable hard drive. There were moments now to spare, and yet some whispering voice, the same sly impulse that had compelled Alice to search every file in those innocuous folders on the laptop, aimed to seduce her once again, assuring her that there would be time for a final search of this last refuge of forbidden knowledge, one last inspection before the boys were finished pacing and smoking and sneaking off to the bathroom for their secret snorts. And if you gaze long into the abyss, the abyss gazes into you, Alice thought, overcoming the call of inner mischief's whisper. She thrust the laptop into the bag like a stone tablet marked by holy writ, zipped it up and slung the device over her shoulder for the journey to the Boatman's brewery.

The migrating procession set out with Alice at the rear, a parade of Justin's fairest fellow travellers and best support acts. Marco flopped a pale damp arm over Justin's shoulder, the two of them taking the lead, while Flipper crab-walked over the uneven concrete of the Chippendale footpath in mid-conversation with Myra, a filmmaker with a silver bob curtaining a broad forehead whose tight-lipped mouth remained closed while her wide blue eyes undressed everyone they fell upon. Behind them was the programmer with the terrible posture whose laugh frightened sparrows out of a fig tree on the corner of Elm Street, and the programmer's partner, Ira, who supplied him offhand with a cigarette, her hair charged with static like a wilful shock of curls. She stopped to show the scars on her legs to that painter Justin had met at a poetry event, whose name was as slippery as the sideways glances she threw at Alice, loaded with grey-green suggestion. Behind the artist, with a copy of the slim red book they were marching to launch, *Songs of Storm and Claw: Chronicles of Greater Crustacea,* was the black-bearded Leon, who was busy scorning the attentions of his companion, Aman, whose tense rock-climber forearms led down to thick calcified fingers, which he gripped and loosened impulsively as they crossed the wide trafficked expanse of Abercrombie Street, on which an old brick terrace house had been newly painted with a rainbow.

Alice began to hear the ascending squeal of braking trains in the distance, and the mumbled rapport of the traffic banging along on Regent Street. She stopped to take a picture of the eccentric marchers, and having fallen slightly behind, paused to let pass three unusual people coming down the footpath on Cleveland Street. The first was a woman in a loose green dress with long dark hair. She was puckering her lips as if at any moment someone would take her picture and she hoped to appear both beautiful and ludic. The woman must have been close to forty, but there was a swirling galaxy of glitter painted around her eyes, across her cheeks, and something sparkling stuck to the centre of her forehead. Alice almost made out what this shiny adhesion was, but just as the two were crossing paths, the glittering woman grabbed hold of a street sign and swung herself around so that her hair whirled, and Alice caught a hint of its perfume. Behind the woman were two men, both narrow-shouldered and pale, and slurring their words and staggering heavily along the bright street. The shorter man was sneering at the other, and snarling 'fucking spastic!' over and over until the younger man grabbed and shoved him stumbling right out into the road, and a passing car swerved to avoid colliding with the little man, its driver sounding a horn, but neither the brawling men, nor their glittered companion, seemed to notice. Alice stood appalled at their brazen carelessness and felt the urge to photograph them as they passed. 'How do people so thoughtless stumble through the day?' she thought, watching the trio meander on, the woman in the green dress again swinging on a street sign up ahead, and the two men bounding into one another and spilling all over the place. Alice felt a kind of dizziness watching those buffoons and she looked around for something reassuring. On the corner across the street was a tavern that had often caught her fancy. The sign above its door was a glowing red symbol, something indistinctly like a set of scales overlain with a sword. The sign had always made her uneasy, there was some flaw in its design, and an irritating urge to correct it sent a ruthless shiver along the muscles in her chest. Through the dark windows, it looked a comforting old pub, like something from a more innocent age. The sight of the place reminded Alice of a scene from a novel where a young man risked his life on an inexplicable whimsy. There was some rule about him entering the pub, she remembered, but he'd done so anyway, out of sheer irresistible curiosity. It was madness to go inside, the young man kept repeating to himself, dangerous, too.

Even from outside, the tavern was noisy, and inside the smell was old sweat and damp, gassy booze. On a small stage beside an empty dance floor, a stocky man with a blonde wig was dancing and singing while lyrics were projected onto an image of a beach behind him. 'Throw donne your gonne, donne be so reck-less!' He sang. Some men in striped blue-and-white jerseys were singing along, in the corner of the room, near the pool tables and television sets of racing horses. An old man in a scooter was muttering to himself beneath a Bulldogs cap, and a large group of women was talking loudly over the music near the games room. Alice followed her own footsteps through the door, and up to the bar. A young girl covered in tattoos poured her a Laphroaig, neat, without a word of conversation. 'Good Irish drink, proper Irish,' said a man with a looming chin who'd come up behind her. 'It's from Islay,' Alice replied, and the man smiled and nodded his agreement, glancing quickly at the tattooed woman working the bar. He wore the same striped jersey as the other men Alice had seen singing in the corner of the room, and she could still hear them over her shoulder as she stepped back a little from her new companion and leaned against the bar with her glass in hand. 'You're a football player?' she asked him, taking a sip of the warm peaty liquor. He smiled, and his teeth were small and neat, like little white corn kernels, but his shoulders were broad, and his arms looked strong and were matted with oily hair. He had a dimpled smile, and the beginnings of a mullet, and smelled of motor grease and salted leather. 'Only local comp,' he said, beaming a rubbery grin. 'Strictly weekenders. We're celebrating a win though, me and the boys. You waiting for anybody? Come join us if you like.' The scotch radiated heat as it dropped into Alice's belly, and the man in the jersey announced that his name was Mondo, short for Monteith. 'Like the beer,' he said with big expectant eyes. One of the older women who'd been talking loudly over the music stepped up behind Mondo and draped her arms around his wide shoulders. He turned and looked at her with an easy familiarity. The older woman had pale blonde hair with fading roots and a weathered face, especially around the eyes, and she investigated Mondo's face with an intensity Alice could scarcely believe, as though she were studying the nature of all faces in this singular instantiation. She cupped his cheek with a bony hand and said, 'You alright, sweetheart?' Mondo assured the woman that he was, and they both turned to cast their mutual gaze upon Alice. 'He's a good man this one,' the woman said. 'I love him.' It seemed to pain the older woman to say so, and she ran her thin jewelled hand up his neck and pinched his cheek very gently, bracelets slipping down her wrist as she let him go. 'You look like my daughter June,' the woman told Alice. 'She's my eldest daughter. She had an accident last year, yeah. She was so depressed you know, so unhappy. She just went and did that awful thing to herself, tried to throw herself into the water. But we got her back now, and she's still with us.' The woman was staring at Alice, and her eyes were grey and blank as grey slate. Mondo stood up and put his arms around the woman and the tattooed girl behind the bar served a glass of rum and coke without a word. 'It was lovely to meet you,' the weathered woman said, clutching her glass in both hands. 'You two have a wonderful night, sweetheart.' The woman wandered over to the table where her friends continued their raucous cackling, and an applause was given to the man in the wig who had finished singing. 'I have to go,' Alice said, suddenly horrified. 'Congratulations on your game, I'm very glad you won.' She put the drink down on top of the bar, and shouldering her laptop, set off for the street. 'You've still got a drink to finish!' Mondo called to her. 'Wilful waste makes woeful want!' he sang out to her as the tavern door eased shut.

At last Alice came to the double-doors of the brewery, over which hung a large outcrop of mossy awning, like the lid of a trap, and above the entrance was a fresco of a ghastly hooded figure, ensconced in a rocking boat, with a yellow lantern held aloft by skeletal hands. Alice stepped inside and beheld a small stage being prepared before which stood sets of tables and chairs in the dingy gloom of glowing red and blue lights. An array of tiny purple lanterns was drilled into the front of the little stage, and black cables coiled and snaked across its scuffed and mouldy surface. The innards of the brewery's ceiling were exposed, and pipes and sprinkler heads and dangling wires twisted round woolly insulation above the bar, where two bald men were slicing lemons and tossing the dribbling wedges into a porringer, and there was a three-tiered shelf of glowing liquor bottles bright as ice behind them. There were hoardings on the walls, plastered with old punk albums, tour posters, psychedelic illustrations, and a statue of an Indian chief in full regalia was guarding the teller machine by the toilet door. 'Ah!' Justin roared. 'There she is!' He thrust his way through a small circle of people as he spoke, and his frightened eyes betrayed great anxiety. He grabbed Alice, held her close and whispered something she couldn't quite understand. Flipper was cheering and clapped along to a song by the Screaming Trees coming through the brewery's speakers, and Marco slapped Justin's back to get his attention and asked a question about the setup on the stage. Several strangers surged between them heading for the bar, and newcomers were pushing through the door, taking seats.

Provisions for the band had begun to be made on the stage now, as guests continued to arrive two by two into the gloom of the brewery, filling the space with their shadowy presence, anonymising in the crepuscular light. An electric burst of feedback struck through the speakers when a connection was made between instrument and amp, and wayward rumblings began to pulse through the DJ's selection. A squad of long-haired strangers was now assembled on the stage, their pale grim faces glowing deathlike in the mortuary shades of the purple lanterns, and Alice moved through the audience, greeting those half-familiar faces reaching out to her from the dark body of the crowd. A hot, stagnant stench bubbled in the air, the reek of mulligatawny beginning to come out of the brewery's small kitchen, steaming into the room and placed onto tables, the damp aroma of hot garlic and onion diffusing in the air. Alice saw heads bent at little tables over steaming bowls, a couple slurping ribbons of wet noodles in splashing gulps, and little trails of rich broth dripped from a hunched woman's chin near the purpled stage.

Eventually, Call Me Ishmael began to play. 'What kind of music is this?' Alice asked Justin, catching him between his tours of handshakes and bathroom trips in the shadowy crowd of new arrivals. He put his mouth so close to her ear she could feel his wet lips moving, and the prickling hairs on his cheek tickling her skin as he replied, 'They're hardcore punk, I think, or metalcore, or beatdown. They're not easy to pinpoint, actually. Hang on,' he said, and disappeared again. When the band's assault was over and the drummer was giving a final pounding to his cymbals to punctuate the space between applause for them and a return to the DJ's more assimilated music, Alice searched through the assembled audience to find Justin. He emerged from the brightness of the bathroom door with an outrageous grinning and snuffling, his mouth hanging open, and Alice could see in his eyes the terrifying bliss of oblivion. 'You've got to be able to read your speech!' Alice implored, squeezing his arm as she caught him, and he looked back at her with a most serious comportment, like an ancient amnesiac on the brink of the familiar. 'I love you,' he said, smiling fully, and produced from nowhere a long plastic rose. Alice took the rose in her fingers and Justin let the momentum of the excited crowd bustle him off to greet more guests arriving in the already cramped brewery. Alice turned the plastic flower up to her mouth, brushed its fine fabric petals against the sensitive skin on the ridge of her lips, and as she closed her eyes against the calamitous noise of the bar, its bawdy blather and its overwhelming music and the brooding red lights and the smell of spices and sweat and smoke, she saw a vast rushing wave, assembling over the surface of her inner eye. She saw a blonde-haired surfer riding the white fins of a limitless sea, balanced flawlessly as any perfection of form, as she cruised gracefully across the water's breaking foam, an infinite blue erupting beneath steady feet.

'Good evening ev'ryone!' Justin announced, slightly swaying on the stage, sheets of paper in his right hand, a glass of scotch in his left, the microphone angled at him in its stand. 'Fucking hell! What an assembly we have gathered here!' he said, and Marco yelled out something inchoate across the room and the hollering began to die down. The DJ dimmed the music, and Justin looked out over the shadow-blanketed audience like Alexander assessing his veterans at the edge of the Indus, the slight sway and lopsided smile the only dampening of his affected authority. 'The metaphor of the author as handmaid to the work they are bequeathing to the world is one I wish most ardently to avoid rehashing this evening. Not because it is a cliché, but because this night is not the endeavour of some mothering author, or a carriage of one particular agent. Though we are here to launch my own single book, we are also present tonight to begin the life of a proliferating organ of greater creatures. We are here tonight on behalf of the birth of Goonbag Press, which begins its being this day, born into the world as a breeding, life-bringer in its own right. I present my work here today – tonight – as but the first in a flurry of ever-preceding hatchlings, which are soon to be assembled on a bright new shore of Australian literary culture. My little book is an individual hatchling, signalling the coming crest of a multitude whose mutual survival will depend not on his or her own particular success, but on the swarming of the countless fellows to come.' There were almighty cheers, and Justin proceeded in this spontaneous fashion, mixing crustacean metaphors with his usual contempt for those gatekeeping Hellfire folk that had been such an obsession throughout the long years Alice had known him, and when his speechifying was done, he froze for a moment, and then recited these words in stark solemnity:

O all fair lovers about the world,
    There is none of you, none that shall comfort me.
My thoughts are as dead things, wrecked and whirled
    Round and round in a gulf of the sea;
And still, through the sound and the straining stream,
Through the coil and chafe, they gleam in a dream,
The bright fine lips so cruelly curled,
    And strange swift eyes where the soul sits free.

Alice's quiet applause was drowned in the crowd's usual hysteria when this recitation ended, and the mood in the room felt strangely transfigured. Justin's tell-tale sway had steadied for the moment. The clack and rattle of the kitchen and some faint few voices at the bar were more pronounced as the cheers died down. Justin bent down and placed his schooner glass, carefully, on the resonant stage, and while bent, groped for a copy of his book, lying beside the microphone stand, with the figure of a great red crab holding up its pincer in triumph on its front cover. A flash of memory at the sight of that image saw Alice transported in a vivid recollection. She was wandering towards a great mound of wet stone forking out of the sand beside crashing waves. 'Dad!' she was calling, and running after her father, and her sister too. They'd taken a short beach walk, not far from their grandmother's house on the Central Coast where they'd spent every summer of her youth. Her father was so much younger, and he ducked down behind the slick wet gorge of rock with a spirited agility he no longer possessed. The spray of a wave blinded Alice, and she cried out to her father with wet hair in her eyes. He laughed, clearing her sight with a wipe of his rough hand. In his other hand he held up a barnacled green crab, and her sister squealed at the sight of it in their father's grasp. The monster's legs preened grotesquely in the sunlight, a deep blue-green claw reaching up into the empty air, seawater spitting from the gaps in its armour, and dribbling down her father's long pale arms. He brought the creature closer to his daughters' faces, waving it before their eyes and smiling at their playful screams. Alice felt the rushing water surging at her feet and leapt away, the smell of clean salt air and the sucking sands tickling her toes. She saw the bubbles foaming on the surface of the rocks where her father was standing, and the girls laughed and shrieked as he waved the crab at them, until he turned towards the sea and tossed the little armoured creature back between the salty rocks. It spun like a disc waving its claws helplessly, plunged down into the great crashing sea and was gone.

Sit Down Young Stranger

Sunset hung over the mountains when Liam stepped off the carriage into the sting of Katoomba's twilight, hoisting his guitar case over the gap and following the evening rush of strangers in black coats and scarves down the station stairs. An electric schedule hanging from the station's awning announced the time in blinking yellow digits, an hour left before the opening, enough time to settle the nerves at a pub up the street, not enough time to become so settled the night's performance would suffer.

A sprawl of graffiti on the walls of the tunnel leading from the station out towards the footpath read 'I've done me self a mischief'. What this meant, Liam couldn't say, but it struck him the phrase might serve as a title, or a lyric that could open into melody. He let that possibility flicker inside the dusky interior plane from which all his songs had come, but nothing stuck in this instance, and all thought of the phrase was forgotten when his eyes fell upon a poster pasted outside the tunnel's arch. The poster read '*Blut und Märchen* – an exhibition by the artist Annie Aver-Mann'. Dominating the poster's arrangement was the print of a painting which depicted a pale, thin girl with long black braids covering her nakedness, standing in the clearing of a leafless forest like something from a fairytale. Along with the title of the exhibition, the advertisement promised a 'free acoustic performance by Liam Henley'. The sight of his name in print was still a giddying thrill, even on this minor scale, disturbing though to see it associated with the haunting figure portrayed in Annie's art.

'I need new friends,' Liam whispered, and looking into that painted face with its alarming dark eyes, he made the sign of the cross, 'father, son, holy, spirit', and kissed his own right hand to seal the prayer, as he had done since childhood.

On the corner by the station there was an old colonial bank building which had been converted into a pub, with a lone security guard out front in a full-length leather coat that only a large, serious man could wear without a hint of theatre. The guard nodded, rubbing gloved hands together as he did so, and nudged open the door with his elbow, giving a sideways glance at the coffin-shaped guitar case Liam was dragging up the steps behind him. The case was cornball, a relic from his youthful heavy metal affectations, but its ugliness helped belie the quality of the rare guitar inside it, made it safer to travel without the threat of being rolled. Now that his name and face meant something to the world, care must be taken; there was always a want for getting one over those who'd made themselves known in this country.

Inside the pub, the patrons were bunched in mounds of coats and jackets on stools at plank-wood tables fastened to wine barrels. Antique lamps with petal rims gave a brazier glow to the bar, and Liam mistook the warm amber light for an open fire somewhere just out of view. A staircase wound its way up to a second floor, behind the bar, which led up to the hotel proper, and from above he could hear the faintest creak of floorboards over the racket and the revelry.

The ruddy scene reminded Liam of the residency he'd undertaken in the English county of Kent, three years ago, and a flood of memories came upon him of that time abroad. The tour had been his making as a musician worthy of the brand. He'd been a fine expat tourist too; had taken time off to see the gold wings of Queen Victoria's statue, high above the gates of Buckingham Palace, and he'd watched the great mechanism of the London Eye, wheeling slowly above the thorny striations of the Houses of Parliament. Liam saw most of London like this: from the open top of a double-decker bus painted in the colours of the Union Jack, with the cockney accent of the tour guide still clear in his ears, pointing out essentials, like the Tower of London, where heads had once been mounted on spikes along the walls, and great men and women had died mad in the darkness made of lime and ragstone. Later on in the tour, Liam took time away from his proper occupation to walk the stony shores of Brighton, watching the grey-green sea foaming and roaring over acres of smooth, flat rocks; in a dank hipster brewery in Ulster he ate a bucket of mussels while England lost their World Cup hopes, and bore witness to a thousand St George flags littering the streets as the locals turned on each other in drunken disappointment. Most cherished of all these fascinations was a day spent busking for hours in the pollen-thick parks of Notting Hill, where his case filled with five-pound notes and white swans stretched out their pinioned wings by the ponds. In the English twilight, Liam sang Gordon Lightfoot's 'The Wreck of Edmund Fitzgerald' and Jim Croce's 'Time in a Bottle' until his fingers puckered and bled.

That memory, above all, was a treasure. A green-eyed girl in a sailor's costume, working a parlour bar in Oxford, smiled at his accent that night. 'I love the beer youse drink here,' he said to her, leaning forward against the too-loud music and the faintness of the light, his heart laced with German lager. 'I'm sure you do, that gassy piss you Aussies drink is rank.' This is English banter, Liam told himself, but for all his efforts he could not become accustomed to its sting. He recalled chatting to an Irish lad at a urinal in a club that same night, who asked, apropos nothing, what part of a woman the Aussie fancied most. They were both pissing into the urinal bowls, a red light coming in through windows frosted against the alley outside. The room stank of bleach, and an ungodly bass pulsed in from the club's speakers and pressed against his skull. Liam took in the Irishman's question, closing his eyes upon the image of a woman's bare belly as it flashed upon his imagination: she, whoever this woman was, was dancing towards him, smooth and brassy as desert dunes at daybreak. Seeing this impression, vivid in his mind, Liam replied with his eyes still closed, 'the thorax'. The Irishman zipped up his splattered jeans, stepped back from the urinal, his skin red from the alley's glow, and said, 'Well that's a word for it! You sure have a way with anatomy there, Mr Vocabulary.' Desperate for some smooth rejoinder, Liam offered, 'You know what they say: *use it or lose it*!' Already half out the door, with waves of sound irrupting into the rank toilet air, the Irishman called back over his shoulder, 'And you obviously lost it a long time ago, mate.'

It was the fault of the rustic insides of this old Katoomba pub, its polished curves like the gullet of a smoking pipe, which had brought these English transportations to mind. 'This tiny slice of England,' Liam thought, and rephrased this near aloud, 'A Slice of Little England.' Would that configuration make for a title? He wasn't convinced, but, for a moment, a line and an image together burst alive in Liam's inner eye, he could see the construction drifting towards him through some second sight, but an uproar of excitement rode over the Dave Brubeck standard the pub was blowing through its speakers and dashed his thoughts to pieces. A large woman in a leather vest had caused the disturbance

– she made a foghorn of her hands and bellowed across the room, 'Hail to thee, blithe spirit!', and a bald, red-bearded man dressed like a lumberjack closer to the bar had called back to her, 'It was an Abyssinian maid, and on her dulcimer she played!' This produced such a calamity of laughter from the entire crowd that Liam came close to covering his ears. These anachronisms rang familiar, were painful sounds, like branches scraping on glass in heavy winds, and whatever game the crowd was at with these mysterious quotations, Liam knew it not.

Most in the crowd were old, Liam saw in a survey of the laughing faces, soft and swollen for the most part, lines around their eyes when they were smiling, the skin hanging under their chins, and it was a relief to realise that whatever song he'd be playing tonight, it would not be for these old drunks and their strange quotations. Lord knows he'd played too often for these types, who were just as likely to chatter through the music as they were to sing along or clap out of time with the beat or stumble up on stage to make a show of it.

There was a brawny woman with short red hair working the bar whose tattoos ran down both her arms from her bare shoulders, and the likeness of a seahorse was inked on her left forearm. It was possible, he realised, as he leant his guitar case up against the bar beside him, a woman her age would know his face and name, now that it meant something, and so when she looked up from the glass of wine she was pouring, he waited for that flicker of recognition to leap from her eyes to his.

'What can I get you?' she asked. There was nothing in her voice but the question, though he tried a question of his own to increase his chances of being recognised, supposing that his voice might help her make an association with his face. 'Do you have pints here?' She shook her head, 'Schooners or middies.'

Liam took a schooner out to the courtyard and found the warmth inside had worsened the evening's sting, and the sun was well behind the mountains now. He sat at a bench in the beer garden and took to rolling a cigarette, hunching over it in hopes its small fire would help to kindle his spirits. Annie would be at the venue already, he knew, checking the hangings with her meticulous eye, half-cut for sure, her wild mane of auburn hair stinking of cigarette smoke and licks of whatever she'd drunk. It amused Liam to think of Greg, the small, anodyne gallery owner who would be doing his best to deal with all the manic energy in that prodigious woman, nervous eyes darting back and forth around the corners of the little shop as Annie stomped around within its walls like a pillaging warrior Hun.

Parades of tourists unloaded from Greyhound buses pulled up by the cenotaph just outside the beer garden's gates, in bright beanies and puffed-up duffle coats that made it hard to tell where these foreigners might be from. Beneath the hanging streetlight, one man with red mittens aimed the long lens of his camera in Liam's direction, and he turned to see if there was something else behind him worthy of the shot, but there were only two teens in black hoodies, sitting at a bench at the back of the garden, near a brick wall veined with creeping vines, both looming over a phone that gave their faces a spectral shade. One of these young men, with what looked like a fish tattooed on his temple, was crying with laughter so completely his wet face was turning red. The other, stub-nosed and grinning wildly, said, 'Did you see that? Cunt's throwing whole raw chickens off a jetty!' This brought a sharp howl out of his breathless friend, who was now clutching his head as tears ran down from his eyes, and drops fell from his nose onto the screen. By the time Liam turned back around, the tourist with the camera was gone into the night.

As Liam looked about for the lost cameraman, Annie, the artist, materialised out of the misty streetlight as though appearing from backstage, tossed a pouch of tobacco onto the bench, and grabbed Liam with an embrace more suited to aikido than affection. 'Oh my God!' Annie cried, hopping backwards onto the benchtop and swinging the mass of her hair away from her face to re-light an extinguished cigarette. 'How are you?' she asked with the smoke between her lips, the stink of sweetened rum cutting through the fog of her heavy breathing. 'Let me get you a beer,' Liam answered, having finished his own and unready to withstand the artist's energies sober.

By the time Liam returned Annie was lighting another smoke, and there was a small stack of posters, just like the one he'd seen outside the tunnel advertising the night's proceedings, laid out beside her on the bench. The central feature of these posters was that same haunted print of the exhibition's titular painting, *Blut und Märchen*, the girl whose penetrating eyes Annie had painted, now looking up at Liam in arresting multitudes.

'So c'mon! What's it like to be famous?' Annie asked. Liam tried to laugh the question away, but Annie pressed it. 'Seriously!' she said. 'If I hear that song of yours on the radio one more time I'm going to drive a forklift through a fucking wall. Makes me sick hearing your voice when I'm at work, with overalls on and all.' She put on a sibilant sing-song voice and recited the lyrics: *the taste of my true lover gone!*

'You can't surely begrudge me my fifteen minutes,' Liam said, half to make her stop, and then to ask, sincerely, 'Why? The song doesn't meet your approval?'

Annie winced and took down half the beer he'd brought her.

'It's a beautiful bit of bedside poetry,' Annie answered. 'It's also the cringiest hipster drool I've heard my entire life. I always said you should have stuck to being a poet, not tried to become Gotye. But don't get me wrong, I still want you to sing it tonight, aye? No one knows any of your other songs, there'll be a riot if you don't give 'em the hit.'

'A fine critic you are,' Liam smiled, only lightly forced, and reached into his tobacco bag to fill some paper, 'Anyway, tonight's about your arty-farty fan-service, not mine. Are you ready for the cavalcade of adoration you're about to be swept away by? Greg's gonna make you out to be Katoomba's answer to Ben Quilty, I bet.'

'I'm foaming in the daks about it – as well you know,' Annie said. 'I hate all this fucking shit. And don't give me that look! It's easy for you. All you've gotta do is sing one lousy song – I've gotta be on fire all night. I've gotta grift.' Talk of the opening made Annie glance at her watch, an old silver thing inherited from a favourite grandfather. 'Fark! Not enough time to get pissed.' Swallowing down the rest of her beer she added, 'Can you sign this shit for me, quick.'

Liam looked over the slim stack of posters, the naked girl, lost in the dark woods, looking back at him with doleful eyes. 'Why would you want me to sign it? You're the fucking artist! These people are coming to see you!' She was deaf to this. There was no way out. Liam signed his name upon them all, though his signature looked unlike itself.

Katoomba's main street had changed since Liam had last been to town. There were Korean cafés, French 'provincial' restaurants, three American burger joints and the air smelt of pizza-smoke and charcoaled meat. Ovens glowed through the shopfronts and couples laughed and clinked their glasses outside of wine bars and whisky joints. Both artist and musician were out of breath by the time they climbed the steep hill up to the gallery, and Liam was relieved to put his guitar case down while they made final preparations before stepping inside for the night's roles. The girl leered out at Liam from the gallery's front display, the disquieting mix of perversion and innocence looked garish in the spotlit brightness of the window. His nerves fired under a coughing fit.

'I need a cigarette,' he said.

Annie started rolling too, coughing and sighing along with him. 'Fuck, we're getting old,' she said with a long hard breath steaming into the air. Liam tried his lighter six or seven times and finally inhaled a lungful of smoke. They both looked in at the crowd and Liam could see Annie's husband, Ian, and their four brunette boys chasing each other around the place, as some older mountains folk with grey beards and champagne flutes in their hands gazed blankly at the various depictions of naked nymphs and lascivious corpses spread on darkling wastelands, and so much blood and gore and sex and fairytale as Annie's art depicted.

'Dude,' Annie said, the word odd in her mouth. 'Just wanna give you a heads-up. Jules is gonna be here.'

'Where?' Liam asked, exhaling a frail stalk of smoke.

'Here,' Annie said, nodding at the gallery.

'Jules is gonna be here? At your opening – here tonight?'

'Yeah. Just thought I'd give you the heads-up.' Annie said,

looking away from Liam and in through the gallery's broad display, checking the faces in the crowd.

'Are you serious? We're about to go through the door; I'm about to play in there! How is this a fucking heads-up?' Liam swore. 'The song is *about her* for fuck's sake!'

'Dude, first, that's precisely what a "heads-up" is – imminent danger, be alert. And I didn't think she'd show, so don't get so mad! She texted me this arvo. She was the model for some of the paintings – the title painting! That's her in the window there – and on the posters! I had to invite her. You gotta respect your models, dude.' Annie gave an apologetic frown, looking at Liam's mortified state, slapped him on the back, flicked her spent smoke into the street and pushed on into the gallery. 'Look at these filth wizards!' she said in a booming voice, hugging a group of dark-haired men with wiry beards, and chains hanging from the pockets of their jeans, and the tall pale women with dyed hair and tattoos who ran over to get in on the hugs and kisses as the gallery door eased itself shut.

'I need another smoke,' Liam said to no one at all, his bent cigarette still lit and half inhaled. For a moment, despite the busy evening sounds of laughter and conversation, and the distant din of rock music coming from the RSL down the street, the only people in sight seemed to be the crowd on the other side of the gallery's glass. Annie was moving amongst them now, stomping between each clique of attendees cramped into the small bright space. Liam watched Annie circulating by the paintings, pointing out their implications, clinking champagne glasses and hugging person after person, her mass of hair flinging into their faces and knocking capers off their salmon canapés. Jules must be among their number, he knew it, though he couldn't see her in the crowd.

Liam's throat was dry, and he began, instead, to see her face assembling itself in his mind's eye, a strange intrusion of panic and memory. He tried to shake the impression but his gaze fell on the painting hanging in the window. It was obvious now that Jules had been the model – the dark hair and shining eyes, her thin, curling smile and dimpled chin. How could he not have known her face the moment he first saw the poster outside the station, when his first glimpse of her in life seemed to renew its impression each time he closed his eyes at the end of the day, or stood silent and alone on an empty street corner, or sat on a train winding its way up into the mountains with a guitar case by his side, staring into the setting distance? It had been a cold night down on the Canberra plains when he first saw Juliana, during one of his shows at the Folk Festival. He'd been stumbling back across the festival field towards the silent rows of tents, tripping on the ropes in the dark, looking half-collapsed in walking sleep, and the moon rolled out from behind a rush of cloud, its pale glow pinning him down like a leviathan's eye in the black firmament. In that shivering moment was his first glimpse of Jules, sitting atop a fence around the tents, her bright eyes bold in the darkness, laughing loudly at two lanky boys who were wrestling for a lighter by the camping ground gates. It had seemed like a waking dream, and when she had caught his eye in the crowd the next morning, as he played 'I Started a Joke' during a festival session titled 'When Good Covers Go Bad', he almost lost the melody, looking into the milky charm of her fixed attention. For the rest of the song, his hands moved of their own accord upon the strings, and he sang only to her, the stranger staring back at him, so that nothing beside remained. When the song was done, she pursed her lips and whistled loudly, her head tilted to the side, like curiously fey folk summoned out of the festival's strange pagan pretensions, her legs crossed, holding up her arms towards him as she applauded.

Liam let the cold Katoomba air and the stage-light shine of the gallery's window transport him back into the present. There was no hope now of playing the song Liam had planned – the song that was about her *for fuck's sake*. Picking up the guitar case and pushing through into the feverish light of the gallery, Liam's mind was awhirl with recalculation: What else can be played? What songs might be sung? Nothing was there in his internal musical catalogue but flashing static and discordant snatches of inaudible confusion.

'Liam!' A small man with slicked-back black hair rushed across the polished floorboards. Greg, the gallery owner. 'I'm so glad you're here – that woman – I know she's your mate – but good grief – I mean really – she puts me in a state! And we're about to start – how can we set you up? Is it just the one song? Are you sure?' Greg put his hand on Liam's back as he asked these questions, the small man's large eyes darting around the gallery as though he were an intruder in his own habitat. Liam answered none of his questions, which seemed to reassure Greg as he led the way towards a stool and a microphone in the far corner of the gallery. A gaunt bald woman was setting up the sound system and she nodded indifferently at the two men on their approach. Greg took his hand off Liam's back and wandered away, still asking questions without answers. The interlude had been enough for Liam to devise a new plan: he would sing a song called 'Redfern Blues' – though its original title was 'Dublin Blues' – by Guy Clark, an American folk singer. The song was one of the covers he'd recorded to fill out his EP – obscure enough so most folks wouldn't know if they were hearing something old or new, especially if he sang it the way he'd done for the album, with local references in place of Clark's originality.

The room was so bright it made for squinting at the paintings on the walls, and Liam took in the many naked bodies and bloody cheeks. He was too nervous now to deal with them as individual objects – instead they formed a kind of enclosure, a frightening wilderness of wild-eyed women and young girls in stages of undress and damnation, shadowy elfish figures being followed by hungry wolves in the darkness between the trees. Inside this strange second world of the gallery was the crowd, an undifferentiated mass of people into which he would soon be asked to pour his music. Only after the first few chords and the amplification of his voice, would he begin to see their unique faces, intense snatches and impressions coming to him throughout the elusive moments of creation.

The tall bald woman was adjusting the cables, testing something – she asked Liam some question and he answered in an absent way, the rare guitar out of its case now and in his arms, and a strange beating of anticipation like a throbbing in his ears. There was sweat on his fingers, they felt hot and clumsy, but when he placed them on the strings, the sounds they made were right, and his hands seemed to know to position themselves. He adjusted the tuning, twisted the small pegs with unconscious calculation. The woman strode across the floorboards in loud heels and handed a microphone to Greg, who was now wearing a blue jacket and a beaming smile as he addressed the gathering, the bright lights gleaming on his oily hair.

'Good evening – thank you all for coming – a characteristically snappy Mountains eve – this is an incredible exhibit – it's my pleasure to be able to present – one of Katoomba's greatest artists –'

What the little man said bounced about the room, re-verb-erating out of the amplification system, through skin and bone, into the empty chamber of Liam's guitar and along the strings like small electric pricks upon the tightening threads of his nerves. The same mysterious energy Liam would need to call upon in just a minute's time. Greg's voice had become a countdown to something absurd – in a matter of ineluctable moments, the crowd would turn to Liam, perched like some sweating foreign specimen pinned upon a stool, and this pinioned wreck of a man would be expected to summon vibrations of the throat and the strings which are called music. No mistakes would be permissible when the fatal time came, and his voice for the entirety of the performance would be forbidden to break, to lose its tune – nor could his fingers miss their mark, his wrists and fingertips must be true to their rehearsal. What barbarism was this expectation of flawlessness! Three full minutes of foul perfection! What madness led such pressures to be thrust on persons made of flesh and blood? Liam dropped his chin into the curve of the guitar, the coolness of its body easing the flush of his cheeks. It would be insanity now to look into the crowd, though he felt their swaying eyes moving towards him, and a trace of sweat rolled from his forehead – why not tears too, he could just let them out.

'Annie is an artist we've hosted here many times – each of her showings hugely successful – people love her work – these strange, seductive and sinister apparitions appeal to us in a way – in my experience – could conceivably –'

God what a folly to aspire, however humbly, to the level of art! Better to be a face in the crowd looking out than a fool on a stool clinging to strings like a songbird wired on a swing in a cage, to be gawked at and mocked, to lose your feathers in front of their hungry attentions! Greg was turning, looking sideways at Liam now with his darting eyes. How slick and cruel that expression was, loaded with the expectation of delivery. The eyes of a butcher bird, carrying a kind of craven desperation too, a co-conspirator's threat.

'And what makes tonight even more astonishing – as if Annie Aver-Mann's art isn't more than enough – we have the incomparable musical stylings of *Liam Henley* here to perform an acoustic track from his latest album – give him a huge round of applause – to perform his hugely popular song – I always get the damn title wrong –'

There was now no time at all, the end of Greg's next sentence led so inextricably into an impossible set of duties that for Liam the end had already begun. 'Ladies and gentlemen' – this was the cue – no sooner said than a force, like a kind of bodily possession, made him light, and when he spoke into the microphone now it was as though another spirit sat inside his body, wore his flesh as a hand wears a sock for a puppet. 'This song is dedicated to Annie Aver-Mann, artist and friend.' Where did this little speech come from? It wasn't planned but it was wise – good to celebrate Annie here – tonight being about her, not music. Some other night would come for that, a night more fit, but if someone in the crowd were to hear Liam's music tonight and decide that it was Liam Henley who was the greater artist, surely he would be blameless?

Liam's fingers took dominion, found their places on strings and frets. They knew their actions better than their master – they could not be willed to miss their mark, they knew only one way to move, the way of song. Liam's body, his arms and legs, his wrists and neck, his thumbs and thighs, felt new and vital and all that was needed from him now was to sing the lines in their order, though the room really was too bright, and the faces of the crowd so very close. Some kids in attendance were tripping over each other, talking loudly to their parents. But the possessing spirit was performing now, and the first chords rippled through the confinement of the room and the crowd was held in place by the energies of song, and the room belonged to Liam Henley, whatever the sorrowful women in those paintings had to say about it.

At the first line of the first verse, he saw Jules in the crowd. She was smiling, the same huge grin she had worn when he played to her that morning at the festival. Still, he had to sing.

Well, I wished I was in Melbourne,
In a chilly laneway bar
Drinkin' rum-and-coca-colas
And not carin' where you are.
But here I sit in Redfern,
Just rollin' cigarettes,
Holdin' back and chokin' back
The shakes with every breath.

The shock of seeing Jules cleaved its way inside him, but he stayed out of his own control, and felt he saw himself performing from a vantage outside his body – guiding the course like a breeze carries a glider through the rushing air. Halfway through the song, a baby started crying, and two of Annie's boys pulled at their mother's jeans to show her something on a phone, and Liam became conscious again of the words he was singing. He wasn't sure if he'd skipped the verses between, or played them unconsciously. The song had played itself and was already coming to an end.

Applause erupted around the gallery, and laughter as Annie put her fingers to her lips for an enormous whistle. Liam felt his face flush anew. He was looking at Jules as the applause rose and fell, and she was smiling, slowly clapping her hands. He smiled back, cool sweat rolling down his body before Annie crashed into him. 'I love you, ya filthy hipster!' She squeezed him hard and her immense hair fell about him so completely it plunged the room into darkness for a long moment – he imagined Jules's attention in that darkness.

'This filth wizard has been a mate of mine since back in the uni days! I love him! But what the fuck was that song, dude! Where was the hit?' The crowd laughed and Annie stepped into her speech, explaining all the ways her art had ended up on the canvases on the too-bright walls. 'To be honest, I'm not an intellectually aware kind of artist, if there's anything going on in these works – you'll have to explain it to me.' There were already red stickers on the walls, and Annie, a champagne flute in her hand as she spoke, flushed with triumph, became so bold and expansive that Greg began to wring his hands.

Liam busied himself with his instrument, making an elaborate ritual of packing it away while Annie talked. An instinct cautioned him not to look back at Jules, though a contrary pull to do so was wriggling in his mind like an itch. 'I want to thank my dad, Teddy Mann – there he is over there – who personally framed every painting in this exhibition.' Annie stopped for a moment. Her arms fell to her sides. 'Jesus Christ!' She laughed, with tears streaming down her face. Teddy, the father, a barrel-shaped man with enormous hands and blacked fingernails stepped out from the crowd and put his arms around his daughter, his own small eyes leaking tears. 'Jesus,' Annie swore. 'I can't believe I'm crying! What a loser!' Greg tried to lead the crowd into a chorus of 'aww', but no one followed.

When at last the talk was over there was wild applause, stamping of feet and whistling – the room relaxed so thoroughly that even the brightness seemed to dim, and all returned to considerations of the paintings they had come to see, some patrons armed with little red stickers, Greg darting about to agree with whatever they were saying about whichever work they happened to be interested in.

'That was good,' Jules said, coming close from out of the crowd. 'But then, you were always a talent.' Her hair was tied back tight, her fine pale cheeks lightly reddening as she stood close.

'You haven't aged a day! You look incredible!' Liam gushed, but there was so much more to say – and the words were close to spilling out. 'You're Annie's muse, so I've discovered,' he said to her, at a loss as to where he might begin. Jules craned her neck around the room as if only just noticing versions of herself in a half-dozen frames. 'What can I say? I've acquired a knack for inspiration.' She smiled broadly when she said this, and Liam could not take his eyes off the shape of that lopsided smile – even the pattern of the teeth! He could not but think: I have kissed her mouth. He had kissed her in his dreams of late. A thin-shouldered man in a grey leather jacket stepped up and loomed into the conversation, his expression as impassive as a mannequin's.

'Liam, this is Manny.' Manny shook hands without turning his eyes from Jules as he announced, 'We really need to get going.' Jules affirmed his statement with a nod. 'Manny's a DJ – he's got a show tonight, too!' She patted Manny on the shoulder as he turned away from them both. 'It was good to see you! Sorry we have to rush off!' Liam tried to respond, but the most he could do was open his mouth and shut it again. He repeated this action twice more and had to use a hand to prevent it repeating for a third time. Jules waved goodbye as she followed Manny out the door, into the dark Katoomba street, passing the haunted version of herself hung in the gallery window, a small red circle beside it now.

Jules had left a half-empty glass of champagne on a table of canapés beneath a painting called *Elfen in nassem Leder*, which depicted several elfish women, nude but for the thinnest strips of leather wrapped around their bodies. These bare figures were wading into a hot spring overlooking an autumnal woodland. It was clear that Juliana had been the model for all three of these luminous beings. Liam took her abandoned glass and sculled it, refilling it quickly from a bottle by the canapés. He swilled that glass too and repeated this action three more times.

Liam hoovered two salmon and caper canapés into his mouth and again, sculled the drink in his hand – and poured another. A man with long thinning hair wrung out in a mess of directions was now standing beside him, looking up at *Elfen in nassem Leder*. Liam blinked at him, there was something familiar about his face. 'I know you!' he said, shocked to recognise the man's face. 'I know you, sure, I know you! You have one of those social media blogs where you go round eating burgers and kebabs. I saw you on television once! You go to Granville and eat chicken, you go to Ashfield for dumplings! You eat those giant burgers at food trucks and drink litre milkshakes with big chunks of ice-cream on the top!' The stranger looked back at Liam as though he had pulled a switchblade on him. 'Yes,' the man confessed, he was indeed the man with the food blog. 'Fuck, dude! That must be a wonderful life! You eat out three times a day, seven days a week, and every café and bar in the country has got to impress you, has to excite your particular fancy, or you tear their work apart with a savage review! What a bloody barrel you've got those businesses over, aye?' The man confessed it was a nice gig. 'Yeah, I'd like to go around stuffing my face all day, it must take a lot of finesse. Where did you eat this evening? You tried the waffle house? The French provincial? You give 'em a good review, gunslinger?' It was his day off, the man explained, and then excused himself and left the gallery. Liam picked up a bottle of champagne and put it to his lips. Imagine a balding food blogger buying a work of art like that! Some rotund sensualist, gazing up at half-nude elves as he strips down on his bed before the mirror! Liam felt the urge to turn the canapé table on its head and kick out the legs. Greg appeared at his shoulder, and put a hand on his back, almost patting him. 'Liam, Liam! You were so good buddy – you consider that Chandon bottle yours – it's on me – least we can do for the song – but please use a glass, okay bud? They'll take my licence away if you get too rock-and-roll!' The small man laughed and scurried away, his eyes darting back at Liam as he did so. Annie now had one arm over her father, the other on her husband, their children huddled together in the corner watching YouTube videos on the phone. There were red circles next to most of the paintings, and the crowd showed no signs of detaching from the artist's orbit. The musician looked over the room one last time, snatched up his guitar case and stumbled out into the night without a word to anyone.

It was bitterly cold but Liam's blood was ringing in his ears as he staggered down the street, passing loud couples drinking outside bars and restaurants with their glowing heaters. There was an image burning bright in Liam's mind of the afternoon he'd spent in Notting Hill, the swan-swept park where he'd played out the day with Gordon Lightfoot and Jim Croce by the gentle hills, under a wide clear sky. The stars were all out now, and the moon was high, and Notting Hill was on the other side of the world, but there was no law against busking at night – he could throw his case open right here, or outside the gallery, and sing like a troubadour. A woman in a Rastafarian hat rolled her eyes at her nose-pierced partner when Liam stumbled on a jag of the concrete footpath in front of them, almost dropping the half-empty bottle of Chandon. The decline of the street made it easy to trip, and distant rock music was coming from the RSL a few streets away. Liam remembered a park at the bottom of the hill where it would be quiet, an amphitheatre in the heart of the park where he could play.

'Kingsford Smith Memorial Park'. This was the place he was looking for, though it was darker than he had expected, and the tops of trees around the archway seemed to loom over the path circling down deep into the strange crater-like depths. By the time Liam lugged his guitar case down to the bottom pit of the empty park the Chandon was finished, and his ragged breath was pulsing steam. There was a dim lantern filled with dead insects near the amphitheatre, and the moon was hidden by the top of an old apartment beside the station. Moths made silent sweeps at the flickering lantern, and Liam placed his open guitar case underneath, so that anyone wandering down the winding path could pay their respects to his work. He slipped into the strap and held the guitar in his arms, swaying slightly. His fingers were cold and stiff, but they knew their place, and their movements gave him the nerve to play into the silence. His hands pulled his voice along, and when the song came from his lips, out into the cold, it rolled around in the wide icy night with a purity he'd never known before.

Long ago at the festival
Under a wide April night
She was the girl I'd love best of all
And I dreamt about her tonight.

We walked the town for an hour
Remembering the people we knew
Then she took me to her tower
I climbed up her hair for the view.

In the morning she's leaving me
As all sweet dreamers will do
She was always the best of me
My sweetest dreaming come true.

She used to roll old gold cigarettes
The taste on the tip of our tongue
Ten thousand years though I'll never forget
The taste of my true lover gone.

Liam played the final chords and let the song disappear into the park's indifference, a little shocked at how intensely he'd pitched the words into living air. Just for a moment, the silence that followed seemed to envelope everything. He felt the hairs rise on his skin and noticed a strange mist had gathered in the trees, so thick he couldn't quite see the lights of the houses or the streetlights near the station. Somebody was moving through the mist. A train passing through the station stirred the silence, and bats squeaking in the trees, and a possum walking unnoticed near the gate was reaching up towards the branches of a twisted tree near the park's arch. Liam's eyes were wide at the figure coming through the mist – it was Jules, her apparition summoned by his song! Liam let the guitar hang from his body and stood silent, and when Jules stepped fully out of the mist, he had to blink hard to see it wasn't her at all, but a man in a hoodie with his head bowed and his hands in his pockets. Then a second hooded figure appeared, following close behind the first. Before Liam could adjust to this transition, the hooded men were standing close to him, the first saying, 'Sick song, bro!' The man was young, with a pale puckered face and small shaded eyes, above which was tattooed something like a fish. 'Thanks,' Liam tried to say, but his voice was dry, and the word was barely audible. 'Hey. You ever seen a three-metre flatty?' Liam looked at the young man, who lit a smoke in his hands so that the flash of the lighter's wheel turned the inside of his hood into a fiery bowl. 'A what?' was the best Liam could offer in answer. Then there was a dull, echoing sound, like somebody dropping a rock on a hollow log.

Soon the park's mist was gone, and the bats and possums had quit, and the early morning light was purple in the sky. Lying in the grass, Liam dreamt of a large stage, his small body in its centre. 'I'm forgetting my lines!' he'd been saying, looking out at the blinding lights and the invisible crowd. When the poor show was over, he came down into the rows to meet his friends and thank them for coming, and a terrible awkwardness fell over the hall. 'I didn't know my lines,' he was explaining to someone. 'I've never known them, never!' He began to sob in his dream, and on the stage behind him he heard Orson Welles announce, 'Well, if you want a happy ending, that depends, of course, on where you stop your story.' Juliana put her hands on Liam's shoulders. 'You'll recover from this,' she said. Liam started to move. There was no stage, at all, only earth, slightly spinning. Sky and tree and wet, cold ground. When the shock subsided, Liam saw his guitar and its case were gone, and he found the strength to raise himself up onto his knees. He knelt there, making a strange choking noise, as close to laughter as the pain allowed. Up in the branches of a tree was a kookaburra, looking down at Liam, rolling its head from side to side, wondering what to make of this strange, wormy thing in the grass below.

An Article of Faith

'I think it comes down to an innate desire to know what is really happening in the world around us, in the lives of those ordinary people we pass in the street, from the old woman in the green floral dress, dragging her trolley load of groceries up the steps of the bus, to the local politician whose lunch with a lobbyist at Vesuvius in Blackheath means an endangered leaf frog is one step closer to extinction.'

Emma had said this to the district manager in an interview for her cadetship, and the manager had smiled and nodded along with every word. The words came to mind whenever Emma noticed Mitch, from across rows of tables in the open plan office with its white walls and silent faces at shared desks, waltzing towards her with his head-swaying, straight-armed poise. 'Em,' he said to her, leaning all his weight on the edge of her desk, talking at his phone rather than at the cadet directly. 'You're on puff patrol this arvo. I'm sending the file to you now.' No sooner had these words been spoken than a little box appeared on the screen on Emma's desk with a demoralising chime. The file mentioned in the pop-up alert was titled 'Bobby Duncan Blacktown Citizen Pap'. Emma clicked it open and glanced back at Mitch while it loaded. He was looking at her now, with grim indifferent eyes, and his spiked greying hair was ringed by an oily sheen ever-present on his bulbed forehead. 'Off you pop,' he said with an edge of urgency, pointing to the door with a nod, and Emma grabbed at her phone and keys and was off and out of the office before she'd even had time to read where she was supposed to be going.

The romance of the newsroom, Emma decided as she blasted

the aircon in her car and typed the subject's address into the map on her phone, was overrated. And frankly, she thought, no course of study on planet Earth can prepare you for calling the families of dead children, asking to speak to the parents, having them come to the phone through their bewildered grief, hounding folks in their moment of deepest despair, chasing after copy with the callous desperation of a meth-head. It was worse, somehow, when the subjects complied, caved into your probing and seductions. It was better to have them hang up on you than listen greedily to them trying to formulate their thoughts. Sometimes you had to see the dead yourself – accidents and suicides. People in the dark with the tops of their heads blending into a mess they've made in the blackened carpet. It's true, she conceded, that sort of thing wasn't common – bothering the families of the dead. Most days Emma was more likely to be busy ringing up local politicians, aggrieved store owners, press agents, art galleries, council members and administrators. There was always a certain give and take with these types, it was an ugly symbiotic arrangement. Journalists are prostitutes and pimps, all rolled into one body, Emma thought. Sometimes they'd call you back, angry, attacking your integrity, swearing, threatening to come into the office. There were plenty of stories about attacks on the newsroom, named-and-shamed crims throwing rocks through the windows at night, shady labourers pounding drunk on the locked doors calling you out – plenty of anonymous death threats and bomb scares. Nothing had ever happened directly to Emma, but the proximity was enough to cause her disturbing dreams of late, and now her bowels had begun to suffer of a morning, just as she was about to walk out the door and head into the office. It was time to go back into academia, she decided as she turned onto the highway heading east for Blacktown. She'd call her old professor, Lynette, that very afternoon – start the wheels of a scholarship in motion. Lynette had tried to warn her, had said directly, 'Don't go into journalism. Journalists are the natural enemies of poets. One defends the terminological status quo, the other wages war upon it.' Emma had been appalled, at the time, offended even. She'd laughed about it with her friends, the sheer elitism. In time the shock had worn away, and Emma realised her mentor had been speaking as a relic of an older age, one where a certain truculence was necessary for an intellectual woman. I'll come back to her like a prodigal daughter, all her matronly fascination will flare up, and I'll bask in its delivering light. 'I'm so glad to hear from you, Emma!' Lynette will say. 'You were always my favourite student!' Well, no. Lynette would never go that far.

The Western highway was bracketed by motley variations of the same flat dry lawns out front of double-brick homes with grey tiled roofs, with two or three cars parked on the nature strips outside each house. Occasionally, palm trees poked their heads from behind the front fences, their bulbous tufts reaching up beyond the extensive powerlines, and Emma saw retirees standing in the afternoon sun by the side of the road at bus stops without shelter, their shopping bags hanging from walking frames. You hate to see an old person forced to stand in the sun, they should have somewhere to sit at least, she thought. There were new unit blocks along the highway too, grey and white and tall, many of them not quite finished, with portaloos on the footpath, hedged in by makeshift building site fences with concrete feet. Closer to Blacktown the signs of dealerships came into view, and the fast-food chains, service stations, tyre joints, random allotments of gum trees blackened by intermittent bushfires caused by tossed cigarettes, and the occasional flame tree in the nature strip between the lanes. An assemblage of shrubs and bushes thrust out from abandoned vacant lots between the homes and businesses. Chewed truck tyres and broken bumpers were left in the long grass on the strips, ad-hoc dumping sites up for sale, and the drains along the highway were peppered with trash tossed from passing open windows, and spare ibis stalked between the folded prams, dirty nappies, mattresses and other signs of life. At the intersection of the highway with Bungarribee Road, a store as old as time was selling enormous rugs, its wares slung across a long pole propped horizontally outside the shopfront. A great black panther was snarling from one rug, and an eagle soared across the American flag on another; a Jolly Roger grinned on a third, and a skeleton dressed as a cowboy was firing both guns from the fourth. Inside the store, behind these displays, were rows of rolled rugs stacked behind the store's glass windows. Who would put such things out the front of their business? Why advertise yourselves that way? Because it catches the eye? Surely it alienates more people than it draws in? Who knows how businesses such as these stay afloat, Emma wondered, and then cringed when she considered the elitism implicit in such thoughts. No, no! Don't be ridiculous, she chastened herself, you're not looking down from some ivory tower! The rugs really are absurd. They're genuinely, objectively hideous. Must you be so neurotic? she asked herself with a smile.

There was a huge shopping centre across the street from the address Emma had typed into the map. An IGA Supa Sava Centre, consisting of a Liquorland, a bakery, a chemist, an Indian restaurant and a vast and spotted car park where three scrawny men in sleeveless shirts and large square sunglasses were huddled together, discussing something concealed in the open boot of an old Kingswood. I should bring a gift, Emma decided, something to sweeten him up for the interview. Not strictly professional, but anything goes with these puff jobs. Background report makes the man sound a genuine sweetheart, plucked out by the committee amongst the other contenders for his selflessness – crossing the street for his neighbours daily, collecting their medications, dispensing them like a one-man Médicins Sans Frontiéres. Apparently does their groceries too, God bless, carries the shopping bags back and forth over the busy street, day and night. They must know him in the chemist there, all his good work. Best to get a quote from them first, some background and leads. Emma parked out front of the chemist and wandered across to the little store, her heels loud on the hot concrete. There were stacks of sunglasses on a rack out front, a bucket of umbrellas for sale in plastic sleeves. A sign by the door read 'Ask your friendly chemist for free medical advice, appointments available for vaccination.' Elaborate respirators wrapped around translucent plastic busts were on display, antifungal ointments, anti-inflammatory tablets, nail clippers on little key chains, electronic BMI meter-readers, home-kit heart monitors, pregnancy tests, a corridor of contraceptives, a sticker on a shelf reading 'From age 35, you should target anti-ageing action!' and at the back of the shop, the chemist in a white coat, two feet above them all, busy behind two panes of glass, his short hair brutally slicked back as he shuffled between his private supplies, glancing down intermittently at his assistant who was working the register. The assistant, a kindly, open-faced girl with long false lashes and a tiny frame, wore a tag above her breast which announced her name as 'Delilah'. 'Hello,' the young girl said when Emma smiled encouragingly at her, and then added, 'How can I help?' Emma felt a flush come to her cheeks as she prepared to play the part of the professional. 'I was wondering,' she began. 'I'm actually here to do an interview with a gentleman across the street. He's just been awarded Blacktown citizen of the year, and my paper has an interview with him scheduled for this afternoon. I was hoping to find out more about him, maybe get some quotes for the article. It says here he comes in and hands over the scripts for the other elderly residents in the housing block across the street, so I thought you must know him if he's always coming in.' Delilah's face changed to one of unbridled joy. 'Oh! Bobby! You mean Bobby!' The slight girl turned around to see if the chemist had overheard Emma's statement of intent, and indeed, the chemist had stopped what he'd been doing and was now looking down with stern eyes, which Emma greeted with her fullest beaming smile, an expression she wore often to disarm those it was her job to impose upon. The expression was easy to fake, and she kept it natural by acknowledging a distant awareness of an honest principle at play, since her deceit was driven by a desire to uncover truth wherever it might lie. Was it really duplicity to smile, to send a signal that says, 'Trust me, all is well'? Is not the face designed with an endowment of complex expressions for just this purpose? What sophistry says that a forced smile is a falsehood? Emma asked herself in the moment, the chemist's severity still on her like a disapproving teacher's scowl. If we all went about wearing our true dispositions on us – would that be more honest? And at what cost?

'Yes!' she said to the young girl at the register. 'That's the one,

Bobby Duncan of Rosencrantz Street. Of course, you know him!' The assistant laughed, a stiff-backed, high-pitched, nervous giggling laugh. 'Oh my goodness, we know Bobby,' she giggled again. 'Oh, yeah, yeah he's a character,' she added. 'We were the ones who nominated him anyway. He always comes in, every day with new scripts to fill for the old people. Everyone around here knows him.' She laughed some more, turning back again to see what the chemist's reaction might be to this discussion. The man had mostly returned to his bottles, shelves and pills, though he glanced back on occasion at the odd presence of a journalist in his store. We have that effect, Emma thought. We're like detectives, they know us from the television, but it's always strange when we step out of fiction, into their lives. The way they gawk at film crews on the street, journos caked in make-up lit by careful placement of the lights, like angels in the transcendental glow, with people passing them, amazed and awed by the presence of famous, haloed faces in their midst. Not always, of course, you get the opposite on occasion too. Kids leaping behind the lens, swearing and gesturing obscenities, little delinquents on display, bragging to their mates about being on the telly.

'Can you tell me anything about him?' Emma asked. 'Anything at all?' The young girl thought for a moment, her eyes darting up at the ceiling as if her memories were pinned above. 'Oh, he's a funny man,' she said, on the verge of giggling again. 'Always has some stories to tell. You should go and talk to him, he'll tell you some funny stories.' I intend to, Emma thought bitterly. I wonder what she really thinks, she's too excitable to say much of use. 'Is there anything you think I can bring him? A gift maybe?' Again, the girl looked around her, as if answers to questions were stacked somewhere in the variety of the shop's bright shelves. 'Oh, maybe ask the bottle shop,' she said. 'He likes to have a drink, does Bobby!' I can't do that, of course, Emma thought. 'Maybe some chocolates or flowers? Something rewarding, to show how much his efforts on behalf of the community are appreciated.' For a while the girl held her mouth open, and seemed to go a little cross-eyed with her contemplation. 'He uses Rexona Sport, the body spray. Buys a double pack about once a month, maybe? They sell flowers and chocolates in the IGA if you want to try in there? And we sell some jewellery and gift boxes, but it's mostly perfume. I don't think he'd like that!' The girl laughed loudly, and the chemist glared over at them. 'It was lovely to meet you,' Emma assured them both. 'And good on you guys for nominating Mister Duncan, it's really wonderful that you took the time. Someone who works hard for his community, being recognised, I think it's really beautiful of you to have done that, and not having met him, I'm sure it must be really important for him too. Lovely to meet you especially, Delilah, and really glad that I got the chance to come out and talk to you about Bobby today, I really can't wait to meet him, he sounds like quite a character.' The young girl waved her goodbye, and Emma left the store, her knee-high boots clopping out into the car park where the afternoon heat was still rising on the concrete. The housing estate across the street, with its bronzed wire fences and uneven box-hedges, patchy banks of weeds in brick-bordered gardens, and old oxidised gates slouching towards the drying lawn sent a slight shiver up Emma's spine, and she felt an anxious dread at what might abide within those shabby silent units.

The number Emma had been given led to a first-floor unit, closest to the bus stop out front of the estate. There was nothing about its appearance – other than a blue-and-white chequer curtain hanging in the window facing the street – to distinguish the unit from those around it, and she could hear no signs of life coming from within as she made her approach. A faint voice called out from the balcony of the unit above. Emma froze, looked up, and saw the top of an old woman's head, then a pair of hands grasping the balcony railing. At first Emma could not quite understand what this diminutive impression of hands and white hair was about, but then she realised it was a poor old thing, slowly pulling herself up from a chair so that she could see over the balcony wall. In a moment, the old darl had gained purchase, standing just tall enough at the balcony proper, so that a pair of orange-lensed sunglasses was visible beneath her wispy white hair. 'Are you a friend of Bobby's?' the old woman asked. 'Have you come to see him? Because that's his lawn you're walking on.' Emma glanced down at the concrete path, then looked back up at the woman, whose long white hair noodled down the sides of her face. 'No, love, I'm a reporter, actually. I'm here to speak to your neighbour about his award. He's been awarded Blacktown citizen of the year, for all his good works. We're doing an article on him for the local paper.' The old woman pursed her lips, muttered an incomprehensible curse, then seemed to be chewing on something very intensely. Without any further remarks, she disappeared beneath the height of her balcony. Poor old thing. She's not all there. Though who's to say? Perhaps her reaction is the correct response to my entreaty – what's it got to do with her? Old people aren't stupid, and only an idiot would assume their eccentric actions are the sleep of reason. They say you get slower at processing information as you age, Emma considered. Not because your computational powers are diminished, but because your accumulated memory requires more time to crunch.

Emma knocked on the flimsy screen and waited. She heard someone groan, and a loud, impatient voice call out, 'Hang on a tick, I'm coming.' She exhaled a private breath, inhaled a professional poise. The door swung open. 'Yes?' A thin man with close-cropped white hair opened the door in a worn grey hoodie, a slightly moist tone to his voice as he asked the question. Emma held out her hand to the old man, smiling, of course. 'Hello, is your name Bobby? Bobby Duncan? I'm Emma Briggs, I'm a reporter from the *Gazette*, and I was wondering if I could have a word about winning the citizen of the year award?' At once the old man reached out and took Emma's hand, shaking it vigorously with an immediate and toothy smile. 'Come in, mate. Come in. How are you, anyway?' Bobby pressed himself up against the door, holding it open for her, and making a small laughing sound to himself as she stepped inside. The single bedroom unit was dark, with a weathered couch and a square coffee table that had survived several inheritances by its condition, an ancient television set surrounded by framed photographs of Bobby, and an elderly, short-haired woman with a wide laughing face in every picture. One was evidently taken at a recent New Year's Eve, you could see the fireworks on the television set in the image, and another friend of theirs was wearing a paper crown on her greying head. 'This is a cosy little place you have here, Mister Duncan.' Bobby gestured towards the couch and said, 'Yeah, mate! It's not too bad, actually. It's a nice place. What can I get you? They called me yesterd'y and they said you'd be coming over sometime this afternoon. I've got some snacks ready for you.' Bobby made his way towards the fridge, there were some photographs on it, but Emma couldn't make them out. There was a framed print of a wallaby on the wall near the door, and a badly faded cutting from a newspaper photograph of a football team – the Saints, probably from the sixties – in a glassless frame in the hallway. 'Oh no, you don't need to feed me, Mister Duncan! I'm on a bit of a dietary abstention at the moment, anyway, trying to cut back on the accumulating mass.' Emma laughed at her own awkward expressions. 'Ah, bullshit!' Bobby replied, coming to the coffee table by the lounge with a tray of cheese cubes, chopped cabanossi, and a corn relish dip, pre-stuffed with crackers. 'There you go, mate,' he said. 'I got the cheese and the cabanossi from the deli across the street. There's a mate of mine working there who knows me, and I went in yesterday – his name's Marcus, Marcus Brown – and I said to him yesterd'y, "Listen, mate, I've got company coming over tomorrow, you reckon you could set us up with something I can put out that doesn't make me look like a tightarse?" 'Cause it's been a long time since I've had anyone over, and I don't eat much myself, so I don't know what passes for finger food in this day and age. And Marcus says to me, "Bobby, I work at a bloody deli. For what you've done for me over the years, if I can't get you something to snack on, I might as well go and jump in the Georges River with an anchor tied to my..." Well, I can't tell you what he said, mate, but you get the idea. Tied to his balls, let's put it that way. He's a good bloke, Marcus. I been shopping there at the IGA since I moved in, that was about fourteen odd years ago, and some of the stories I could tell you about him. Well, I suppose I can't tell you, unless it's strictly off the record, if you know what I mean, mate?' Emma was swallowing a cube of cheese and nodded her head enthusiastically at this sudden rush of generosity. 'I hope you don't mind if I have a drink?' Bobby said. 'We're early openers around here on Thursdays. Not one to stand on ceremony, if you know what I mean. There's a cold one in the fridge if you're thirsty, or I can get you a soda water or some lemonade.' The old man cracked open a green tinny and the froth splashed a little on his hoodie. He swore under his breath. 'No, no thank you, Bobby. We're not allowed to drink on the job, and I've just had a week's worth of coffee back at the office so I might burst if I have any more liquid.' He raised his can and winked at the reporter. 'No worries,' he said. 'I'll get you a cold glass of water anyway.'

Emma took out a pen and a little notebook while Bobby was busy at the sink, and when he placed the drink on the table beside the cubes and crackers, she pointed at the paper cutting with her pen. 'You a Saints supporter, Bobby? My father followed the Saints.' It was somewhat true, but the slightly cloying nature of the comment made Emma squirm once she'd spoken. 'Yeah!' Bobby said, as though genuinely perplexed by the reporter's powers of deduction. 'That photo is the St George premiership team from 1956, with Tommy Ryan, Norm Provan, and Peter Carroll on the front row with Billy Wilson. That was the beginning of the eleven-year-long winning streak, 1956 to 1966. That's what they call the golden era for St George, back in the day. They won that year, eighteen to twelve against Balmain, at the Sydney Cricket Ground, on September 8th, 1956.' Emma at first thought he was a former player, but the dates didn't match up, and then she noticed several trophies stacked up on the kitchen cupboards, for snooker, tenpin bowling and cricket. 'Oh my goodness, I didn't realise you were a sportsman and a sports historian!'

The old man squinted round at the trophies behind him and

scratched his wiry thighs. 'See that middle one there, that was for playing billiards with a man named Greg Hellman. He and I used to play every Saturday down at the Albion Park Hotel. We were the immortals, as we like to be called, but people used to call us the pisspots.' He took a steady drink from his can as if to illustrate the origins behind this moniker. 'We played, one night, on the same table, for six hours straight. Nobody in the place could beat us, so we kept the table for about six hours. Back in those days, if you were winning, you kept the table in play until someone came along to beat you. That's just how we played in them days, I dunno if they still do that or not, but that was the way it used to be. If you win, the table's yours until someone comes along and knocks you off, sort of thing. Anyway, to cut a long story short, one night Greg Hellman and me were playing doubles, down there at the Park Hotel, and we must have had the table for, oh, I dunno, maybe, six or seven hours at one point. We'd played everybody in the room, at doubles, everyone and his dog had had a go, and then this bloke comes over.' Bobby took another drink, looked into the hole in the can to check the remaining depth and continued. 'He was a short bloke, but about seventeen stone, and as wide as a proverbial rhinoceros. Had a head like an anvil. Anyway, he comes over to me and he says, "Excuse me." And I look at him, and I say, "Yes, mate? What can I do for you?" And he says to me, "Listen. I've been watching you. Watching you play all night. And you know what I reckon? I reckon you're a bit of a smart-arse. You think you're a real smart-arse, don't you?" And I held my arms up to him, I said, "No, mate, no I don't think I'm a smart-arse. I don't think I'm better than anyone else, you know. I'm just here playing doubles with my mate, Greg Hellman." And he says, "No, you're a smart-arse alright. I've been watching you all night, and you're a smart-arse," he says. "And you know what?" he says. "I'm gonna play you. In a game." I said, "Okay, sure, sure. Just get your partner over here and we'll give you a game, no worries." We're playing doubles, Greg and me, so we're happy to have a game against this bloke and his mate. "No," he says. "I don't want to play doubles. I want to play a game, just me, against you." I said, "Well, I'm sorry, but we're playing doubles." Well, I can't tell you what he said next, but then he says, "No you're effing not." If you know what I mean. And then he said, "You're not playing effing doubles. I'm playing you right now, me against you. And what's more, I'm gonna beat you, and when I do, I'm gonna take you outside and break your effing neck." Well, I'm starting to sweat now, if you know what I'm talking about. Greg Hellman, he's looking at me, just saying, "Well, you've got no choice now, Bobby." Greg gives me a wave, and he walks off and goes and sits at the bar. I'm thinking, thanks very much. With friends like Hellman! So, to cut a long story short, would you believe, this bloke breaks, and two balls go in. He sinks another ball. Then another ball. I'm looking over at Greg, and I'm thinking, "I'm done for here. He's gonna sink every ball in the table, then he's gonna drag me out by the scruff of my neck, and off me in the alleyway." Well, would you credit this, he pockets every ball but one before the black. His last shot, before the black, and the ball comes to a stop, one inch before the pocket. And I haven't even had a shot yet. And Greg Hellman comes over to me, and he says, "Good luck, mate, I hope your last will and testament is up to effing date," and I said, "Yeah, thanks very much." The bloke is glaring at me, and I take the cue for my first shot, and then..." Just as Bobby seemed prepared to unfold the miraculous part of this pool-hall legend to Emma, a knock on the screen door broke in on the monologue. The old woman who had appeared on the balcony above was standing at the doorway, looking in through the fly screen. 'Christ almighty,' Bobby said. 'Brace yourself, she'll talk your bloody ears off, this one.'

'Good morning,' came a faint and breathless voice from the obscured figure. Bobby opened the screen door and revealed the elderly woman, whose large watery eyes peered into the darkness of the unit. It's that old sweetheart from the balcony upstairs, Emma thought. In her hands was a Tupperware container of crumbling biscuits. 'I thought the young lady would like to try some of these, I made them last week for my daughter, but I forgot she's not eating sugar.' Bobby took the container of sweets and looked at it from every angle, as though he'd never seen something like it before. 'Thank you, Grace,' he said, in the same impatient tone Emma heard when she'd first knocked on his door. 'Now, Grace, listen mate. I'm sorry but we're just in the middle of an interview here. This young woman, if she doesn't mind me saying so, is from a newspaper, and she's on a tight schedule.' The old woman, who was wrapped tightly in a light blue dressing gown, her small feet tucked in purple slippers, shuffled inside without a word and placed a trembling hand on the arm of the couch nearest Emma. 'Don't listen to him,' she said with a heavy, coughing breath. 'He goes on.' Old Grace then looked at Bobby, pointed at him with an involuntarily wagging finger and asked, 'Does Magda know you have a visitor today?' Bobby took a swig from his tin and his head quivered as though he was enduring a sudden electric shock. Before Bob could give an answer, Grace turned back to Emma. 'Magda's Bob's special lady friend.' Bobby put his hands on his hips and shook his head with a foul expression. 'She lives round the way there, number 16.

All the old people here are in a special relationship of one sort or another. You get lonely, at our age. Anything goes.' Bobby waved at the old woman in obvious disgust and said, 'Don't get taken in by this idler, mate. She knows only too well that Magda's no such thing as my special lady. Don't pay the old so-and-so any attention, mate. She'd talk the ears off an antenna, if you know what I mean.'

Grace put a hand on Emma's arm and said 'You're about the same age as my son, Blake. He's a mechanic out at Rydalmere. He was in the news, too. Like you. They shot him and my grandson outside his house, five years ago it was now. Blake survived, after surgery at Blacktown, but he has a bag now, and my grandboy was killed at the scene. He died in the driveway and they had his funeral in Rookwood. Believe it or not, I had seven grandchildren before that, but Stephen was the first one to die, in the shooting, and then Lillian got leukemia, and she died about a year later. It was a terrible thing, she was a pretty girl. I have pictures of her in my place, near the phone, so I can think about her when I'm talking to my sister. And my youngest son, Wayne, he was run over just down the street here, on Buttress Parade, near the lights. A truck hit him in the dark while he was crossing the road and he was killed right away, just crossing the street. I had four boys, and only two are left now, and the girls are doing okay except for their husbands. I had one of them come round here last week, a drug addict. My daughter was staying with me, because he bashes her and calls her names in front of the kids, but then he was banging on the windows, calling out for her to come outside or he'd set himself on fire. He puts cigarettes out on the kids.'

Bobby was rolling his eyes wildly and making a wheeling motion at his temple as Grace spoke, shaking his head and smirking over her shoulder. 'I'm so, so sorry you've had so much loss, Grace. That's heartbreaking.' Emma said. 'Each one of those terrible incidents must have been incredibly traumatic for everyone involved. I'm so sorry. Have you spoken to the police about the son-in-law? The one who came around here?' Emma put her hand on Grace's.

'Yeah, there was a lot of news about my Blake when they done that shooting to him outside his house, but it wasn't ever brought into court. Can you imagine? They shot him dead in front of his own father and nothing ever came of it and nobody ever talks about it anymore. Not long before it happened, him and his boy came to visit me, before Christmas it was. His boy was such a lovely one, he had his mother's long hair and he'd always help his dad out round the house and everything, and they were thick as thieves. Worked together at the mechanic shop Blake bought from his father-in-law, and they came round here with fruit cake and presents for me on my birthday. Fruit cake is my favourite, ever since I was about half your age, and they had a bag of presents for me. Bobby can tell you, he saw them when they come round to visit me that day, didn't you, Bob? You saw what they brought me? He remembers, don't you worry. Bob helped me set the telly up afterwards. They brought me out a bag of presents and a new telly, too. The old one was like Bob's. Actually, that's it there! That's my old telly, isn't it, Bob? Yes, it is. Now I remember, I gave it to you, didn't I? Anyway, my Blake told me that day, he said "Mum, I'm worried about things," and I said, "What sort of things are you worried about? What have you got to worry about? With a beautiful boy like yours and a wife and your own shop? What are you talking about?" He was always a private boy, even when he was a little fella and he'd come home with a black eye, he wouldn't speak one word about his troubles.

And now here he was telling me "I'm worried"? Well, I said, "Tell me what's going on, Blake! I'm your mother! I want to know what's the matter." He was looking out the window, staring out the window like he was trying to see something far in the distance.'

Just when the old woman seemed to be coming to the pivotal detail of her story, there was a crashing knock on the flimsy door and a loud baritone voice called out, 'Hello? Bob? Hello?' The newest arrival knocked again, aggressively, before anyone had a chance to react. 'Oh no,' Grace said, completely out of breath. 'It's that bloody Cypriot.' Bobby shuffled towards the screen door, and an old man with a square face and his mouth hanging open to reveal a great red tongue lolling over toothless gums stepped into the unit, hunching his way in past Bobby holding open the door. 'G'day!' he said, very loudly, and stared a moment at Emma as though he couldn't make sense of her, then glanced a moment at Bobby, and in a booming voice said, 'Bob, you never toll me your daughter so beautiful? You never toll me you have a beautiful daughter? Why you not show her to me all these years?' The man panted when he'd finished speaking, and ploughed forward to shake her hand. 'My name's Bob, like him,' he said pointing at Bobby. 'But everyone here calls me Cypriot Bob. Fucking racists, aye!' Emma assured him it was a pleasure to meet this second Bob, and asked about the origin of his epithet. 'I was a merchant marine, a fisherman, sailed all round the world. I seen every island and country on one side of the world. Every one, believe it! And you know, out of all the countries you can name, Greece is the most beautiful of all countries, but there are other places I like. You been to Malta? Lebanon? Egypt? Tasmania? Armenia? Greece?' Emma, smiling, shook her head at each of the destinations the new Bob rattled off, and he raised his arms up in amazement. 'She's not been anywhere!' he shouted. 'Bob, you not take your daughter anywhere! She like you, been nowhere and seen nothing! Typical Aussie.' He made these remarks with a wink at Emma, while the original Bob looked at her over the guest's shoulder, making the same wheeling motion at his temple. Grace was making her way towards the door, having complained loudly to herself about the second Bob's volume, and slapped the first Bob across the mouth as she went by, 'Watch your bloody manners with a young lady present, you dirty dog. We're in no mood for your carry on.' When she reached the door, Grace turned and called out to Emma with her faint frail tones riding over the old men's interchange, 'You might as well head home, love, you're wasting your time with these mongrels.' When the door shut behind Grace, the second Bob quietened considerably and said, 'You owe me a beer, Bobby,' and his host complied, shuffling quickly over to the fridge, handing his guest a can of cold beer and grabbing another for himself. Both men cracked open their cans, saluted each other and took a long sip. With a sigh of refreshment, the second Bobby announced, 'Okay, I go now,' then he looked at Emma and explained, 'I only come 'cause I see her come in here. She talks, talks, talk, but she hates me, so I come over whenever I see her, and she goes home right away.' He emphasised this by clapping his hands loudly, and gesturing with one hand in the direction Grace had gone. 'Okay, Bobby, I'm going,' he said again, walking quickly out the door with another long drink from his can of bitters.

When Emma and Bobby the first were alone again, a sense of wasted time impinged upon the visitor. 'Tell me a little about yourself,' Emma asked, as she prepared to scribble quotes in her book that might serve to stich up two hundred words of copy for a piece about a local man given the nod by council committee. The old man was expansive, discursive, circuitous, but so many subjects were alike, and Emma knew her craft well enough to shepherd even the worst offender towards the salient topic, and Bobby was nothing if not accommodating. What work had he done in early life? Public servant. What was his outlook on life? It costs nothing to say 'please' and 'thank you'. How did it feel to be recognised for his good deeds? It was only what he'd been raised to do, far as he was concerned. It stung a little, each time Emma urged the old man along, or took him down a different path at the expense of another more urgent, or reined in any talk of his youth, like tales of catching mud crabs under the rocks of the harbour's waters with baitfish on hooks near the timber yards, meeting local football legends in pubs and discussing the minutiae of long-forgotten grand-final controversies. That's what he wanted to talk about, but Emma couldn't spend much longer listening. What choice did she have but to keep him on the straight and narrow, so to speak? She thought of herself as playing the role of Virgil, guiding the old man through the wilderness of his own memories. It was a pretentious and self-serving conception of her job, Emma saw that as soon as it came to her. She repeated the words in her mind, 'The role of Virgil'. Not only self-aggrandising, but clichéd. Fatuous. For a moment Emma saw herself sitting in the dark of the unit listening to the old man, the encouraging smile on her lips, the scribbling notes, her patronising nodding. The thought arose in her like a phantom: what would Lynette think if she could see into this dark room? A shiver rippled up the back of her neck. She felt for a moment as if she might make a run for the door. For one full second they sat across from each other in silence before Emma realised Bobby had stopped talking. On a burst of impulse,

Emma pointed to the photograph of the smiling woman in the New Year's Eve portrait. 'Your neighbour mentioned a lady friend, Bobby. Is that her? Is that Magda?' The old man turned his thin, veiny neck and frowned, as though he'd been insulted. But it wasn't that. Emma saw he was struck by a sudden overflow of emotion, and as he sat a foot from her on a chair perpendicular to the couch, she watched the old man struggling madly to gain hold of himself. He looked bent by the burden of his struggle, and Emma put a cautious hand on his bony knee. 'Bob, are you alright? I'm really sorry if I've upset you.' This only disfigured the old man's expression more fully, and he looked at the reporter with eyes mangled with upheaval, his mouth in a twisted grip against his chin. 'Nah, mate,' he said with spongey, quivering lips. 'Nah, it's no worries, mate. Just an old fool, I am. I was a bachelor most of my life. Never had much luck with the ladies before I came here. But then when I came here, Magda and me became best mates, sort of thing. And then a few years later they found some sort of shit in my guts.' Just as the old man seemed to be regaining his composure, he froze again, overcome by memory, and Emma patted his knee and assured him they could change the subject. 'They cut me open,' he said abruptly, pointing to his stomach, his fingers shaking. 'They cut me open along here and they took my guts out, and they chucked them on a table beside me like a bunch of sausages, 'cause there was a cancer in the middle. Then they stuck the guts back in, and stitched me up, and I woke up in hospital.' Bobby looked over at the photograph again, with a stream of tears coming down his cheeks. 'She was the only one who came along to visit me, while I was in there. In the recovery, you know? She used to catch the bus in, used to catch it just outside here, actually. The 421 bus from Rosencrantz Street to Blacktown hospital. She'd bring me some of her cooking, and I ate it, even though I knew my bowels wasn't ready for her food cause she's always putting spices in there that an honest man's never heard of. Anyway, long story short, we're still good mates to this day.' Emma found a box of tissues near the couch and handed a couple to Bobby, who blew his nose hard. She rubbed his bent back as he apologised for losing his cool. 'You get older, and it gets harder to keep yourself together, I reckon.' He laughed with red eyes, and they sat together talking for a while, Emma abandoning her urgent duties, listening and sharing stories of her own.

They hugged each other in the doorway when Emma said she had to leave. 'Sorry, mate,' Bobby repeated, and she told him not to be ridiculous. 'You're a wonderful man and listening to all your stories has been an absolute treat. I can see why the council honoured you, Bobby.' He told Emma to drop by anytime she wanted, that he had plenty more stories to tell. 'Don't make fun of me, whatever you do!' he called out to her. 'Don't tell anyone that I used to haunt houses!' Emma assured him she would keep his secret, though she had no idea what the old man meant. 'Someone will be here tomorrow to take your photograph,' Emma told him. 'I hope they've had experience shooting fossils!' he yelled back, and Emma waved goodbye as she crossed back into the car park of the Supa Centre. In the hermetic silence of her car, Emma sighed and pressed her head back into her seat, closing her eyes to keep out her troubling inner censures. At the office they'll want me to write like an automaton with generic phrases. 'Good manners are said to be out of fashion in a culture obsessed with the self, but Bobby Duncan is living proof that a sense of community is alive and well in Blacktown.' She could already feel the clichés itching to leap out of her fingers. But that is not what it all means to me. That is not what these old folks taught me at all. She started her car and headed back onto the main road towards the office, her thoughts disorganised except for one – journalism was not enough, not enough to feed her hungry soul. It would be better to be a screenwriter than a journo. She could set the film of Bobby's life in some apposite splendour, have it open on a scene near the city's bays. It will show him standing astride a crooked footpath parallel to the river's edge as a boy, an immense spectre of cloud imposing itself against the pale blue skies of the Australian inner city. Jane Campion can direct, Emma thought. She does landscape so well, and men. Who would play him, what actor? Hugo Weaving's son, what was his name? Tall and lanky, like a foal squeezing its stallion-esque form down into a boyish package. What would he say, in that opening scene? There could be a voiceover, saying, 'Ah, now I know where I am! I know these streets and pathways, I used to scrape a living here, as a boy, pulling metal pegs out of railway timbers to be melted down and sold for pennies by the pound, and up the street my father spliced steel wires with his bare hands, until his bloody fingers yellowed with rust, and I jumped behind him, hobbled by scarlet fever, my head shaved and painted purple, callipers up to my hips.' What would he say next? Looking directly into the lens. Emma had no idea, and what did it matter? I'm not a screenwriter, she confessed. I haven't the faintest idea how to swell a progress, set a scene, shape a hero's journey. But what if I wrote the most essential article instead, the most incredible article ever written? I am no Joan Didion, nor was meant to be. But I have seen the Bobs and Graces of this world enough to know how to speak to their intrinsic natures. I can sing the song of my people, she thought. They won't print such a thing in the *Gazette*.

They won't accept such an article from me. Imagine it, Mitch reads it over. 'I have to hand it to you, Em,' he'd say, closing his laptop slowly to absorb more fully his delight in skewering her on the spot. 'You certainly have a Rabelaisian predilection for wallowing in the more grotesque and unrefined reaches of contemporary life.'

What did it matter to her now? What men like Mitch thought about her? Emma could already see her place was not amongst the constant compromises of the journalistic trade. She would return to her open-plan office, with the hum of monitors and the smell of coffee cups with rubber caps, sit down at her desk, and unfold all she had seen at the old man's unit, capturing all the Baudelairean riches of an Aussie fugue passing through the ordinary excess along the way – all this Emma would evoke in her article, having captured her experience in a prose sparkling with its desire to reveal, and she'd toss the copy to Mitch at his desk, hardcopy, a triumphant light of knowing in her large green eyes, as he sneered and told her it was time to pack her desk. This will be a romantic tale to tell Lynette, she thought. My old mentor, clapping in delight at my last-gasp rejection of the mendacity of the journalistic trade, going out not with a whimper, but a bang.

A scarlet twilight was eating into the shadowy mountains of the west, currawongs were flapping in the tops of the tall ghost gums along the highway, powerlines like stitches between the houses crossing the highway with dead bats and shoes hanging from them. Emma was grinning as she passed the tyre shops and service stations, a billboard crowned by sulphur-crested cockatoos, picking parasites from their claws atop an enormous advertisement for some new reality television show full of celebrities. She began to write the words inside her mind, each sentence seeming grander than the last, each image more imbued with an unexpected resonance than the one before. Prose came to her, as if she were the amanuensis of some greater broader mind, whose thoughts were dictated to her without hesitation. She could almost see the whole thing now, and by the time she parked outside the office, she found it necessary to run, with clopping heels, in order not to lose one word of her inspiration.

Some days later, the following article appeared in the *Gazette*, without attribution. 'Everybody needs good neighbours. They say a good man is hard to find, but not for one public housing complex in Sydney's west. Bobby Duncan is living proof that the old virtues still cling on in our local communities.

'For over a decade, Bobby Duncan has played the saintly man of service for whatever his neighbours might need, many of these pensioners being unable to make the perilous journey across the street to gain access to the medical centres and chemists located there. Bobby has made his message clear, "I'm only ever a phone call away," the former bookmaker's clerk assures his friends at the Rosenthal complex. "Giving anyone a hand is the way I was brought up. I was always told that it cost nothing to say please and thank you, and even less to say hello." Saint though Mr Duncan might be, he still enjoys the occasional punt, but admits it had never made him much of a profit. "A wise man once told me, the only way you'll turn a quid following the horses is with a sugar bag and shovel," he said.'

A Night at the House

'This may be a little cold.' The nurse squirted a dollop of gel on Pam's abdomen, right near the talisman tattoo she got on a whim, at age nineteen. Martin held her hand, and she bit her lip as the nurse pressed the transducer against her bare skin, swirling the gel. The little monitor showed a ghostly pouch, and a pale spectral thing contained within. There was a long silence except for the muffled echo of the device. 'I'm sorry,' the nurse said, wiping the mess she'd made on Pam with a disposable towel torn from a roll by the door. 'I need to do an internal scan. I can't see clearly from the outside.' Martin and Pam looked at one another, they sensed already what this might mean. Martin kept his eyes on Pam's expression. She looked pained, and her hands were damp. The nurse apologised each time Pam shifted on the bed, her brows knitted tight. The procedure seemed to last a long time. 'I'm so sorry,' the nurse said, already cleaning the probe, 'but there's no heartbeat at all.' She patted Pam on the shoulder, spoke a few words of comfort, and wheeled her instrument outside, giving the couple a moment. A long, private moment. Eventually a doctor came in to see them, and with an empathetic expression, made a list of recommendations. Pam would agree to nothing, and sensing there was no point persisting, the doctor repeated her condolences and left.

The long white halls of the hospital, with nurses pushing patients on their bed trolleys, and old people moaning in darkened doorways, and parents cradling children who wore casts on their arms or leant into vomit bags with their hair hanging down, led out into the brightness of an overcast street, and they walked with Pam's head resting on Martin's shoulder. Two old women in wheelchairs were smoking outside the hospital doors, and a large man with a brace on his neck was being unloaded from a van with green checkers on its side. The street beyond was busy, and grey. 'What do we do now?' Pam asked, once they were sitting alone in the car, the noisy day around them strangely abstracted. 'Have you ever noticed that place in Tempe called Manhattan Superbowl?' Martin said, rubbing a hand gently along her thigh. 'I think we should go bowling, honestly.' Pam sighed and placed her hands across her belly, edging his affections out of the way. 'You're serious?' she asked. For a moment Martin felt he might blush, looked out at the construction across the street and saw two men in hardhats guiding a truck into a fenced yard. 'I don't want us to go back to the house, whatever we do. It will feel worse there,' he said, and then started the car, putting on his blinker without any further thought. 'Why don't we go to the beach?' Pam asked. Her eyes were closed, and the expression on her face was pale and pained. 'We can have a drink at a bar near the water, I'll even drive you home if you want to tie one on.' That settled it then, as Pam knew it would.

They parked near a renovated pub beside the beach and sat at a plastic table under a blue-and-white umbrella. It was mid-afternoon now and music was coming from the pavilion, and the smell of wood-fire ovens cooking pizzas and the salt of the surf was strong in the air. There was a children's birthday party under a canopy of red and blue balloons at a table inside the pub's pavilion, the kids were laughing and squealing over soft drinks and chips, while their parents wrangled them and kept them from wandering outside. The air near the beach was cool, and a chill breeze pushed its way across the sand behind them, whipping occasional stinging gusts across the tables. 'Maybe we should go inside?' Martin asked as Pam shuddered. He could see the goosebumps on her arms. 'The music's a little obnoxious in there, though,' Pam said. 'I'll ask if they can turn it down,' Martin offered, but Pam shook her head. 'It's fine. Just get us a beer.' He got up and followed her instruction, not sure how else to proceed with her, not sure how to read the moment. From inside the pub, he turned back and observed Pam sitting on the curved plastic seat, leaning on the table, alone before the passing joggers and dogwalkers crossing the paved stones of the promenade. Her head was turned towards the breeze, hair trailing in a constant stream of motion, and she was squinting into the horizon over the water, her feet angled inward, rubbing her hand very gently on her belly, again. She looked so unlike herself in that moment, though Martin could not say what produced the strangeness about her.

It was noisy in here, as Pam had said, but it wasn't the music that bothered him the most. Closer to the brightly coloured mess and noise of the children's party, the kids looked animal, almost rabid. They scoffed their chips and screeched at one another, spilling their plastic cups and dropping half-eaten slices of pizza to the floor. One little boy was standing on his chair, sticking packets of sugar in his nose and waving his arms like a bird and screeching something at the top of his lungs. There were little torn-up bags of sweets and toys tossed across the table, spilling everywhere an explosion of primary colours. Their parents seemed oblivious to the noise and the wreckage. They were mostly mothers, some had babies clinging to them, but there were fathers too, fat and balding and quiet. They were all dull-eyed, like beasts in a field, some of them in the process of being milked by tiny, shrouded bubs. The party spilled over into the nearby games area, a section of the bar with fake grass and musical notes painted across yellow walls. There the children were playing with a giant chequerboard, an air hockey table and, to Martin's amazement, a miniature bowling alley. Most of the children were ignoring the bowls and pins, and making little games of their own, and Martin could see that it would be possible to shoo them away from the little lanes and have a game if Pam was so inclined. Surely it would work to change the tone of the day to have a little fun, and if the presence of the miniature alley in this pub wasn't a sign that he was right then he didn't know what was.

'I got us Stellas,' Martin said, sitting down at the table with an exaggerated grunt. 'You always said you like Stellas during the daylight hours.' Pam dug her fingers hard into the flesh of her thighs and tore her attention away from the grey clouds moving over the sea. They were enormous assemblies of steely grey and incandescent white, billowing and shifting across the sky. Pam gave Martin a weak smile, which he took as disapproval, and she put the dark bottle to her lips, taking a long swig. 'Thanks for bringing us here,' she said, and clinked her bottle to his. 'You know,' Martin said. 'You won't believe this, but there's a bowling alley inside there. Some kids are playing it now, but maybe we could have a game later?' Pam turned around to look at a woman with a large greyhound walking by. The dog was horribly thin, and there was a cage around its narrow head. 'I really don't feel like bowling today,' she said. 'But if you want to, by all means.' He looked inside the pub for a moment. He could just make out a mass of the children rushing and sprawling around the games area, and the blonde bartender who had served him pouring drinks for some men in suits, and he said, 'No, I'm just as happy sitting and talking.' The sun moved out from behind some cover and bleached the world around them with an intolerable glare, just as the cold air tossed a scattering of dry leaves from the trees in the park. Martin closed his eyes against the sudden uptake of wind. The sudden shift in the light seemed to sink Martin out of the present and into a vague remembrance of his childhood. He'd been a sullen boy, painfully shy and malcontent. There'd been no parties at pubs with bowling alleys. If he'd been invited to one, he'd have sat at the table and watched in a kind of dejected fascination. The earliest years of his life had moved around him without leaving much of a concrete impression. It was as though he had grown up out of the ground, like a plant emerging from the dirt, overlooking the same barren corner of life, receiving occasional sustenance, being addressed by changes in the seasons, but otherwise in solitude as silent and empty of companionship as the deepest wilderness. It made him shiver to think on the past. A nauseating feeling began to boil in his stomach, and a kind of nervous tremor in his chest began to beat.

'I dunno why she felt the need to say that,' Pam said, thinking of the doctor. 'Telling us we'd get on with our lives like that? Sure wasn't what I needed to hear from her so quickly. We'll get over it, of course, but would a little tact go astray? Give folks a moment to grieve without urging them to think forward. To process the shock of it. She's right, we'll recover, but what is it in *Macbeth*, "I must first feel it as a man"?' Pam laughed at the thought and looked over at Martin. He nodded in agreement. 'It wasn't the time,' he said, his face a kind of brooding mask. 'I'll have to call everyone and tell them what happened,' she said to him. 'And the ones who get upset, will make me more upset, and the ones who don't get upset will make me angry, and then tomorrow we'll all feel a little better. Everything we do today though, well...it's a complete write-off.' Martin grimaced at hearing this and screwed his eyes closed tight. A foul mood had descended on him. He could not recall one single pleasant memory from all his childhood, now that he was bent upon it. There had been a pall over the whole of his early life, an endurance he'd hoped vaguely to outgrow. He could recall no flying kites, no games of cricket, no camping trips, no board games at the kitchen table, no giant chequerboards. That such things happened, he was sure, but all he could think of was the constant bickering, the drunkenness of the parents, the sleepless nights and ostracism in the schoolyard. Spending days befriending pigeons on the playground and watching the ants march along weeds in the driveway beside his house. A blue-tongue lizard moving slickly through the bushes, watching it move like a disembodied organ near the crooked concrete by the fence, going under a crack in the paling. He remembered fighting in the house, most nights, grown men belting each other and knocking tables and chairs down, spilling beer bottles all over the lino and the general din of shouting. The breaking glass and screaming women, slamming doors waking him in the middle of the night. He remembered seeing his mother dragged by her hair out into the yard and her red face covered in welts. The neighbour's boy threw stones at him one morning, Jackson Bally. His father was a mechanic who worked in his yard, the sound of power wrenches and engine misfires rang out over the evenings. Later that week in the playground Jackson and Martin fought each other behind a demountable at recess. Two hits on the chin and Martin fell to the grass, his head all but busted. Dad will have me for fighting, he had thought, still lying there with the beginnings of a swelling pulsing on his jaw. He had never had a single birthday party, let alone one with a bowling alley by the beach!

'I wouldn't worry about making any phone calls just yet,' he said. 'Let's deal with that later.' Martin's expression was stormy now, and he was staring at the table as though something appalling was placed upon it. Pam turned her whole body towards him, reached out across the table and put her hand on his wrist. 'It's alright, I'm just thinking out loud.' Pam said. 'I know that. I know it.' Pam looked at him very keenly, as though trying to calibrate her next move. There was an ambulance stopped at the traffic lights at the intersection behind them, its lights were flashing but there was no siren. It seemed to be in no hurry. The lights caught Pam's attention. 'You don't need to think about the future, honey,' she said. 'You don't need to think about anything right now. I'll get us through it,' she said, turning to watch his face very carefully. 'You know though, they might have to clean the miscarriage out of me in the next few days. Did you hear her recommending it to me back at the hospital? I told her I'm not agreeing to anything without seeing my doctor first. I don't trust the system. I like my people. I like to have people I can trust take care of me. Evacuation of remains. Sounds morbid. They should give it a spiffier title, for goodness' sake. My doctor's very particular about these things, as you know, and I'm not doing anything without his express say-so. We've been trying at this for too long to have some new complication arise at this stage in the process, and we'll need to get back to business right away, obviously.' Martin saw how she was looking at him. A slight smile on her face. 'It's going to be tough for me if he says we should have the operation. You know I don't like the sight of blood,' she said. 'I faint, like a woman from a Victorian novel. Did I ever tell you about the time I fainted at the hospital ward, in the toilet? My mother had to carry me, and the sight of blood got her too, and we were both lying down on the floor, together, up against the hospital bed. When my dad walked in, he started screaming. The nurse came running and he had to sit down, he was shaking so bad. Mum and I woke up, like we'd just had the sweetest sleep ever, right there in each other's arms. But Dad was a wreck for days.' Martin stared at Pam for a moment, his expression blank, 'That's ridiculous,' he said. 'I don't know if I quite believe you.' Pam shrugged and looked back over her shoulder at the traffic on the street.

'Listen,' Martin folded up his arms and cleared his throat. 'I know it's like you said. This today, it's just a near miss. We'll get over it. But it's got me thinking, y'know? Like all those parenting things, your dad, your mum. How they fuss about you all the time. All that shit they do that I don't know anything about. All that shit I never had growing up.' Pam folded her arms, too, and she sighed loudly. 'What do you mean? Your parents raised you right. You turned out fine.' Martin turned the bottle in his fingers, the condensation running down its sides. 'I'm just telling you, it's kinda frightening. That's all. Only I'm not just afraid for me, and for you. I'm afraid for everybody. You know what I mean? Every single person. All those people walking there, and in the cars, at the lights, and the people in the park, and the people swimming out in the surf.' The sun was sharply retreating behind its clouds, and the brightness drained from the world around them. 'Martin, I'm going to ask you a very direct question. Are you trying to tell me you're afraid to have kids, Martin?' Pam looked straight into his face, but he'd closed his eyes again and seemed to be holding back tears. 'It's not just that,'

Martin said, and managed to open his eyes without crying. 'Of course I'm afraid to have kids, for fuck's sake. I'm terrified. Don't tell me you never get that feeling? Just this feeling like something terribly sad is gonna take place, something tragic, it might happen right now, somewhere? Like you think some poor kid must be out there right now, right this minute, being just crucified by it all, and there's nothing anyone can ever do about it?' Martin took a deep breath and pressed his chin against his chest. 'You're having a panic attack,' Pam said. 'I'll get you a drink of water, you just wait a minute.' When Pam came back outside she was carrying two tall glasses of water and ice, with a wedge of lime, and she kissed his sweating brow before she sat down. 'Last week,' Martin said, 'I didn't tell you but I was out at Broadway, going down the escalator there. And there was this little boy, maybe six or seven years old, and he was waving like crazy to his mother from the balcony they have there. His mother was coming up the other side, coming up to the same floor as the kid. You never saw a happier face than that kid's face. He was this pudgy kid, waving at his mum, and she was coming up the escalator towards him, and he had the happiest little smile. And there was this couple in front of me on the escalator, this ordinary couple. The woman, in front of me, she nudges her boyfriend standing beside her, and you know what she says? She points at the little kid, and she says, "Fuck, I'd hate to have a ginger kid like that." Can you imagine? A grown woman! Just hating on this kid! And that's nothing at all, on the scale of things. And yet here we are, trying to bring a child into this?'

For a moment Pam was silent, studying her partner as if trying to recognise some physical transformation to go along with his sudden distress. 'I know you're upset,' she said, 'but you can't talk like this to me right now.' Martin swallowed some cold water, letting the condensation drop from the side of the glass onto his shirt, its touch soothing as it soaked into him. His eyes were open, and he watched the traffic lights change from orange to red in his silence, a new set of people in different cars halting behind them, and a mass of cockatoos descended into the moving branches in the park beside them, hanging from their beaks and claws and whipping their wings around the leaves in frightful screeches. 'I know it's not right, but it's the truth! If I don't say it now, then I don't know if I ever will. And that terrifies me, too.' Pam closed her eyes to conceal the anger she was feeling, and said gently, 'I know this moment is difficult for you, and I know you struggle sometimes, but, please, I need you to keep it together for just a little while, okay? Just for today, and then we can talk about all of this tomorrow, please.'

'Alright, yes!' Martin said with a hiss. 'I know the timing is barbaric, but it's true. I'm scared to have a baby. What kind of mad person isn't afraid of that? What kind of self-absorbed lunatic wouldn't be?'

'Martin, be careful now,' Pam said. 'I know you're struggling but don't abuse me. Don't you lash out and call me selfish for wishing I hadn't lost a baby today!'

Martin burst out laughing, 'Jesus, you are ridiculous, Pam. You are an absolutely ridiculous woman,' he said, and then tears ran down his cheeks. 'I'm not saying that about you, and you know it!' he said. 'You know that's not what I'm saying, so don't try turning me up in knots when you know I'm not thinking straight and getting my words muddled. I'm telling you that you're the only one on the fucking planet who can't see the writing on the wall. I know it's a fucking cliché, but look at the situation we're in, for heaven's sake!

The country's on fire every summer, and then its these constant floods, and the pandemics, and everything the doomsayers were crying about the ice caps melting is coming true, and there are wars all over the place, and microplastics in our lungs, it feels like everything is just on the brink of complete and utter collapse, and there are kids stabbing and shooting each other in the street. The old ways are dead, and the new ways are shit, and I'm not sure I even want to go on living myself half the time.'

Pam's face was pale and hard, there was pain in her eyes, white hot. 'Martin,' she said, very slowly, 'Martin, you don't mean any of that. You're spouting nonsense, you don't mean anything you're saying. You're saying things you don't really believe. Don't pretend you're telling me something about the world. You don't know the world, Martin, because you don't want to. You've never cared about the world, not one bit. You're concerned for yourself, you always have been, and you were frightened long before I ever met you, which was long before there were children to pretend to care about. The world is too big a subject for a man like you, so, please, just stop, stop attacking me because you're spinning out of control. Just let me get through this afternoon without dragging me down with you, please! I promise everything else will be fine if you'll only stop!' The melting ice rattled in the glass that Martin held to his chest, and still tears came to his eyes as he laughed and growled, 'There's not going to be any fucking tomorrow! How can that be fine?' He placed the glass on the table with a long slow motion. He stood up, and began to walk off towards the park across from the beach, swarming with birds and the trembling limbs of trees. Pam watched him wandering over the uneven ground, holding his head as he sobbed and cursed, and she exhaled. She closed her eyes for a moment, conjured up the sight of the waves, and in her mind, she saw herself as a young girl. It was abnormal, the level of clarity Pam had for the earliest things. She'd learnt to read before kindergarten, and could still remember the sticky sweet smell of her mother's breast milk, though no one believed her about that. She could remember the purple colour of the walls in her preschool, eating slices of orange at naptime while the teachers cleaned up the toys on a rug near the door. Those memories were filtered in a kind of golden haze, as if dipped in an oily light. She saw herself sitting in the shade of a paperbark tree, in a circle with her friends at the school, playing with a stone in the dirt and singing a song to herself. She couldn't remember the melody, but she recalled pretending the stone in her hand was the family cat, Trim, who had belonged to her grandmother. She told her friends about the cat as she played. He was jet-black, with a starry patch on his breast. Her friends weren't really listening, but she told them how they'd needed to save Trim from a bushfire one Christmas, out in the fields past Penrith. The rushing fire front loomed over her grandmother's property, a skyline of smoke and pulsating heat just below the mountains. They'd packed her grandmother up and fled, but the cat was nowhere to be seen. Weeks later, amidst the black char and ash of the bush near the property line, they found him, still alive. That night Pam had washed him in her grandmother's basin, though he thrashed and squealed and whipped the soapy water in every direction. 'Keep still, Trim, keep still!' she sang at him. She had always been good with little creatures. She had an understanding. His little heart was trembling, she could feel it through the wet fur. How thin and frail he looked, all soaked and shaking. A tiny, pitiable thing.

Pam finished her drink and walked towards the car. She sat inside it with her hands on the wheel, just watching the passing parade of people against the shifting movements of grey cloud over wide, green sea. It was calming, the motions of the waves, and warm inside. At the far end of the park, a man with long ragged whiskers and a black trucker's hat was hammering stakes into the earth, a small boy beside him running a rope along the tops of the stakes, and a large truck began to reverse onto the grass. There were clowns and acrobats and horses painted along the side of the truck. 'Well,' Pam said to herself, smiling sorrowfully. 'Looks like the circus is back in town.' She watched the man with the beard hammer away, his efforts drowned out by the piercing squawk of cockies in the trees. The back of the truck opened slowly when they'd finished their fence, and another man with bare arms and a square face led a line of piebald ponies down a ramp and out into the park. Blonde-haired little horses, with small squinting eyes, their muzzled faces low to the ground as they hunched around in a circle. They had such sorrowful faces. The sun was beginning to go down, and the waves turned the colour of the darkening sky. Still, it was warm and quiet in the car, the constant pulse of the sea and the movement of people and animals and traffic seemed somehow far away. Pam remembered a night at the house not long ago, when they'd come home from a show at the State Theatre, half drunk, and she'd pulled Martin into a hot shower and stripped his soaking clothes off in the water's stream. She wrapped her naked legs around him and pushed her body against his with such force that they knocked the shampoo bottles down around them, water surging in a heavy spray along her back, her hands slapping at the slippery surface of the steaming glass, and their heavy gasping breath filled with soapy vapour, clean sweat on wet bare skin, turning slick and rosy in her soft pink body, swollen tender under the steam's discretion. They became a slippery envelope of heat, swallowing and sucking, and making such a greedy rubbing against each other that they filled up with a rush of passion, so that even the jets of hot water shooting down at them was numbed by the waves and pushes of tightness pulsing through them. They tasted sweet and sticky to each other, Martin's lips on a tingling red nipple Pam stuck into his mouth, its stiffening sweet and full, and his tongue was warm and soft as creation on her tingling skin until her thighs began to shake and cramp and shudder harder under the lapping tongue, like sea water spilling over ocean rock. They rocked back and forth inside one another in this private heat until it spilled out of them both and washed away in the warm waters, and they collapsed in each other's arms afterwards, sopping wet on the wide bed with the lights on till morning, steaming and seeping unseemly on sticking sheets under a mess of covers.

After a long time, the passenger's door opened, and Martin sat down beside her. His face was blotched and red, his eyes bloodshot. 'I'm sorry,' he said. Pam said nothing, she started the car and headed for home. 'I've always hated the circus,' Martin said as they drove past the ponies. Pam turned the radio on but kept the volume low. Martin looked over at the small tattoo of a star on her neck, partly hidden behind her ear. 'You know,' he said. 'You can have a smoke now, if you'd like? When we get back,' he finished, uncertainly. Pam made no reply, she didn't seem to hear, and Martin looked out over the waters to the east. There was something floating on the darkening horizon, and it seemed to Martin, that it was coming on – moving rapidly towards them from a great distance. 'What is it?'

he said aloud to himself. It was something closing the impossible distance. A bird erupting through the branches, scattering the cockies and sparrows into the air with a shrieking and flapping mess of wings. A vast crow, cutting through the air, dark and final as an ending.

Acknowledgements

I am overrun with gratitude to Ivor Indyk, Evelyn Juers, Nick Tapper, Aleesha Paz, and the rest of the superlative crew at Giramondo for working with me on this collection.

Blessings to my fellow-travellers in the life of signs and symbols – Felicity Castagna, Fiona Wright, Lachlan Brown, Catriona Menzies-Pike, David Henley, Alice Grundy, Hugh Newton, Ian Van Gemert, Milissa Deitz, Ben Muir, Peter Cartwright, Sue Crawford, Mihaela Cristescu, Oliver Mol, and Luke Johnson.

More than any other companion on this lonesome road of dreams and desolations, my thanks to Augusta Supple, whose indefatigable dedication to the arts and its inhabitants made this work possible, amongst so many other things.

To my beloved family, thank you all for your love, support, and understanding – and for bestowing upon me a fascination with the inner-lives of others. You are all such extraordinary and wonderful people – under an influence such as yours, I could do no other but to write.

And finally, to Leroy Carman, whose love and laughter is a northern star that shines through every darkness.

About the author

Luke Carman's debut work of fiction, *An Elegant Young Man*, won the 2014 NSW Premier's New Writing Award and was shortlisted for the ALS Gold Medal, the Steele Rudd Short Story Prize and the Readings New Writing Award. His essay collection *Intimate Antipathies* was published by Giramondo in June 2019.